TO DIE FOR

THE EIGHTH BOMBER HANSON MYSTERY

DAVID CHAMPION

ALLEN A. KNOLL, PUBLISHERS

SANTA BARBARA, CA

Allen A. Knoll, Publishers
200 West Victoria Street,
Santa Barbara, CA 93101
(805) 564-3377
bookinfo@knollpublishers.com

First Edition

09   08   07   06   05   5   4   3   2   1

Library of Congress Cataloging-in-Publication Data
Champion, David.
  To die for : a Bomber Hanson mystery / David Champion.- 1st ed.
     p. cm.
  ISBN 1-888310-71-5 (alk. paper)
  1.   Hanson, Bomber (Fictitious character)-Fiction.   2.   Landlords-Crimes against-
Fiction.
3.   Women college students-Fiction.   4.   Attorney and client-Fiction.   5.   Trials
(Murder)-Fiction.   6.   California-Fiction.   I. Title.
PS3553.H2649T6 2005
813'.54-dc22
                                                                2005014273

Also By David Champion

Easy Come, Easy Go
She Died for her Sins
Too Rich and Too Thin
Phantom Virus
Celebrity Trouble
Nobody Roots for Goliath
The Mountain Massacres
The Snatch

"I'm here to see Bomber Hanson," he said with a self-importance that would have made Attila the Hun blush.

Bonnie Doone, our clueless secretary, frowned and feigned looking down at her appointment calendar.

"Your name?"

"My name is Fabrizio Franceschi."

I could see him from my cubicle off to the side of the central reception room. My door was open. It was hellish hot. We had air conditioning; Bomber just didn't like to turn it on. Saving money to put gas in his Chinese red Bentley, no doubt.

"This house was built in the 1800s," he had said in his own defense—not to be confused with defensively, which has never happened. "In 1880, air conditioning wasn't even a gleam in anyone's eye. They built these places to stay cool in the summer."

Easy for him to say. He managed to get himself ensconced on the north side of the building. I was on the southwest in a room the size and temperature of a sauna.

"I don't find your name here…" Bonnie said to the visitor.

"You don't *find* my *name!*" he puffed up his chest to make him seem taller, more august.

"No…"

"Well *put* it there, then. F-A-B-R-I-Z-I-O F-R-A-N-C-E-S-C-H-I," he spelled it for her, his emphasis suggesting capital letters.

"What is this in regards to, Mr. Franceschi?"

"Life or death is what this is in regards to, Miss," he

1

mocked her, and shot her a stare that would have wilted a more delicate flower than our Bonnie Doone.

"Whose?"

"Whose what?"

"Life or death."

"My *daughter!* Pia." I thought I saw smoke coming out of his ears, but on closer inspection it was only great clouds of hair. "I *have* to talk to Bomber—"

"How do you know Bomber?"

Franceschi stood back and poked his chest with both hands in the gesture of self-evidence. "I'm a detective," he said. "Where is Bomber?" He looked around the central waiting room of our Victorian house in Angleton, California, a comfortable distance north of Los Angeles.

"Well, if it's about Bomber representing you—"

"—My daughter."

"Or your daughter, I'm afraid you'll have to talk to Tod first."

"*Who?*" The contempt for the substitute *couldn't* have been clearer.

"Tod Hanson. He does the first interview for Bomber."

"First interview?" he was aghast. "Like *screening?* Listen, Miss, I'm an important man in this trade. Don't trifle with me."

"I'm just telling it like it is, Mr. Franceschi. Do you want to see Tod or not?"

Fabrizio Franceschi looked over at me through my open doorway, no effort made to hide his disdain.

When I looked at Franceschi, I saw a guy who made a constant effort to look imposing. He wasn't very tall or physically impressive in any detail, but he held his head like a peacock holds his tail feathers. His every gesture said, I'm important and don't you forget it. Of course, in my experience, the guys who tried to look important, weren't.

"Do I need an appointment for that too?"

Bonnie was about to laugh, but, God bless her, she said, "Let me check with him."

She got up and walked into my office with that sway that could have sent any red-blooded male into traction. Franceschi didn't take his eyes off her back.

She entered my steaming office, leaned on my desk to further tantalize our visitor and rolled her eyes.

"Hear that?" she whispered.

I nodded. Her body was hiding me from Franceschi—not that he would have been looking at me if I had been visible.

I scrawled on a piece of paper: I'll see him in a few minutes (cool his heels) have important assignment to finish for Bomber first.

She picked up a pencil and wrote on the bottom: *What assignment?*

I rolled my eyes.

She smiled—this was one of the definite high spots of my relationship with Bonnie. The enemy of my enemy is my friend.

Bonnie about-faced and returned to her desk, which sat behind a chest high U-shaped cubicle wall with a counter on top, put there, I suppose so the fellas could get comfortable ogling Bonnie Doone.

I began writing assiduously on a blank piece of paper. Intelligence such as, the quick brown fox jumped over the lazy purple dog, the nonsense flowing from my pen with alacrity.

Fabrizio Franceschi stared and shifted his weight from foot to foot. Just as I was about to go out and greet him, he said to Bonnie, "You know, if everyone around here is too busy, maybe I should go somewhere else?"

Bonnie, in rare form, said, "Suit yourself."

"I mean," Franceschi snorted, "this is ridiculous. How much time can it take?"

"I expect most lawyers in town prefer you make an appointment, Mr. Franceschi."

"Call me Fab," he said.

"Fab," she said, and hid a snicker behind her hand.

"What's so funny?" he asked.

"Oh, nothing," she lowered her hand and smiled from ear to ear, "I just had to sneeze."

Bonnie looked over at me, and I signaled for her to send Franceschi in.

He had that well-it's-about-time attitude as he strode toward me. I stood and offered my hand.

"Tod Hanson," I said.

"Yeah, well," he said, taking my hand as though it were a great compromise of his principles. "Fabrizio Franceschi. Call me Fab."

There are two kinds of prospective clients: those who are insulted that they have to see me before Bomber will deign to even *consider* their case, and those who are disappointed, naturally enough, that they have to be vetted by an intermediary, but who make the best of it.

Call-Me-Fab was a standout in the former category.

He was a guy with a large personality. It would crowd you out of the room if you let it. He tried to be a hail-fellow-well-met with that "Call-Me-Fab" business, but the easy manner eluded him. Everything he did, every move he made branded him indelibly as uptight. He was uptight even as he sat in the sole chair in my "office".

Had he been the victim of a cheap facelift? Or was it one of those newer operations where they store the skin cells of a dead pig under your skin to make you look as young as a dead pig?

"My God, man, it's hot in here," Fab said, pulling on his necktie knot to loosen it and unbutton the top button of his shirt. Somehow he looked like a man more comfortable in a soft, open collar without a tie. "Why don't you turn on the A.C.?"

I lifted my palms. "This is an old house—"

"—What? You don't have air conditioning? We in the dark ages or something?"

"Dark ages, yes," I said, letting him assume the worst. "Definitely dark ages."

"Short of cash?"

4

"That's a question you may put to the boss—if we get that far."

"So what do you have to do to get his ear?"

"Talk to me."

"I'm talkin'—"

"What do you want Bomber to do, exactly?"

"Okay," he said. "Here's what happened. Saturday night—just the night before last, you understand?"

I don't know if he was looking for an answer, but I nodded just in case. His eyes rolled over to the door, and he leaned closer to me. "This is confidential," he said, mixing a statement of fact with a question.

"Want me to close the door?"

He jumped back in his chair. "Good God, no!" he exclaimed. "It's a friggin' steam bath as it is." He got an idea. I thought that might be an unusual occurrence from the look on his face. He flipped his head behind him toward Bonnie Doone, "You and Miss America out there ever take off your clothes and sweat up a storm in this hot box?"

"No," I said.

"No?" he looked disappointed. "Looks to me like you're missing a bet."

"Ugh," I said, "It would be incest."

"Yeah? She related?"

"Not by blood," I said, "by sweat and tears."

"What's that mean?"

"Shall we get back to what happened Saturday night?"

"Yeah, sure," he said, "If you insist. Anyway, Saturday night, Pia—that's my daughter—came home from a party and found her landlord in her bed," he paused and I could tell he was milking it for effect—"Dead.

"He was a scumbag that one, a real nuisance around the place—came in at all hours without knocking. Nobody liked him. So somebody shot him—I don't know who. I'm just sure it wasn't Pia."

Fab was hard to understand. It was a combination of his

rapid-fire speech, his accent, and the way he arranged his words.

"Shot, you say?"

He nodded.

"They find a gun?"

"Not yet—but there's the rub here. A month ago I gave Pia a gun to protect herself. She protested she didn't need it, but I insisted. The gun is missing."

"Did you tell the police?"

He pulled himself up to full height. "You kidding me? Once they convince me they're on our side, then maybe I'll talk."

"That might not be too smart. Cooperate and they may come to your side."

"From the police you don't have to tell me nothing. I worked the LAPD, Long Beach. You name it, from cops, I know from straight up."

"Where's your daughter now?"

"Pia? She's in school. I told her to just carry on as though nothing happened. But I know they're just waiting to nail her. I want to be prepared. The police kicked everyone out of the house. Her housemates are staying with friends. Pia and I are at the Motel 6 on Camillo Street."

"The police question her yet?"

"I wouldn't let them. Said I'd get a lawyer to be with her. You know how they can trip up the most innocent person. I told them I was hiring Bomber Hanson—they backed off—said they'd give me the rest of the day. So fella, what are my chances of getting in to the man himself? Today?"

"Well, I'll pass it on. I know he'll have to see your daughter before he commits to anything."

"That I can arrange." His head swiveled as though he were looking for a clue. "So this is what you do here? A go-between?"

"More or less."

"Not too taxing, is it?" he said with a self-satisfied smile. "So is it more or less?"

"Whatever you want," I said.

"So there's more? You a lawyer?"

"Yes."

"Well, I'm not settling for *you*, no offense," he said.

"Don't worry," I said. "I don't try cases."

"Just do interviews, huh?"

"Some investigation."

"Investigation!" he pulled himself back again in that I'm-shocked-out-of-my-mind mode. "That's what I do. I don't need any help on that score. I plan to handle this one myself. I don't want any screwups." He looked at me as though he had just shrunk me on his importance meter. "Brother, it's hot. You ought to have some A.C."

"Good idea," I said.

"This a penny ante operation?"

"You might say that."

"Then the fees must be reasonable."

"You might *not* say that."

"So what is it with this intermediary stuff? You guys elitists or something?"

"Just the efficient management of time, so Bomber can concentrate on winning cases."

"Well, you can tell him he can win this one, no sweat. Guaranteed. And he'll have me on his team—and that's one of the top investigators in this profession. And if he takes the case, I promise you this, he'll never see a bill from me."

"I'm sure he'll be glad to hear that," I said.

"Yeah, well, you get him to take the case, I'll see you get yourself some air conditioning in this hellhole. That's a promise."

I took his phone number and bade him goodbye.

2

I don't think Bomber was listening to me when I gave my subtle pitch to stay as far as he could from Fabrizio Franceschi. He was preoccupied with some matter which had taken control of his desk, and he barely looked up as I stuttered through my spiel. You'd think the stutter would diminish if he wasn't looking at me, but no such luck. No one else made me stutter, just Bomber. If he'd paid me a living wage I'd have gone to a psychiatrist.

"Um, yeah," he said. "Well, I guess we have to see the girl. She's the defendant."

"Okay, I'm only saying *he's* a handful."

He waved me off—"She's the one we'd be working with. Set it up. Can't hurt to talk to her."

And that was that. If I hadn't wanted to believe better of him, I'd say the preoccupied insouciance was an act. Bomber smelled a high profile sensational case—lots of press, as he liked to say (disparagingly, to be sure). Tabloid cases I called them. Class against class, plenty of sexual innuendo. Rich landlord *(hiss)* shot dead in the bed of pretty, poor student tenant *(ahhh)*. Though he often took low-profile, even pro bono cases, there seemed to be only one person in town who thirsted for publicity as much as Bomber. That was Webster Arlington Grainger III, our conscientious district attorney—defender of truth and guardian of our fundamental rights to life, liberty and the pursuit of happiness.

I set up the appointment with Call-Me-Fab, and promptly at three he showed up with a pouting, reluctant daughter in tow.

Pia was making her debut at the Bomber Hanson

Victorian Theater in tight low-waist jeans and a tee shirt, advertising some beer, which could fairly be characterized as clinging. The boys would say she was "built." They'd also say, "If you got it, flaunt it," so flaunt it she did.

She had black hair and flashing eyes and her body language bespoke a filly who was itching to get free of the fence and the overbearing stallion.

She hadn't wanted to come. That was obvious. We all settled into Bomber's palatial office with the walls smothered in celebrity testimonials, plaques and anything that the facile mind of man could conjure in the service of ego.

With Fab champing at the bit to say his piece, Bomber opened the festivities. Introductions were made—"Call me Fab, and this is my daughter Pia—"

"So, young lady, why don't you tell me what happened?" Bomber said, addressing Pia.

"Nothing happened," she said.

Bomber raised an eyebrow at Fab, who stepped into the breach. "She came home from a party and found her landlord shot dead in her bed."

At times like that I was glad I was sitting behind the players, and the smile on my face could not be seen by anyone but Bomber, and he seldom looked at me. The ridiculousness of the rhyme gave me a perverse inspiration for a musical composition: Shot Dead in Her Bed. It would be a rhyme. The local free newspaper would feature it on its cover on Thursday. Even the Los Angeles freebies would pick it up.

Since my beloved Joan, stellar violinist with the Los Angeles Philharmonic, had come into my life I'd been writing more violin pieces. What could be better for a composer than to have an in-house violinist?

"I appreciate your help, Mr. Franceschi—"

"Call me Fab."

Bomber sent him a withering glare that didn't wither—"If we are to consider defending…" he paused to look at Pia and consider what he might call her, "the girl," he finally said, "we're going to have to hear it from her." He turned to Pia. "Now, young lady," (striving for a smattering of political correctness, a concept that was foreign to the great Bomber) "please, tell it from the beginning."

She shrugged, "I got home, and there was that creep, in my bed. I thought he was asleep."

"What did you do?"

"I freaked out. But I was totally wasted, so I passed out on the couch in the living room. I just couldn't deal with it."

"That creep have a name?"

"Izuks," Fab chimed in. "DeWitt Izuks."

"Would you let her answer the questions, please?"

"Well, but she wasn't."

"The police aren't going to invite you to participate in their questioning. They resent *me* being there. Now can you be quiet, or shall I exclude you?"

"Yes, no, fine, I'll be quiet. Sure. That's what you want, no problem."

Bomber's glare hung on Call-Me-Fab longer than absolutely necessary. He turned, finally, back to Pia.

"Go on," he said.

"He was such a creepy guy, and like, you wouldn't put anything past him. He thought he was God's gift to women."

"Had he ever been in your bed before?"

"Hey!" Fab couldn't contain himself any longer. I could see the muscles at the back of his neck tensing in hard knots. "I resent that!"

Bomber slammed his hand on his desk causing Pia to jump, and I even saw an involuntary twitch from Fab.

"That's it!" Bomber boomed. "Out!"

Fab was not one to be cowed by *any* man. "This is a free country. We have freedom of speech," he said. "You can't take that away from *any*body."

"No, but I don't have to listen to it. Now, out!"

I saw an amusing reaction from Pia. She seemed pleased. It could have been because she saw an out to an unpleasant business or because someone was standing up to her father.

"But…but…you haven't heard the facts yet."

"And I'm not going to hear them from you," Bomber said with a respectable sneer. "You have two options—either you leave alone or you leave together."

"You don't understand," Fab said earnestly, as though it were in his power to make Bomber understand anything he didn't want to. "I'm a private detective—LAPD, Long Beach Police, the Simpson case. I'm looking for Tyrone Power's missing great granddaughter right now. I'm not *just* some bum you can toss out like an empty cigarette pack. I can save you a *bundle* on investigation. I'll work right along side of you, and it won't cost you a dime."

Bomber stood, getting all he could out of his elevator shoes. "Are you going to leave, or am I?"

"You'd leave us here?" Fab was confused.

"Long enough to get the police to forcibly eject you."

"No, wait," he said.

"Alone or together," Bomber reiterated.

"I'll go, if that's what you want."

Bomber stared at him. He didn't move.

"The thing is, Pia is innocent—she knows it, so she isn't taking things as seriously as she should. I just want to help you out. Answer the questions she doesn't want to bother with."

"That is one of the judgments I have to make, Mr. Franceschi."

"Fab, please," he said, so softly Bomber might have missed the detective's foray into humility.

"I must decide what kind of client she would make—cooperative or uncooperative—serious or not. I may well decide I don't *want* this case. It's a decision I'm willing to consider for another half hour—but not with you in residence, answering the questions."

"Okay, okay," Fab said with a hanging head. "I'll wait outside."

When he closed the door gently behind him, I actually felt a little sorry for him.

Pia shrugged. "That's my dad," she said, not an apology, not an explanation exactly, more a statement of irreversible fact.

"Okay, Pia," Bomber said when he resumed his seat. "What was your relationship with this DeWitt person—your landlord?"

"He was a creepy guy. He was always walking in and out of the house, hitting on all the girls. He told me I was, 'To die for'."

"I guess you were."

"Yeah."

"So he thought you were special."

"He told all the girls that. He was a joke. He's forty years old and trying to be cool, and it only makes him look ridiculous. So we started, like, saying it for everything. Clothes, food, movies—"

"Drugs?" I asked.

"She don't do drugs," came the voice of Fab from the other side of the door.

"Oh, Fab," she said to the door, "*Everybody* does."

"You don't talk like that! It'll get you into trouble."

"You don't think I'm in trouble now?"

Bomber moved without a word to the door, opened it, ignored Fab and strode over to Bonnie Doone's desk.

"Bonnie," he said, "Mr. Franceschi is going to sit down over there. If he makes the slightest move toward the door, you call the police and have him arrested for trespassing."

"Yes, sir," she said in a lovely military fashion.

Like a whipped dog, Fab took his seat. Bomber returned to his office, locked the door and sat down.

"Is he always like that?" he asked Pia.

"Always," she said. "Actually, he's usually much worse—a nightmare when I still lived at home."

"Tell me," Bomber said, his interest piqued.

"Oh, you know," she said. "In high school, he used to lock me in my room at night, 'To protect me,' he said. I'd climb out the window, so he put bars on the windows. He's paranoid. Thinks everyone is going to *despoil* his little girl. Even my mom told him it was ridiculous. She tried to convince him to give me some space."

"Did your father have any reason to be so overprotective?"

"Kind of," she said.

"DeWitt apparently had some interest in you."

"Oh, he's a nutcase. He's got houses up and down the beach, and he only rents to girls. Freshmen mostly. Of course, we didn't find this out until after we had signed a year lease. Now we're stuck there till next January."

Bomber nodded. "Pia, can you think of anyone besides yourself who might have wanted to kill Mr. Izuks?"

"Sure, lots of people hate him, but I don't know anyone who would actually murder him."

"Do you have a boyfriend, Pia?" he asked as though his mind were elsewhere.

"Ex—" she said, hanging her head in a morose reverie.

"How long has he been ex?"

"A few weeks."

"What did he think of your landlord?"

"Hated him. Thought I was *interested* in him. That shows how far-out he was. DeWitt is the *last* person any girl would be interested in."

"Where is this ex now?"

"I don't know."

"You don't know where your boyfriend lives?"

"He lives next door to me, but he's not there. I tried to call him yesterday but no one knows where he is."

"When did you see him last?"

"When we broke up a few weeks ago. He just disappeared after that."

Bomber continued to seem distracted. It was as though

he were asking questions but not listening to the answers.

Pia must have sensed his insouciance. Her interest seemed to lag right along with his. Several times I was about to cut in, but I was pulled up short by not wanting to stutter in front of Pia.

"So, tell me how you discovered DeWitt Izuks was dead," said Bomber.

"Well, we all slept in pretty late Sunday morning. I got up around eleven and went to my room thinking he would be gone by then, but he was still sprawled out on my bed. I was so mad, and then all of a sudden, I saw there was blood all over my pillows. I screamed and screamed until Veronica and Erin came running in. I think Veronica called the cops.

"They came right away and made us stay while they took pictures and stuff. They let us call our parents and asked us all kinds of questions. We were all pretty freaked out. I called my mom and the next thing I knew, Fab was there telling me not to say anything.

"Finally, they took the body away and now none of us is allowed back inside the house. The police say it's a crime scene. They also told us not to leave town," concluded Pia.

"Okay, I've heard enough. I'll represent you if the police want to question you. We'll see how you do there. Your story is a good one. How it will hold up is another matter. I don't mind committing some of Tod's time to the enterprise. The first order of business would seem to be to find your boyfriend. What's his name?"

"Lance Ludlow."

"Tod will meet with your roommates. Let him know where he can find them."

"They are all staying at friends' houses until their parents get here. Do you really think they could arrest *me* for this? I had nothing to do with it, you know."

"We are proceeding on that assumption. Could they arrest *you?* Certainly. He was shot in your bed, probably with your gun that is missing. Any thoughts on anyone who might go to these lengths to frame you?"

She seemed startled at the idea. "Frame me? Why?"

"I've no idea," Bomber said, a little testily. Sometimes he liked to play judge. Traditionally we mortals are constrained from asking a judge a question. *He* asked the questions. And so did Bomber. Here and now Pia Franceschi asked him two questions in a row.

"So when the police call, get in touch with Tod. Oh, and Miss Franceschi, the agreement is only good if the fabulous Fab butts out. Is that understood?"

"Well, sure," she said. "I understand. I just don't know how I can guarantee anything where Fab is concerned."

"Up to you," he said, "and him. If he cares for your welfare, he will stay out of this. The cops are touchy enough without going out of your way to aggravate them."

"I understand," she said, but I could tell from her expression she wasn't optimistic.

He stood. "Tod will give you our phone number. He will have to talk to you more so we won't have any surprises with the police. Can he talk to you without Fab?"

"I can try."

"Tell him it's his choice—this or get another lawyer."

"Could you tell him for me?" she pleaded.

"No," Bomber said, and that ended it.

3

Before we left Bomber's office I suggested Pia and I go alone to the waterfront fish and chips shack—without Fab. He protested, but finally agreed to let us go so long as we were at the motel by seven o'clock.

At the fish and chips place she was a different person without her father on her back. It was as though an albatross had flown from around her neck.

"Any ideas where your boyfriend might be?" I asked her.

"I don't want to have any ideas about him anymore." She shuddered. "He is *so* insanely jealous."

"The obvious question is, could he have been jealous enough to shoot your landlord in your bed?"

"Lance?" she frowned as though considering the proposition for the first time. "Well, somebody did it—Lance, the mailman...all I know is, I didn't do it."

"When did you see your gun last?"

"When Fab gave it to me—I should say forced it on me. I didn't want it."

"Why not?"

"I didn't think I'd ever need it, and if I did I'd never use it—I'd probably shoot myself before the intruder."

"So where did you put it?"

"I didn't touch it. Fab put it in a drawer in my dresser. I made it a point to never open that drawer."

"Did anyone know it was there?"

"Fab told my roommates."

"Tell your boyfriend?"

"Probably," she said. "I've been known to be less than

discreet sometimes."

"And there were bullets in it?"

"Fab said so." She shrugged. "I never looked."

"When did you discover the gun was missing?"

"The police opened the drawer and it was empty."

"Who else knew it was in there?"

She shrugged.

Our order was taken by a curly redhead who looked like it was his first day on the job.

"What can you tell me about your roommates?"

"What do you want to know?"

"How did you meet? Where were they at the time of the murder? Any of them hate DeWitt enough to shoot him? Any of them want to make you look guilty?"

"We met the usual way, I guess—class—one has a friend—you just get together, you know. You talk about houses and find out how expensive it is and how everyone, like, has to share. We thought it would be cool to live right on the beach. This guy was advertising—his ad said women only. We thought that was because he thought women would take better care of his place. Hah! Romeo. You know he doesn't have the slightest idea of how repulsive he is—was."

"So you didn't really know one another before you all moved in together?"

"No, but they all turned out to be really nice. I can't imagine any of them killing someone."

"You said DeWitt owned other houses?"

"Yeah."

"All girls?"

"Of course."

"Know any of them?"

"A couple," she said.

"Any rumors of any kind about DeWitt and any of the girls?"

"Oh, there are lots of stories," she said.

When our fish and chips came—what else?—I prodded

her for the stories.

"Well, the upstairs shower leaked, and he came out to look at it. I don't understand about those things. He looked, and then asked the girl to get in and turn on the water. She was outraged. 'Why?' she asked. 'I want to see where it leaks—' She pointed to the place that coincided with where the water was running down below. 'I want to see how it hits your body and what happens.'"

"Did she do it?"

"Of course not. He must think we're pretty stupid."

"Who was the girl?"

She blushed. "Me," she said.

"Tempt you to go for your gun?"

"Never thought about it."

"What can you tell me about your boyfriend? How did you meet?"

"We had a class together. I could tell he was into me from the moment we met. It took him so long to come up and talk to me, but when he finally did, it just felt meant-to-be, you know? He's a theater major. Gets small parts in plays and stuff. He's from San Diego—in his third year here, but at the rate he's going he's got at least two more."

"He know anything about guns?"

"Not that I know about."

"If he disappeared and you had to find him, where would you look?"

"I don't know. Never thought about it. I guess San Diego—his parents' house first."

"Do you have their phone number?"

"Yeah, in my cell phone." She pulled it out and read me the number. I'd call them in the morning.

My theory about restaurants on the sand is they don't have to serve good food to stay in business. Or, as they might appear in one of those media food-rating articles, five stars for atmosphere, no stars for food.

I paid the tab like the gallant gentleman I aspire to be,

and while she used the restroom, I called Bomber on my cell phone. He did not think going to the police to show them Pia's hands was a good idea. "Like the army," he said. "Never volunteer anything. The burden of proof is with them, remember?"

On the way back to the motel, we drove past Pia's house on the beach. The houses were only seven or eight feet apart and if any architect was employed in any of the projects, he'd never admit it. The focal point of most of the stucco structures (all painted a shade of beige) was the garage and jammed parking area in front. For anyone to get a car out of some of them would require the moving of six other cars.

The place was still taped off with yellow caution tape warning people to stay away from the crime scene, and a black and white police car was parked where normally cars jammed in the driveway.

"DeWitt locked the front door and didn't give us a key," Pia sighed as we drove past. "We had to use the sliding glass door, which faced the beach at the back to get in and out."

Arriving at the motel, we found two cops waiting for us in the lobby, watching the courtesy television. My immediate thought as they looked up at Pia was we represented an intrusion.

I was disheartened to see it was old Mike Venegas they'd sent to do the job. Sarge Venegas was not a happy camper. In fact he was one bitter puppy, putting in his time for a retirement pension that never seemed to come. It couldn't come too soon for the wellbeing of the populace, as far as I was concerned.

Mike Venegas had sheered gray hair that topped a puffy face that had seen better moons. I was always drawn to the wart on his chin. Somehow it seemed to define his character. If you painted his portrait, warts and all, you'd only need to paint the wart.

When he could put it off no longer (was it a commercial break?) the sarge sighed and hoisted himself from the couch, and with some effort, said, "Pia Franceschi, we'd like to ask you a few questions." He looked at me with a crooked eye. "Can't say I admire the company you keep."

"Oh, lighten up, Mike," I said, with a bravado I didn't know was there. "You aren't talking to a hardened repeat offender here."

"Thank goodness for that," he said. "One murder is enough. We're gonna see she doesn't repeat it."

"You arresting her?"

"Up to the district attorney. We're going to question her."

Fearing Fabrizio would soon discover us—as it was nearly seven, I suggested we all go down to the station.

"So call that hotshot dad of yours to meet us at the station," the sarge said.

"Okay," I said. "I'll go along."

He gave me that evil eye he was so beloved for. "*If* I say so," he said.

"Oh, you wouldn't want to deny her her right to counsel, would you?"

He gave me his patented look of disdain. "You?" he said. "You stepping in for the big man?"

"I'll pinch hit until he gets to the station."

Mike Venegas smirked. "Afraid we're going to torture her? Not read her her rights?"

"Now, Mike, you know *everybody* has implicit faith in you."

He bristled and shot me his murderous look of uncertainty. He wanted to take that comment literally, but he wasn't sure he could.

I didn't recognize his sidekick, so I introduced myself in the absence of that grace from the sarge. I saw his nametag on his breast said Kelly. "Officer Kelly," I said, "I'm Tod Hanson."

Officer Kelly nodded and we shook hands. "You're new on the force?"

Officer Kelly looked at Venegas as though he needed permission to answer.

"Yeah," Venegas answered for him, "he's new."

Who else would work with that unhappy lug, I wondered.

"Okay, let's get a move on—we won't cuff you, honey," he said. "Just don't try any funny stuff."

"Oh, Mike," I said. "Really."

"And you shut your trap if you want to accompany the suspect."

"*Suspect* is it?" I said. "Suspected of what?"

"I'm warning you," he said with a menacing glower.

I called Bomber.

4

As it turned out, Officer Venegas, the grouch, did most of the questioning at the Police Station. It's unusual to have the officer who picks up the suspect also be the one who does the questioning. We usually got a better shake. I suspect Grouchy heard there was an attractive woman involved and he wanted to see for himself.

Bomber breezed in a few moments after we did—as though he were lying in wait behind a bush in his Chinese red Bentley, waiting so he wouldn't have to be the first on the scene. He was much too important for that. I had to give him credit—he didn't mind coming out after dinner to protect the innocent.

We sat on one side of the table in the interrogation room. Pia was between us. Grouchy entered carrying a paper bag, which he dropped with a thud on his side of the table. Then he sat with an eerily similar thud. The grouch was no Charles Atlas, more of a Santa Claus in training. He was followed by a guy in a patrolman's uniform who must have been there to play the part of the good cop. He sat beside Grouchy. Our side stared at the paper bag, then tried to look blasé.

No small talker, Grouchy went for the meat: "So the victim was found dead in *your* room, in *your* bed. Want to tell me how he got there?"

Pia glared at him. I was proud of her. Just as quickly she established she would not be pushed around. "I wasn't in there with him," she said.

"We'll get to that," he snapped, as though he wanted her to realize he was in charge and he wasn't going to give up trying to intimidate her. "What do you know about him?"

She told him the landlord story, leaving out the incriminating part about the shower.

Pia handled herself well amidst Grouchy's snarls of derision. He put me in mind of our nemesis, the district attorney, who snarled when he was trying too hard to make an impression.

"Where were you on Saturday night—from six o'clock to midnight?"

"At the party."

"What party?"

"In the park."

"How close to your house was that?"

"Two doors away."

"Go back to your house during the party?"

"No."

"To use the bathroom—get a snack?"

"No."

"Before the party, what were you doing?"

"Nothing special. Had dinner—maybe read a little for my Spanish class."

"Weren't you earning your rent?"

Bomber cut in. "Do you want to explain what you mean, officer?"

"Sure, glad to. It's no secret DeWitt Izuks slept with his tenants in exchange for their rent. You did that, didn't you?"

"Not me."

"Can you tell me what he was doing in your bed?"

"No. He was a creep. He was probably hoping he could sleep with me. He wasn't in the bed when I left for the party."

"What time did you get home?"

"Around midnight, I guess. A little after."

"What time did you get your gun from the drawer?"

"Didn't," she said.

"Come now, how could you shoot him without a gun?"

"I didn't shoot him."

"Why didn't you call the police when you found him

dead?"

"I didn't know he was dead. I took one look in my room, and when I saw that creep, I turned around and went straight to the living room to sleep on the couch."

Bomber said, "Have you established the time of death?"

Grouchy nodded.

"It was while my client was at the party, wasn't it?"

"If she *was* at the party. I don't mind telling you the time of death has been established between eight-thirty and ten-thirty Saturday night. At the time, by her own admission, your client was steps away from her lover in her bed."

"Oh please, officer, that is rank speculation. Perhaps even wishful thinking on your part."

"We'll see about that."

Throughout the questioning Grouchy would carelessly caress the paper bag, running his hand top to bottom and back again. Then he would fold the top and nonchalantly glance inside as though to see if what he'd put in it was still there.

Finally the sarge said, patting the bag, "You know what's in here?"

"No," she said, "I don't."

"Yes, you do."

"No, I don't."

"I think you do."

Bomber broke in for the first time. "Okay, Officer, that's enough fun and games. Pia Franceschi is not a clairvoyant. Why don't you show her what's inside and question her about it?"

"Not so fast," he said, running his hands along the crease as if to seal the contents against unfriendly eyes. "Tell me again about your missing gun," he said pointedly. A third grader could have grasped he was trying to imply the gun was in the bag—from the thud it made it could have been. I expected if he had the gun in the bag he would show it before we left—possibly detaining Pia.

"I've told you all I know," she said.

"Tell me again."

"My father gave it to me for protection—"

"From this...landlord?"

"I don't know—ask him."

"When did you see it last?"

"When he gave it to me."

"When was that?"

"Sometime after school started."

"*When* sometime?"

"I don't remember."

"Could it have been yesterday?"

"No—we've been in school a couple months."

"So he gave you the gun a couple months ago?"

"Maybe six or seven weeks?"

"Where is it now?"

"I don't know."

"Did you ever handle it?"

"No."

"Tell the truth."

"Just a minute, Sergeant. Pia is cooperating, there is no need to badger her. If you have the gun, run a print test on it. Get the ballistics. See if her prints are on it. This girl is innocent of this crime. So if you have the slightest evidence against her, let's hear it."

"Expect me to tip my hand, counselor? Like I'd fall for that trick—like this is my first case."

Grouchy was getting defensive.

"Show us what's in the bag," Bomber said.

"When I'm good and ready," he lifted the corner of his lip.

"Not the gun, is it?" asked Bomber.

"Why don't you tell me?" he said to Pia.

"I don't know what's in the bag."

"I'll tell you," Bomber said. "A stone or some other heavy object that is supposed to make us think it's a gun." He looked at the sergeant. "You can show it, we have nothing to hide."

That was a flush of red that clouded Venegas' face and vision.

"Now let me understand this relationship with your

landlord. Your housemates told me you were friendly with him."

"Not especially," she said. "I'm a friendly person. I try to be nice to everybody."

"*Real* friendly—to Izuks?"

"Not especially."

"Did you sleep with him?"

"Ugh—no! Never!"

"Yet he was in your bed?"

"I didn't put him there."

"No? How did he get into the house?"

"He just came in. Whenever he felt like it."

"Just walked in the front door without knocking?"

"He came in the sliding doors at the back. He locked the front door and never gave us the key."

The sarge raised an eyebrow. "And you all just let him?"

"Let him? It's his house. What were we supposed to do?"

"One of you must have been sweet on him. Your house-mates couldn't stand him—that leaves you."

"I couldn't stand him either."

"So you say." He was not convinced.

"Okay, Sarge," Bomber said. "You can save the sarcasm. Tell us what you have. How do you plan to make a case out of thin air?"

"Thin air, huh? I got a lot more than thin air."

"What?"

Sarge said nothing.

"What's in the bag, Sarge?"

"Wait here," the sarge said, and scooped up the paper bag. "I'll be right back." The silent cop stayed with us, then he too got up and left. Bomber held up his forefinger and touched his lips with it. He took a pad of paper from his inside jacket pocket and wrote the word BUGGED on it.

"How're you holding up to all this questioning, Pia?"

"Okay," she said.

"He's trying to scare you," Bomber said. "I wonder if

he could be so naïve as to think you had anything to do with it?"

"Well, I didn't."

"I know that, you know that and the cops know that. It's what we call a fishing expedition. He's fishing, they have zilch. They have to do something to make it seem like they are doing something."

Bomber put his finger back to his lips. When the cops were satisfied nothing more incriminating would be said, they returned. This time with a cardboard box of a variety of pistols, and no paper bag.

With a macho swoosh, he banged the box on the table. Then he took the guns out, one at a time and placed them on the table.

"Okay, Pia, do your recognize any of these firearms?"

She looked blankly at them and shook her head.

"Look closely," he said. "We have reason to believe one of these was used in the murder of DeWitt Izuks."

"I don't know anything about guns."

"I'm not asking for a scholarly paper, I just want you to tell me which one looks like the gun your father gave you."

"Sorry," she said, and shook her head again.

He lifted the first of the four guns. "This look like it?"

"I don't know—"

"Here," he said, handing it to her. "Lift it, feel it—see if it's at all familiar—"

Bomber shot out his hand and intercepted the gun between the sarge and Pia. "Don't touch any of them," he said. "You know better, Sergeant. That's a trick you might bring off without a lawyer present."

"What?" Pia asked.

"He's trying to get your prints on a weapon. You know, Sarge," he said, turning to the cop, "you can fingerprint my client anytime you want to. Be a lot clearer prints than you'd get on any gun."

"Okay," the cop said, lifting each in its turn and saying, "This look like it? Or this one? Or this?"

To each she shook her head and said, "I don't know *what* it looked like. I never even touched it."

"You're fishing in a dry stream," Bomber said.

5

The next day, I was conferring with Bomber in his office, when I heard a distressed cry from Bonnie V. Doone. I looked up to see the door to Bomber's office fly open and the nightmare visage of Call-Me-Fab burst through it, the voice of Bonnie Doone crying in the background, "Stop! You can't go in there."

"Who do you think you are," Fab demanded of Bomber, "to take my daughter to the police without telling me? *I* know how to handle cops. I've made a career of it." Fab was leaning with both hands on the supplicant's side of Bomber's super-sized desk.

I felt at that moment, the eyes of all the celebrities on Bomber's ego walls looking down on the scene without appreciation or approval.

In the measured tones Bomber reserved for such contingencies he said, "You know how to handle the cops? Fine. Handle them. I wash my hands of the whole thing."

"Not so fast," Fab said. He had a way of making himself seem dominant in any situation—especially unique with Bomber, who, of course, wasn't buying it. "Why isn't anyone looking for the missing boyfriend? Why, it's almost a cliché in murder. And he's *gone. Missing.* Out of sight. And what do the cops say? He's not *technically* a missing person because he's an *adult!* Put your boy on it," he demanded. His tone, I'm bound to say, did not resonate any respect for my capabilities as an investigator.

Bomber turned the page on the legal tablet in front of him and with a pen still in his hand he scrawled a note, then tore the page out and waved it at Bonnie, who was still hovering in the doorway as though she were on call as an extra security force.

Bonnie came forward to Bomber's desk, took the note between Bomber and Fab, who was still leaning threatening-like on that desk, glanced at it and left the room.

In Bonnie's absence, Fab filled the air with his pontification, another reprise of his background on the LAPD and sundry police forces around the country and made a renewed demand for Bomber to marshal all the forces at his command and hunt down the boyfriend, Lance, who by his very absence was calling attention to his guilt.

Finally Bomber had had all he could take and he slammed his palm on the desk with a force that threw Fab back into an upright position. "That's *enough!*" Bomber growled. "I don't want to hear any more of your claptrap. You have the temerity to burst into my office unbidden, and I want you to burst out just as suddenly. I don't take orders from you or anyone else for that matter. I have given my services to your daughter because I believe in her innocence. She has not been charged with any crime that I am aware of. If she has any further need of my services, that will be an arrangement made between her and me and contingent upon the exclusion of your person in every detail and facet. Otherwise, you or she may locate another attorney better able to cope with your asinine shenanigans."

Fab was beginning to sputter when Bonnie Doone waltzed in with a sheet of paper she handed to Bomber who glanced at it before he thrust it at Fab, who was still upright before him.

"What's this?" Fab asked, glancing at the paper, then doing an exaggerated double take. "Five thousand dollars! What?"

"That's your bill for my services to date."

"B-but that's outrageous!" he stammered. It made me happy to see someone else stutter in the presence of the great Bomber Hanson, but it was short-lived.

"That may be," Bomber said, "but you want the best, you pay for the best. Should your daughter have further need of my services, and you find yourself able to stay out of my sight, I might mitigate that invoice."

Fab stared down at the bill in his hand. "You can't be serious," he said.

"Oh, yes I can," said Bomber.

"But what about her missing boyfriend, Lance?"

"Find him yourself. You're a hotshot detective—" Bomber said, standing. "Now I'll thank you to leave my office, and should you ever show your face on these premises again, I will have you arrested for trespassing."

"Well," Fab said, startled at Bomber's audacity, "we'll see about *that!*"

"Yes, we will," Bomber said. "Now *out!*"

Fab looked helplessly around from me, to the photos on the wall, to Bonnie Doone who was still guarding the inner sanctum as though one of us would come to his aid. When it was clear to him that none of us could do anything for him he marched out in a faux huff, his head still held high, but his spirits were low.

6

After Franceschi left Bomber's office, Bonnie Doone returned to what was laughingly referred to as her workstation. Bomber shook his head and said, "What do you make of that guy?"

It was a measure of how unsettling the experience was for Bomber that he asked my opinion.

"Strange," I said, building slowly to the stutter I suffered only in Bomber's presence. "Maybe he j-just l-loves his daughter."

"Yeah—you buy all that malarkey about the LAPD?"

"I c-could check."

He waved his dismissal hand. "No need," he said. "We aren't going within three hundred miles of that turkey." Bomber looked at me as though he had a sudden idea. "Now don't tell me *that's* politically incorrect—disrespectful of turkeys?"

My stutter caused hiccups in my laughter.

I returned to my "office" and planned to watch the clock for the rest of the day. I was looking for the window when Joan might call between her rehearsal and performance with the Los Angeles Philharmonic. Joan was my pretty new girlfriend (also she was my pretty, new girlfriend) who fiddled with the Los Angeles Philharmonic while I burned in Angelton.

When we connected she told me about her rehearsals— she called the guest conductor a time-beater. She meant all he could do was beat time with his baton without adding any soul to the music.

I told her about Pia and her dad Fab.

Joan said, "I knew a father just like that at home." Home was Chicago, where I met Joan on a case I wrote with the title *She Died for Her Sins.*

"He had two daughters and a son. He locked the girls in their rooms, and he didn't care what the son did."

"What became of them?" I asked.

"I don't know," she said. "I could find out."

"Oh, no need," I said. "I don't think the girl is going to be charged with the murder."

It's a good thing I don't give séances, because within twenty-four hours a visitor came to the office to see Bomber, but Bomber was not there. He was at the courthouse appearing on a civil case motion, for which my presence wasn't required.

The visitor was, of course, Pia. If being shunted off on me ruffled her feathers, I couldn't tell; she was pretty ruffled when she arrived.

"I'm starting to get a bad vibe," she said. "The police are everywhere, talking to my housemates and their parents. And everyone is, like, acting really strange to me all of a sudden."

"Because of something the cops said," I asked, "or something they said to the cops?"

"Yeah, well, I don't really know. I mean, everything was normal until the cops came around and, like, started asking everybody questions."

"Any speculation?"

"Not really," she said, then plunged into what I thought was a thoughtful silence.

"Okay," I said, "if you were using your wildest imagination about what they could be saying bad about you, what could you come up with?"

She frowned. I knew there was something there, it just wasn't coming out.

"Well, I don't know, like, maybe they would try to say DeWitt and I had something going, you know." She sighed. "He's such a creep. Like, even if I were fooling around with that creep, would that have to mean I, like, killed him?" She shuddered at the thought.

"Of course not," I said, trying to be reassuring and consoling at the same time. "Why don't you just ask your room-mates what the cops asked them—what they talked about?"

"Yeah, but they're just acting too weird. I can hardly say hello without getting that *look* in return. I mean it's just too *weird.* "

I nodded. "All the more reason to clear the air."

She wasn't clearing anything then. I'd already come to the conclusion she did have something "going" with the late landlord, and it could have been a plausible motive for murder. It wasn't proof positive she was the culprit, but it *was* incriminating.

"Your father thinks your boyfriend killed DeWitt out of jealousy—"

"Oh, he was jealous all right—" then she seemed to catch herself—"about *any*body. All I had to do was, like, look at a guy and he'd flip out."

"Did you ever have a discussion with…Lance, is it?"

She nodded.

"About your landlord?"

"Well, sure," she said. "He thought I had something going with every guy in the universe."

"Did you deny the landlord to Lance?"

"Well, of course I denied it."

"Did Lance accept that?"

She pouted. "Not really," she said.

"Your dad says we should find Lance. Any ideas?"

"I told you he's from San Diego—but don't listen to Fab, he's insane."

"I think Bomber agrees with you on that score. In fact he feels so strongly about Fab, he doesn't want anything to do with your case, if it comes to that."

Pia became suddenly anxious. "But…if I could, like, keep him away?"

I shook my head. I couldn't encourage that fantasy. "I don't think Bomber…or I… or *you* for that matter thinks that is possible."

"Yeah," she said. "I guess…"

She sat there a long time without contributing anything significant to the fund of knowledge, afraid to return to the motel. Perhaps that demonstrated a prescience of which I didn't think her capable.

We went over the details of her case again, and after she left, I spent hours typing up my notes and planning my investigation to prove Pia's innocence.

I had scarcely been home five minutes when the phone rang. I thought it was Joan. "Hi," I said, with the *bonhomie* of high expectations.

It was the answering service. They had a Pia Franceschi on the line who was desperate to talk to me. My inclination was to tell her to call tomorrow. Then I softened. "Okay," I said, "put her on."

"Tod," she said with that crackly cell-phone voice which came at me from the depth of despair, "I need help.

"I have this big, big favor to ask," she said. "Can I stay at your place? Just tonight...?"

"*My* place?" Could I have misunderstood her? "*My* place?" I asked again as though the repetition would solve everything. "My place is small. One room. I have a girlfriend."

"*Please*, Tod, *please!*" She pleaded. "At least let me come over and talk to you for a few minutes. You're the only one left on the planet I can talk to, and I'm *scared!*"

Call me soft-hearted—soft-headed is more like it. I just couldn't resist the plea of a damsel in distress.

I don't know how Pia got there so quickly, or how she snuck out of the motel. She must have been calling from the corner. I was glad to see she came with only the clothes on her back—jeans and one of those short tops that bared the midriff of the young ladies of the day—some who would be better advised to cover as much as they could. Pia was not one of those. Her skin fairly glistened between her low top jeans and her high bottom blouse. If I hadn't had a girlfriend, I would have had little trouble being attracted to Pia. Those eyes were trained on me as two dark, shallow ponds, bleak, still, and all liquid.

She looked around the room as though for a place to perch. She found the lone chair and deposited her dispirited bones on it. "Thanks for having me," she said.

"I'm not *having* you," I hastened to correct her. "You were just coming to talk, remember?"

"Oh, yeah, well, sure."

"I'm making spaghetti, would you like some?"

"Oh, no thanks," she said. "I can't eat in the mood I'm in. But you go ahead. I can talk while you eat."

I cut a piece of bacon in little squares and fried cut up celery and onions and some garlic in the fat. I put the pot of water on to boil. Then I opened a can of diced tomatoes and added it to the bacon mix. All the while there was not a peep from the chair. I wanted to get it over with so she could go back home. She wanted the opposite.

I put my dinner on the table and waved to the silent Pia to join me in Joan's chair.

She hoisted herself from the chair with great effort and slid into the dining chair (first cabin folding chair).

I began to eat. "Mmm," I said. It was good, but not like mother made. "So," I prompted her—"What's on your mind?"

"Oh," she said, "like *every*thing!"

I brought my palm down on the table Bomber-like. "Darn it, Pia, stop *playing*. Do you want to tell me or do you want to go back home?"

She jumped. "I'm sorry," she said when she settled down. "It's just, like, I don't know what to do. My roommates are ganging up on me—my father is running around like a crazy man—playing detective and asking all these questions—then," she said, so quietly I wasn't sure I heard her, "there's the police."

"Police?" I said, perking up. "What about the police?"

"They're going to arrest me."

"Were they at your motel? Is that why you called me?"

"I…it's like, I'm scared. My roommates are telling them *lies* about me."

"If the police want to talk to you, you can't hide-out here."

"No, I..." she stumbled over her tongue. "You just have to let me stay the night. Until this all blows over."

"Murder investigations don't 'blow over'. I can't keep you here—it's a crime to harbor a fugitive—"

"Is that what I am, a fugitive?"

"That's what you are if the police are looking for you."

"Oh, Tod," she said, reaching across the table to grab my hand, "*help* me."

"That's the only way I can help you—take you in—see what they want. If they want to charge you, what evidence they have..."

"Will you defend me if they arrest me?"

I shook my head. "That would have to be Bomber," I said, "and Bomber is up to here with Fab—" I held my hand just below my chin. "You don't suppose you could communicate that to your father, do you? That Bomber won't touch your case unless Fab stays away from him."

"Are you kidding? My father has been controlling me all my life. You think I can wave my hand and suddenly, like, reverse all that?"

"I understand. Okay, Pia, we really don't have any choice. If what your roommates are saying is untrue you have nothing to worry about."

Her lips were quivering. "What if it is true? I mean," she said suddenly, "like, hypothetically."

"If it's true—that you had an affair with your landlord, who wound up shot in your bed, probably by your missing gun—it doesn't look good. Not because that's a solid case against you, but the fact you lied about it..." I didn't have to say more. She got the picture.

"Excuse me, but I have to go to the bathroom. When I come out I want you to be gone. If you don't want to return to your house, that's not my business—but you can't stay here— that *is* my business. If you are still here, I'm calling the police. Clear?"

She stared at me then looked away.

"Is that *clear?*" I insisted on an answer.

"I guess," she mumbled.

I went into the bathroom and closed the door. After a minute the phone rang. To my astonishment I heard Pia pick up the phone and in a cheery voice say, "Hellooo—Tod Hanson's house. How may I help you?" Then there was silence. "Hello?" Pia said, "hello?" again, then she hung up the phone.

When I came out I asked, "Who was that?"

"I don't know," she said. "They hung up."

It was Joan—I knew it.

8

Quickly, I dialed Joan's cell phone. Just as quickly she answered.

"Tod?" she said.

"Joan—did you just call?"

"What was that all about?"

"I can explain—"

"I hope so." She didn't sound convinced.

"She's a client—"

"You have clients now? Opening up in competition with Bomber are you?"

"Well…no. She's Bomber's client."

"You take them home now, do you?"

"No…I…" I was sounding foolish. The more I talked, the more foolish I sounded. "Here," I said, thrusting the phone at Pia. "You tell her what happened."

Pia took the phone and giggled into it. "Who's this?" she asked. When she heard the answer she said, "He sure is cute, isn't he?"

I grabbed the phone back and said, "Joan?" but there was no one there. Further attempts to reach her met with a busy signal, then when that cleared, her answering message.

"Thanks a lot," I said to Pia who turned her face into a mask of innocence. "Who was it?" she asked. "She wouldn't tell me."

"That was my *girlfriend.*"

"Oh, geez," she said, with faux sympathy. "I'm sorry. I guess I didn't have to, like, giggle… and say you're cute."

"No—"

"But you *are* cute. If she dumps you, I could get interested."

40

"Thanks," I said with the opposite spin on the meaning. "Now you're going to have to leave here. Would you, please?"

"Sure, sure," she said. "Do you have someplace for me to go?"

"Do *I*? Go back to your motel."

She shook her head with a resolute and solemn air. "No can do."

"It's your call," I said with a shrug meant to convey indifference, but apparently failing at the task.

While we were arguing about whether she went or stayed, "It's only for one night for gosh sakes. I'll sleep on the floor—in the bathroom if you like—I just can't leave right now. I'm not going to molest you or anything."

"That's a relief," I said, shooting my sarcastic arrow into the air.

"But you are awful cute," she said.

And just as she said it, there was a knock on the door—almost unprecedented that any huckster or proselytizing Christians could find this place.

"Who's there?" I asked, looking at Pia with a question. She shrugged.

There was another knock, stronger this time.

"*Who is it?*" I demanded.

"Fabrizio Franceschi," the inimitable voice answered. "I know you have Pia in there so open up or I'll kick the door down and have you arrested for kidnapping and white slavery."

"Oh, my," I said, opening the door to the fabulous Fab looking through the viewfinder of a small camera and clicking off a raft of flashbulb shots, like a cliché detective in search of a couple *in flagrante delicto.*

"How did you find my place?" I asked, "And what's with the pictures?"

"How did I *find* you?" he boomed. "I'm a private detective, that's how."

"And the pictures?" I said, nodding at the tiny camera. "What's this all about?"

"That's privileged information," he said with his

patented want of clarity. "Are you all right, sweetheart?" he asked Pia.

"Yeah," she said. She didn't seem that surprised to see her dad at her secret hideout.

"He didn't hurt you or…anything?"

"No." Now she seemed to be getting exasperated.

"All right, Fab, thanks for coming. Now take your daughter and leave my home, please."

"Oh, yeah," he said waving the camera as though it were a weapon. "Look who's suddenly a big shot. It just might be to Pia's advantage to stay here awhile."

"Sorry," I said.

"Sorry?" Fab said. "What do you mean, sorry?"

"Can't be done."

"Looks to me like it was already being done when I surprised you in the act."

"Oh, Fab," Pia said. "Really…"

"Don't you, 'Oh, Fab' me. Now listen to me, young fella," he said, turning to me, "Here's what is going down here. I have an attorney-client relationship here. Pia is in trouble—you're going to help her. The police want to arrest her on the thinnest of grounds. Transparent—you can see right through it. She is innocent! *Innocent*, I tell you—and it's going to be your job to prove it—"

Apparently the fabulous Fab didn't understand the presumption of innocence. I wasn't about to enlighten him—he was so amusing on his own.

"I don't mean to burst your balloon Fab, but if you think you have established any kind of relationship with Bomber you're sadly mistaken."

"Don't you tell me I'm mistaken. Wasn't I in his office? Don't I have a bill to prove it?"

"Any relationship you think you *may* have had has been abruptly terminated. Bomber won't touch this case with a ten foot pole."

"So get him an eleven foot pole."

I shook my head. "No way," I said, "Now, get out of my

house—I want to go to bed."

"Oh, bed?" Fab said with a cocked eye in Pia's direction.

"The damage is already done," Fab said, "Pia *has* to stay here."

"What damage?" I asked.

"You know very well what damage—to her virtue."

"You really are crazy," I said, and as I said it I realized that was just what Joan had thought.

"Listen, if we're going to be your clients, we don't have to be enemies. It's really a simple thing," Fab said with a touch of the old plea slipping into his voice. "All signs point to the boyfriend. These crimes, and I've seen hundreds of them, are jealousy inspired. Look at the facts: the gun I gave her is missing. The stiff was most likely shot with that gun. The boyfriend is missing."

"Ex-boyfriend," Pia corrected him.

"If we put our heads together I *know* we can smoke him out. I don't want her sullied by even one night in jail. You know there is no bail for the charge of murder."

I knew of a few exceptions, but I didn't want to confuse the issue.

"So where's the skin off your nose if Pia stays here a night or two until we can find Lance?"

"Okay, I'll just call Bomber and if he says it's okay, it's fine with me."

"Bomber?" Fab was flustered. "I'm talking to *you.*"

Charming, I thought, the way he kicked and screamed when he had to talk to me instead of Bomber.

"He's the boss," I said, picking up the phone. Believe it or not, Fab made a grab for the phone. I was able to divert his hand, pushed my speed dial button for Bomber, and after two rings he picked it up. I told him the whole story—Fab had his wary, watchful eyes on me all the while.

When I finished the tale I heard Bomber building up to his full volume outrage, so I took the phone from my ear so Fab could hear Bomber's response.

"You tell that idiot to be out of there in two minutes or *I* will call the police and tell them where to find them both. Fab can cool his heels in the slammer for trespassing, blackmail, obstruction of justice, conspiring to harbor a fugitive—and I'm just getting started."

Fab grabbed the phone—"You can't *do* this to me," he said. "I'm your client!"

"Two minutes!" Bomber boomed. "If Tod doesn't call me in two minutes to tell me you are gone, I'm calling the police!"

"But..."

The sound of Bomber slamming down the phone startled Fab.

Pia glanced a question at her father. It set him off on another tirade. I watched the clock.

"You have one minute left," I said.

"He wouldn't *dare* call the cops," Fab sputtered.

"Wanna bet?"

"Oh, I don't care," he said, with thirty seconds to spare. "I wouldn't hire Bomber to defend Pia if he were the last lawyer on earth."

"Bomber will be pleased to hear that," I said, and both Franceschis made their exit, but not without a healthy slamming of the door.

9

After Fab and Pia finally left my apartment I began concentrating on the clock. I expected Joan's concert to be over by ten, at which time I would begin calling her to explain the faux pas.

She would have her cell phone in her violin case in the locked room with a custodian. You couldn't be too careful in downtown L.A.

I expected her to turn it off. I hoped she remembered to turn it back on.

To the first message I got I said, "Hi Joan, please call when you get a chance."

To the second, ten minutes later, I said, "Hi Joan, call me tonight, please. Pia is gone. Her father took her." In desperation, I added, "She's *not here.*"

To the third, five minutes after that, I said, "Hi Joan, please call, it's urgent."

Then I waited, and the longer I waited, the more my imagination ran amok. I visualized my Joan in some downtown barroom with a lecherous bassoon player, or engaged in an adulterous affair with her married stand mate in the first violin section.

It was a long night. I called once or twice more (okay, maybe three or four) but left no message. I became more obviously distraught, and I didn't think that was a good face to present my dear girlfriend.

I dozed off in the chair around eleven-thirty that night. The phone woke me up. I jumped for joy at it.

"Tod?" a hushed voice that was not Joan's asked.

"Who's this?" Even at that juncture, I thought this was

someone calling to say Joan missed me—or she was in an accident; she's okay, but couldn't call; wanted me to…

"It's Pia. He's got me hostage in Pomloc. Help me!"

"How?"

"Come get me…"

She'd presented a rather unappealing request. Pomloc was inland from Angelton—about fifty miles north. The round trip would take two hours. Apparently Fab didn't like the accommodations at the Motel 6.

"Pia, I can't do that," I said. "It's late," I added lamely. "I was asleep."

"I have to get away. He's going to keep me in this seedy motel. It's worse than the first one. They'll think I'm guilty because I'm hiding out. I want to turn myself in. I have no one but you to turn to. Please!"

I looked at the clock again as though that would turn it back to a more reasonable hour. It was midnight. I considered her plight. It was true; the district attorney would consider it guilty flight. If Bomber did take the case, I could see the time we'd have convincing the judge it was Pia's crazy father's idea. She wanted to turn herself in but he kidnapped her. "Umhmm," District Attorney Webster A. Grainger III would say, stroking his chin—"and butterflies give milk".

We bantered a bit more. Each exchange caused her more distress. She finally sounded so desperate I repressed my better judgment. I never could resist a woman in distress—

"Where are you?"

"I'm hiding out back—behind the garbage dumpster. If he wakes up he'll be on the warpath. There's a coffee shop on the corner of Grant and Maxwell. You could pick me up there. I'll hide somewhere just in case Fab gets awake and comes looking. I'll watch for you—"

She broke the connection abruptly.

I was committed. I forgot Joan momentarily, and when I remembered her, I realized it was too late to call again. She didn't want to talk to me, she was playing hard to get, or she didn't get the message.

When my mind finally turned to the subject at hand, I realized I should not be on this goose chase without Bomber's permission. Sure I was an adult and all but I did work for him, and he made all the decisions. He would surely consider this safari of mine the work of a hopeless romantic, and I could just see the meeting in his office and hear him saying, "Fine, you want to represent her, you have my blessing. You're a lawyer licensed to practice in the state of California. Go get 'em."

He knew perfectly well I didn't want that. But I knew just as perfectly well he was not about to take the case, not with that nutcase Fabrizio Franceschi hanging over us.

Well, at least I could be there with her when she turned herself in. I can't imagine a more forlorn feeling for a young woman than to turn herself into the police for something she didn't do—that is, I assumed she didn't do it. The police and the D.A. seemed to have other ideas. They must have had some evidence I wasn't aware of.

Wearily, I got in my car and pointed it north on the 101—fifty some minutes later, I pulled into town.

Pomloc was what was cavalierly referred to as a nothing town. It was dead flat, had only the stuff a town needed to get by, including this coffee shop and motel, as well as an ersatz shopping center, a couple of simple restaurants and a Wal-Mart. The federal government had blessed Pomloc with its leading industries: an air force base and a federal prison. Fab must have considered it an ideal place to hide—no one ever went there. Besides, the motel rooms were cheap.

I eased into the parking lot of the all-night coffee shop, but I didn't see Pia. I sat in the car a few minutes then got out. I feared I was being set up for something. That, or Fab had awoken, discovered Pia missing from her bed and set out to find her. Maybe he found her and took her back.

I looked in the windows of the coffee shop. One lone man was at a table nursing a cup of coffee; I went in, just to be sure. I asked the waitress if she had seen a young woman—eighteen-years-old or so in the last hour. She said she hadn't.

Now what? I decided to go back to the car and drive around the neighborhood. But what could have become of her? Fab finding her was one thing. Some miscreant on the prowl taking her was quite another. I couldn't very well knock on Fab's door and ask if Pia was in. First of all, I didn't know what room they were in, or if they were in this motel at all.

I got back to the car. I opened the door and jumped back—Pia was hiding on the floor of the passenger side.

"Let's go—" she whispered hoarsely.

I sat in the driver's seat, turned on the ignition, threw it in gear, took off the brake all in one motion. I uncharacteristically burned rubber.

When we were finally underway, Pia got up into the seat. "I saw him," she said shuddering.

"Who?" I asked, but I knew.

"Fab," she said.

"Did he see you?" I asked.

"No, or I wouldn't be here."

"Why is Fab doing this?" I asked. "Surely he knows flight is considered a sign of guilt."

"He says it's not flight. I haven't been arrested, so I'm not fleeing anything. He says I can say I didn't know the police wanted me. It was only a rumor. Whatever," she looked at me, her eyes on mine imploringly. "You have to help me."

"I'm helping you all I can. I'll go with you to the police, but that's it."

"But I'll need a lawyer."

"There are a lot of them in town. You could even find one in L.A. if you want."

She shook her head. "I want you—"

"I don't do that kind of work."

"Well, okay, Bomber."

Now I gave my head a good shake. "Your dad has put the kibosh on that," I said.

We drove in silence for awhile, until I asked her, "So

how did this all come about—Fab taking you to hide out?"

"My housemates told the cops I invited DeWitt into my bed; that I slept with him to get free rent."

"Did you?"

She shrugged her shoulders, giving me the answer without technically committing. "Fab keeps me on a tight budget," she said.

"How much is your share of rent?"

"Six hundred dollars," she said. "He's like, made the same offer to the other girls."

"What's the offer?"

"You know—a trade. We negotiate. Like, he wants every week, I offer once a month. We settle on twice a month."

"I guess we have to admit under the circumstances, with DeWitt getting shot in your bed and you lying about it—it doesn't look good."

"No," she admitted.

"And Fab didn't know?"

She looked at me, shocked. "Of course not. You think I'd tell him that?"

"But he found out?"

"Probably from my housemates. He's always playing detective."

"Isn't he really a detective?"

"Couldn't prove it by me. My mom supports him. He tries to be the boss and make it look like he's the big support of the family, but he doesn't do anything."

"What's this he says about being in the LAPD?"

"Oh, that! He was a cadet, or whatever they call it—riding in patrol cars at night. Playing cop. Fab lives in a fantasy world. It revolves around making himself look macho—important. And, like, controlling me."

"Why doesn't he want you to go to the police?"

"He thinks they'll put me in jail. He says, like, he knows Lance did it and if he can just keep me out until he finds Lance, everything will be all right."

"What do you think?"

"I don't know what to think—other than I didn't kill DeWitt—" she stopped to giggle briefly— "We called him DimWit—"

"So you slept with him for free rent? Or was it a choice?"

"Fab kept me on a piddly allowance. Said no one ever sent him to school. He earned his way since he was fourteen, blah blah. Like, he isn't even earning his own way today. He takes mom's money and controls me with it. He gave me barely enough to pay the rent. Wanted me to get a job."

"Did you?"

"I had some jobs—babysitting, companion to an old person, stuff like that. But I can't slough off school, I'm not smart enough to pass without studying. Like, I'm no genius or anything, but I do my work. It doesn't leave me time for the kind of full-time job Fab thinks I should have."

"You know where he's going to look first for you, don't you?"

She nodded.

"He's liable to be there when we get there. So I better take you in first. You okay with that?"

She frowned. "I'd rather have a night outside of, what do they call it? Custody. It's so late. I'd sleep on your floor. I just know I wouldn't sleep in jail. Couldn't we go in first thing in the morning?"

I didn't like the idea. I realized she would get the bed and I the floor, my chivalric impulses being so strong and all, and I wasn't keen on sleeping on the floor. But it was agreed that in the morning I would call Bomber for instructions. If he didn't have strong objections to me accompanying Pia to jail, I would do so. Otherwise I would drop her off—or at her option, find another attorney to do the deed.

"I don't want another attorney," she said flatly.

"Suit yourself," I said.

As we approached my apartment above the garage, Pia

became more nervous—fidgeting in her seat, looking all around. "He's going to be here," she said, "I just know it."

We both looked for his car. I tell myself that is the reason I didn't see the other car. So the surprise was saved for when I opened the door.

On the way up the steps Pia had apparently found something funny. Perhaps it was just a nervous reaction to getting this far without her father pouncing on her—a nervous laugh—whatever it was was too loud for that hour of the morning, and I told her—which only made her giggle all the more. I couldn't wait to get her inside.

So I quickly opened the door and grabbed her arm and pulled her inside.

Suddenly my heart dropped through the floor. Seated in my big chair, staring at the scene implacably was my beloved Joan.

10

"Don't tell me…" Joan said, raising a hand against any unstated but visible protest, "you can explain it."

"Yes, I…I can…yes—" I stammered. "She's a client."

"So you said. I'm having trouble connecting a giggling teenybopper staggering up the steps at three in the morning with the word *client.*"

"She needed a place to stay—her father kidnapped her—he doesn't want her to go to jail. Look, there's *nothing* between us that way. Believe me."

Joan looked to Pia for confirmation.

"It's true," she said, nodding vigorously.

"Where are you spending the night?" Joan asked Pia.

"Well…like, here," Pia said.

"I guess I'll be going along then," Joan said, standing abruptly.

"No…" I started.

"That's okay," Joan said, tempering her sarcasm, "this is a nice place and all, but there's not room for two women."

"I'll sleep in the bathroom," Pia said, suddenly coming to my aid.

"Oh, you should be comfortable on your last night of freedom," Joan said. "I'll just trundle on back to my cozy apartment in L.A. Toodleloo, Tod. Sweet dreams."

I stood flatfooted as Joan shot out the door and slammed it with a crack.

"Oh man," I lamented, sinking into the chair Joan just abandoned. It was still warm from her body. Was she really driving over an hour to her Los Angeles apartment at three in the morning?

"Go ahead," I said to Pia, gesturing, "take the bed. I'm going to sit in the chair here and mope."

"I can't *do* that," she said. "Like, I've caused you enough trouble as it is. I can sleep on the floor."

"No, no," I insisted. "Starting tomorrow your accommodations won't be deluxe. I know this isn't the Ritz-Carlton, but enjoy it while you can."

"No can do," she said, and stretched out on the floor. I stayed in the chair until I heard the even breathing that told me Pia was asleep. I had started to doze myself when I heard an insistent knocking on my door.

I was about to open it, but a sudden foreboding held me in check— "Who is it?" I asked.

"I know you have my daughter in there," the voice of Fab tore through the door. "That's kidnapping, and I want her back, or I'll throw the book at you."

Only the fabulous Fab would make such an idle threat.

"Please leave my premises, Fab, or I'll call the police and have you arrested for trespassing and harassment."

"I want my daughter," he said with a whining, insistent voice.

"Come back in the morning," I said, "and I'll help you find her."

"She's in there, I know it—and I want her. Now *Pia!*" he said at the top of his voice. "Come out here this minute!"

I put my finger to my lips at Pia who was sitting up on the floor.

"Please be quiet, Fab. I have neighbors. If I hear from Pia I'll call you."

"Call me where? You don't know where I am—or do you?"

"You're at my front door now," I said, "but unless you leave me alone, you're going to be at the police station."

"You give me my daughter, and you won't have any trouble—open up. *Show* me you don't have her."

"That's enough, Fab. I'm in bed. You wake me up with demands. One more word from you, and the police will take you in. Up to you—"

It worked. To my amazement I heard what I thought were footsteps slinking back downstairs.

I put my finger back to my lips and waved a hand to indicate she should take the bed. Pia shook her head and lay back down. But sleep did not come easily after Fab.

I expect I slept off and on without knowing it, but by the time the sun rose, so did I. When I came out of the bathroom, Pia was sitting up on the floor, rubbing her eyes. Neither of us had compromised our deference by using the bed, though I expect Joan had visions of us frolicking there together.

I hadn't planned on a visitor for breakfast, but I didn't think going out under the circumstances was an intelligent thing to do. I threw together some cereal, milk and bananas, and Pia allowed as how that would be just fine, though I sensed she would have liked to have some of the all-American breakfast beverage, coffee, which I didn't have. I thought the lockup would be able to supply her with that stimulant-depressant.

We both seemed propelled by the big event at hand and consumed our food in less than leisurely fashion, mostly in silence. One exception was my observation that, "Fab is probably waiting outside."

"Yeah," she said. "Like, he doesn't want me to turn myself in. Can he stop me?"

I expect there was an ounce of hope in that question. After all who *wants* to go to jail? Then I had to call Bomber to get him to bless my participation, not a sure thing by any means.

When I reached him and laid out my plan, he boomed into the phone, "Are you *crazy?* If the cops get the notion you kept her overnight, I'll be defending *you* for harboring a fugitive—that is, if you can afford my fee—so save your money, I don't come cheap."

I didn't have to tell him I was suitably chastised, but there were practical considerations.

"What should I do now?" I asked. "T-take her in, call the p-police and have them p-p-pick her up or j-just d-dr-drop her off?"

"I don't want anything to do with that moron father of hers. You say he might still be there?"

"L-likely."

"Impossible."

"P-Pia needs h-help."

"Yeah," he said, "Does she ever. I'm just afraid the kind of help she needs, we can't give her: protecting her from Call-Me-Fab. All right," he said. "You've gone too far. Look *more* suspicious if you don't follow through with this harebrained scheme. Take her in. Make like you're her attorney of record, see that her rights aren't trampled by some bozo at the station. We'll do a substitution of attorney as soon as she finds one. Make that clear to her. Your taking her in is a courtesy, not a commitment. Understand?"

"Yes, sir."

After I hung up the phone, I explained the drill to Pia. Poor kid. She nodded her understanding and sighed her disappointment.

I looked out my windows for a sign of Fab. I didn't see any, but neither did I expect to. He was, after all's said and done, a hotshot detective, and you wouldn't expect a man of that consummate sophistication to be doing a covert surveillance and be in plain sight.

"Ready?" I asked Pia.

She sucked up her courage with a bellyfull of air and nodded.

"If Fab gives us any trouble, I'm calling the police, and they can take you in. I'll go along to see everything is above board." I checked my pocket for my cell phone or, as Bomber calls it, my celery phone.

The homeowner, my landlord, used the garage under my digs to park his cars. I was obliged to park in the street.

Pia followed me down the outside steps and across the driveway to the street. Before I was halfway to the street I saw Fab sitting behind the wheel of his car. He looked like he had not gotten much sleep in that position. But alert or groggy, Fab was not a face I wanted to see.

We had the advantage—my car was on our side of the street and Fab's was across the street and down three spaces.

"Run for it!" I said to Pia and we ran toward the car as Fab leapt out of his car.

"You had her, you liar!" he shouted. We reached the car and dove inside.

"Lock the doors," I said, and we locked ourselves in before Fab reached us.

Fab was at my window signaling for me to roll it down. I shook my head and started the engine.

"I'll have you arrested for kidnapping!" he yelled to penetrate the glass of my window. I began to maneuver to get the car out of its space at the curb. Fab held fast, putting his hand on the door handle as though he could stop the car by brute force. When he realized my determination to drive off, dragging him if necessary, he ran back to his car, hopped in, started the engine and U-turned in time to give us chase.

I am not much of a driver, certainly out of my element as an evasive racing driver, but Fab didn't seem much better at it. As a result, he was more reckless than he might have had to be.

I headed toward the police station—only two or three miles away, driving more sensibly than my pursuer. It was quickly obvious, that was a losing battle.

"I thought Fab was going to grab you outside the station," I said to Pia, "But it looks like he doesn't want to wait that long." Fab had seemed content to follow me on the short residential blocks leading to the stretch along the beach. There, with hotels on one side of the street, a park strip, bike path and beach on the other, Fab shot out to the oncoming lane and tried to run me off the road by nosing his car in front of mine.

A biker was crossing the street in the crosswalk to get from the sidewalk to the bike path. Fab grazed him and sent him flying onto the asphalt like a swimmer doing a racing drive. Fab didn't stop—hit and run—and I couldn't afford to, but it did send Fab back behind me. I slowed for the next stoplight, and went through on the end of the yellow—Fab ran it and pulled again beside me as if to pass. A car came toward him—he forced me to the right, denting my left fender. He swerved and accelerated and got in front of me. I threw my car into reverse just as he was backing up to ram me. I did a three-point turn amid the traffic on Magellan Boulevard and zoomed up a side street. Fab was right behind me.

I was dealing with a desperate man. It looked like Fab was willing to give his life in the cause of keeping his daughter out of the hands of the police. I was about to call 911 when I felt a crunch and my car limped to a stop between a telephone pole and Fab's accordion car.

I grabbed my cell phone and shouted, "Don't open the door!" as Fab was approaching.

I gave the dispatcher my location and said—"I'm trying to bring Pia Franceschi in—her father has rammed my car and he's coming toward us. Need help A.S.A.P.!"

Fab grabbed the door handle on the passenger side— "Open up!" he shouted. We were beginning to attract a sizeable crowd. Pia was petrified.

"He isn't going to hurt us," I said, as he pulled his pistol from beneath his jacket. As if to appease the crowd, he barked, "Police officer! Open up!"

"Don't open," I said. "He isn't going to shoot us." But from the look on his face, I wasn't sure.

He didn't shoot us, but he shot through the side window and out the windshield.

It left two neat bullet holes. So Fab took the butt of his gun and smashed the passenger window. Pia screamed.

Reaching for a miracle, I tried to start the car again. No luck. Fab was reaching to unlock the door. I was trying to fend him off by reaching across Pia to keep her father's hands from the locks, which were recessed inside the door.

Not even the sound of the siren in the distance fazed Fab. He continued to grope for the lock, while I continued to swat his hand any time it got close to his goal.

Irrationally, as the siren got closer, I was thinking how I could mimic that sound in a musical composition. French horns and clarinets? Perhaps a few strings?

Suddenly, in my irrational reverie, I saw the business end of Fab's pistol starring me in the face.

Circumstances like that speed up my learning process, and I quickly withdrew my hands. He kept the gun trained on me and demanded, "Pia! Get out of the car!"

"No!"

"Get out of the car or I'll put a bullet-sized hole in your boyfriend here!"

As the first squad car pulled up he undid the lock and opened the door. With one motion he undid Pia's seat belt and yanked her out of the car.

Two cops leapt out of their police car and using their doors for shields yelled, "Drop the gun!" simultaneously. The gathered onlookers ran for cover.

I thought Fab was considering shooting it out until the second car came. He still had Pia in the position of a shield. Two policemen jumped out of the second car, using the doors as shields, covering Fab from two angles. "Drop it!" the driver of the second car said. "The girl gets hurt, you're history."

"Hey, wait a minute," Fab said, waving his gun over his head. "I was just trying to save my daughter," he said. "This man was kidnapping her. I'm a private detective. I have a license to carry this weapon."

What a nice story, I thought. Could it possibly fly?

"That's very nice," one of our cops said. "So put down the gun. Nobody is kidnapping her now."

Fab considered the logic, then nodded, curtly, and laid his gun at his feet.

Kick it towards us, was the command. Fab waited a beat—could he really have been considering options? But he finally complied and that luckless pistol slid across the asphalt like a leaden hockey puck.

Angelton's finest cuffed the reluctant Fab Franceschi and pushed him into one of the squad cars, while Pia and I got in the back of the second car.

The last thing I heard from Fab before they closed the door on him was, "This is a big mistake—will you guys have egg on your face when you find out who I am—I'm a private detective. I worked the LAPD and…"

11

Angelton's Police Station was in the Spanish architecture mode, like the courthouse down the street and most of the other government buildings downtown.

The planning commission liked conformity, and what better way to conform than to pay tribute to the culture the gringos ran out of town a couple centuries ago.

In time, the gringos became gentrified and too good, or too lazy, for manual labor, so they welcomed the Mexicans back with open arms, to keep the economy humming.

If you weren't on your guard, the cutesy Spanish buildings could get cloying. But there was no easier way into the hearts of the planning commission than to submit a beige stucco house with a red tile roof for their approval. It was failsafe. Arches and pillars were helpful too, but the police station was simple white stucco with the red tile roof—as though the architect was making a statement; the design may be *partially* Spanish but don't get the idea only Latinos get arrested.

The two patrol cars pulled up in the lot behind the building. I got out of one car with Pia, and two uniformed officers helped Fab out of the other. He was talking nonstop, and I expect he had been pontificating the whole trip. How could they make such a mistake? He was one of them. He was only trying to save his daughter from kidnapping.

Fortunately, the cops all knew Bomber, and I rode his coattails, so claiming I was kidnapping Fab's daughter Pia was a tough sell.

That was another thing about Bomber's reach in this small community. The cops were deferential to Bomber, in the hope, I suppose, of his not making a fool of them in court.

The dynamic was clear to the desk officer—Roscoe Nelson by name. I was with Pia, not with Fab. Pia got the preferential treatment. He almost apologized for having to lock her up. A matron came to take Pia back to a holding cell. Pia was placid, going with the flow. I told her I'd be in touch. She nodded fatalistically.

When Roscoe turned to Fab, he was still filling the air with the pulsations of his tightened vocal cords.

"This is an *outrage!*" he croaked. "I'm an officer of the law myself. I demand my rights. I demand a phone call to my attorney if you are to persist in this travesty of justice."

"You have an attorney?" Roscoe asked him.

"*Bomber* is my attorney," he said, with a force not warranted by the circumstances.

Roscoe looked at me. I rolled my eyes.

"I caught that," Fab said. "Bomber will get me out of this. He and I are close. Ridiculous as it is, I'm in trouble, and that's Bomber's shtick—he helps people in trouble. It's no secret he and I met just yesterday. We're practically brothers— he respects me. It's mutual."

Roscoe Nelson looked to me. I closed my eyes in forbearance.

Roscoe kept making attempts to get the requisite information from Fab, but it was a long haul between his self-serving declarations and his birth date, full name, and address.

"Listen," Fab said to me, "get Bomber over here. This is too many questions."

I looked at the desk officer—he nodded. I took the phone he handed me and dialed Bomber at home.

"What's up?" he asked. "I was just on my way to the office." This was his code question for, why are you bothering me at home?

I told him the story and ended with, "Fab w-wants you to come down here and b-be his attorney f-for the ordeal."

"Jesus Jenny!" was Bomber's response. "Does the man

have no shame?"

"No," I said.

Fab sputtered an expression of mirth, "The kid *stutters* when he talks to his dad!" as though he had just discovered America. In the silence that followed, Fab was the one to disturb it—"So when can he be here?"

I turned to Fab. "I don't think he is coming."

"What are you talking about? We're practically brothers. I help people in trouble. So does he."

He spoke so loudly I didn't have to repeat what Fab said to Bomber. Bomber said, "Yeah, that's right. I help people in trouble, not people who *are* trouble."

"Here, give me the phone," Fab, still handcuffed, demanded.

I gave it to him. Bomber hung up just as Fab was reaching awkwardly for it.

"He got cut off," he said.

"No," I said, "he hung up. You're going to have to find another attorney."

"But—but this is such a travesty. I try to save my daughter from a kidnapper and this is what it gets me—" he held his handcuffs aloft and shook his head.

"May I have a word with Pia now?" I asked. Roscoe picked up the phone and asked someone to take Pia to the conference room. Then he nodded his head in the direction I wanted to go. Fab was still at it, though I don't remember exactly what he said. It was all starting to run together.

We reached the windowless room with a table and chairs—we took two of them. The matron tactfully waited outside. It didn't take long to size Pia up as low flight risk.

"What a morning," I said.

"Yeah," she said, sitting facing me across the table. "What's going to happen to me?"

"Let's hope you are going to be inconvenienced for a short while, until the enemy comes to his senses. I don't see any kind of strong prosecution case here. I don't see anything but circumstantial evidence, and that seems pretty thin. These high profile cases often bring out the worst in the establishment. Lot of pressure for results."

"Will Bomber defend me?"

"We'll see," I said. "Your father didn't make a very good impression on Bomber."

"No," she said.

"Bomber will ask me for a logical scenario to counter the state's claim that you shot DeWitt with the gun your father gave you a month or so before. You were sleeping with the landlord for the rent, and you couldn't take it anymore?"

"Yeah," she said, "like, it doesn't look good."

"Do you know where the gun is, Pia?"

She shook her head.

"If we could find that we could rule you out."

"No idea."

"How about your boyfriend—Lance?"

"Ex," she said flatly.

"I called his parents in San Diego. They haven't heard from him in a few months. Where else should I look for him?"

Pia looked at me a long moment, as though I had inadvertently and surprisingly struck a nerve. Then she looked away.

"It's important, Pia," I said, beseeching her. "With your life at stake it won't help you to cover up anything."

"My life…?"

I nodded as solemnly as I could. Though the death penalty would have been remote in her case, a hefty prison sentence would certainly alter the quality of her life.

Without looking back at me, Pia opened her mouth, then closed it again.

"Why are you protecting him?" I asked. "He left you, didn't he?" I prodded.

Absently, her hand drifted to the back of her dark hair, and she began to twist it between her fingers. She was becoming adept at wordless answers—I only wished I had been as perceptive about understanding them.

While Pia was twisting her hair, I thought of Joan. I should have kept my mind on the business at hand, but the subject of breakups was too close to home for me to ignore.

"Did you mean that?" she finally spoke as though spooked.

"What?"

"That my…life…you don't…" she stopped twisting her hair, "could they actually, like, put me to…death?"

"In a murder case—" I began, then decided it was to my advantage to leave it at that. I just shrugged.

She took a deep breath, sighed and went back to twisting her hair.

"Pia…?"

"Okay," she said. "Like, sometimes he goes up to the mountain—Lopez Flats—old hippy place…sometimes…" she said and trailed off.

I knew where it was, and I went.

12

Through it all, I couldn't get Joan out of my mind. I called her at every opportunity, leaving contrite messages, while realizing she wasn't going to answer. I gave up. This is not to say I planned to sacrifice her, I just realized I would have to pay her a persuasive visit.

Joan was approaching her busy spate of concerts, which were usually Thursday night through Sunday matinee. I planned to surprise her after the Sunday concert.

In the meantime, I found myself driving up the mountain seven and a half miles to a quaint commune settled by the original hippies some fifty years ago. The area of basic shacks and derelict trailers had been spruced up somewhat, but the modest residences were still without electricity, gas, or city water. There were perhaps ten to fifteen living units of every stripe. The closest communities were about eight miles away on one side and fifteen on the other. Not too convenient, but the prices were right for these latter-day hippies, some genetically connected to the proud founders of the movement.

I passed some cars without tires and a fuchsia colored Volvo, the ancient paint crying for help. It had a fading bumper sticker that said, "Practice random kindness and senseless acts of beauty."

The first guy I came to was glaring at me as though at an undesirable. Then I realized I had been thoughtless to wear my suit. He had a large and unruly salty beard that came to a point like a corkscrew. He wasn't very tall, but he made up for it with his condescending attitude.

"I'm looking for Lance Ludlow," I said, with what I

thought was a quiet humility. It cut no ice, melted no hearts. This dime store Santa glared at me still. "Never heard of him," he said with an attitude that told me he had and dared me to do something about it. Nor had I missed the sidelong glance at my suit and tie. He wore a ratty uniform of T-shirt and jeans, the former carrying a mélange of antiestablishment fervor, and his reception indicated I was part of the same establishment.

I looked down at my own clothes, thanked him and left.

At home I rummaged through my spare, few drawers and took out the dirtiest looking T-shirt and rattiest jeans I could find. I put them on and checked myself in the mirror. Could I pass? I wished I'd had time to grow a beard. My landlord was kind enough to let me park my bicycle in the garage below my apartment. I took it out and gave it a quick once over. It wouldn't fill the bill as a bike some homeless guy might ride, but it would have to do. Pulling the quick release lever, I took off the front tire, opened the trunk of my car, and put the bike in, then the tire. The bike stuck out a couple of inches so I had to tie the trunk lid to the latch.

I thought of Bomber's Chinese red Bentley and wondered how the bike would fit in the trunk. I quickly put the ridiculous notion out of my head.

I headed my car to the hills and in a few minutes was winding around the foothills, leaving the town behind, every mile leading to the thinner housing density. I started up Glacier Road, passed the Episcopal monastery, and in another two miles the houses began to thin to none. I parked the car in one of the cut out parking areas a mile or so from my destination. I could have gotten closer but the idea that I could bike up this mountain was fanciful enough so that I'd better work up some perspiration to legitimize the ploy.

I put my bike back together, took a look at the commanding view of Angelton far below and then at my antiquated bike. I thought it would pass muster in this neck of the woods. Lopez Flats was around three thousand feet above sea level—where I lived. A number of local bikers were able to make it up this mountain (and another one thousand feet to the top), but I wasn't one of them. Even this mile, all of it up, was a challenge for my heretofore-sedentary bones.

The road at that altitude was pothole city. Drastic evasive action was required to keep your liver from jarring out of your body. I envied those with shock absorbers on their newer bikes. But had I had one of those, I would surely have been greeted again in this hippie Heaven as an enemy.

I had, with a great effort, made it to the yawning mouth of the infamous Flats. Fortunately, I didn't see the bearded gent who greeted me on my prior visit.

On my bicycle I was more aware of the dirt road beneath me. It made the rutted main road seem like a piece of glass. I employed the better part of valor and got off the bike.

The first person I came to was a young woman who had sacrificed her shape to the infant she was carrying in a sack on her chest. The woman wore a tie-dyed dress that looked like one of the earlier attempts of one not too adroit at the procedure. It was a blur of blues, reds and greens.

I smiled at her. She smiled back. Behind her were a mess of shacks, mobile homes and even a couple of sizeable tents. A quick calculation of the area led me to believe the population hovered between twenty and fifty.

"Hi," I said in my most down-home, devil-may-care voice, "Lance around?"

From the startled look on her face I speculated she was surprised that anyone knew Lance was there, or defensive in her protection of him from the prying public eye, or surprised that I should ride my bike all that distance in search of someone who wasn't there.

Before she answered, I switched gears, "That a baby in there?" I asked.

She smiled. "Yeah," she said.

"May I see him or her?"

"Her," she said, proudly taking the child from her chest and holding her out for me to see.

"Oh, she's gorgeous!" I said, and the new mom beamed.

"What's her name?"

"Tiffany," she said.

"Oh, that's nice," I said.

"And I'm Calico."

"Wow, another special name. Where did you get it?"

She beamed again. "Mom and Dad liked it. They were looking for something special."

"Well it *is* special. They live here?" I asked, waving an arm around the flats.

"Yeah," she said. "I was born here."

"Wow, three generations now."

"Yeah."

Lance had slipped out of our conversation, and the tenor had changed. Fascinating as she and her child were, I'd come on business.

"Well, that's great!" I said with an enthusiasm that could have fooled me. Then, as an afterthought, I casually slipped in, "Er, you think Lance is around?"

"Lance? Well, I don't know. He has been—" she waved toward a tent at the far end of the dirt road, "Check it out, the tent."

"Thanks," I said.

I pushed my bike down the washboard road to the tent, which looked more like a wigwam. Laying the bike down, I moved with some becoming stealth to the opening—a flap that lay over on the tent wall. There was a fellow inside, lying on an air mattress, his hands beneath his head, staring up at the apex of the wigwam.

"Lance, my man?" I said, as I thought the hippies might speak.

His wary look at me told me two things: he didn't want to be called a hippie, and he was less than happy to see me.

Lance Ludlow was a lanky lad. Dark and brooding, there might have been some Mediterranean influence in his background. His anthracite eyes were glued on to me like a pair of blood sucking leeches, and he seemed to want nothing so much as for me to disappear.

"Yo," he said without much enthusiasm, and without moving a muscle. "Who are you?"

"I'm Tod Hanson. I'm an attorney representing Pia Franceschi."

"How'd you find me?"

"Pia said you sometimes come up here. She says hello, by the way."

He looked up, hopeful.

"She misses you," I ventured, as I stepped into the wigwam and sat down on a rug.

"Fab still around?" he asked as though he couldn't have cared less.

"He's in jail."

That bit of news energized Lance. His head snapped back in my direction and he sat up and stared at me. "You kidding me?"

I shook my head.

"How come?" he asked as though he were afraid of the answer.

"Long story," I said.

"I have time," he said. So I told him the ugly tale.

"Pia couldn't have killed that guy. She just wouldn't be capable of doing something like that."

"That's why we're trying to help her."

"How long can you keep Fab in jail?"

"Don't know. Why?"

"No reason," he said, trying to fake an insouciance he didn't seem to feel.

"Pia misses you—" I said, I don't think he realized I was speculating.

"I didn't kill that guy," he said.

I hadn't asked.

13

I let Lance hold that volunteered thought—that he didn't kill DeWitt. We looked at each other with a sense of foreboding. I had the suspicion he had protested too much. Lance had the same notion.

"Why don't we start from the beginning," I said, with a gentle prodding in my voice.

"I hardly remember where the beginning is," he said, staring blankly. "I guess I first saw Pia in class—Introduction to American Lit. I fell in love right on the spot without ever talking to her. After that I couldn't concentrate in class, I was staring at her all the time. It was weeks before I worked up the nerve to talk to her. It was at the break. I was so nervous I was trembling. But she didn't seem the least bit nervous—she hadn't been sweating about the first meeting like I was. She didn't even notice me. Like I was just part of the furniture."

"But she came around?" I asked.

"Reluctantly," he said. "She was scared of relationships, she told me. I didn't find out right away. I took her to coffee and there was chemistry there, we could both feel it. We started going out, and I was never so happy in my life. Like I was in love, man."

"Was she?"

"That was the funny thing. She seemed to be, but then she would pull back, like she was afraid of something. As time went on and we got closer, I found out she *was* afraid, and what she was afraid *of*."

I knew the answer, but I asked anyway, "What?"

"Fab—her father."

I nodded. "Did you ever meet him?"

"Yeah," he said, his features brooding darker, then he fell silent.

"And?"

"It was not a happy meeting. Fab was furious, as though I were public enemy number one, molesting and abusing his precious daughter. He told me he wanted me to back off—Pia was too young and inexperienced in that way, and he thought our relationship would interfere with her education, and that was the most important thing. He had scrimped and saved to put her through school, and he wasn't going to stand idly by and see her throw it away on some bum."

"He called you that? A bum?"

"Yeah."

I shook my head, clucked my tongue and made all the appropriate sounds of sympathetic disbelief.

"Piece of work," I contributed.

Lance nodded and sucked in some air. "I loved Pia, but I couldn't take Fab. For a while I stuck it out. Then he made my life so miserable I folded. She was always short of cash—Fab hardly gave her any money—so she found a way to get her rent comped."

I could see it in his eyes, and posture, and on his mouth, but I asked anyway, "Bummed you out?"

"I was *wrecked.* " he admitted.

"Miss her?"

"Terribly. I'd stake my life Pia didn't, wouldn't and couldn't kill anybody."

"Fab says you did it," I said. "Jealousy."

"He would," Lance said, deflating. "Pia would be a lot better off if that buzzard buzzed off."

"You won't find a lot of sentiment on the other side of that issue—" I said. "In the meantime, your absence creates suspicion."

"What do you want from me?"

"Just the truth—something helpful. Where were you on

the night of the murder?"

"Oh, yeah. That night there was a party in the park—that little patch of grass down on the ocean—between a couple of houses. I was thinking Pia and I could get back together."

"Did you?"

"No, I didn't have the nerve."

"Why, was her father there?"

"I didn't see him."

"Did you go to the party?"

"No," he said, "But Pia did."

"How do you know if you weren't there?"

"I didn't say I wasn't there, I said I didn't go to the party."

In my time as Bomber's investigator I'd heard some convoluted logic, but that one, you might say, took the cake. My expression telegraphed that sentiment to Lance Ludlow.

"Well, see, like I wasn't *at* the party, I was *watching* it."

"*Watching?*"

"Yeah. A friend had a place overlooking the park. That's where I was—full time."

"What was the time frame?"

"I got there about seven. People started showing up around about seven-thirty. The band started at eight. That's when it got crazy."

"What time did Pia arrive?"

"Before the band started, say ten of eight or so."

"Do you know her housemates?"

"Yeah, sure."

"Did you see them?"

"Off and on. But I mean, I was focused on Pia that night."

"What time did Pia leave?"

"Around midnight, when the band shut down."

"She didn't leave the party before?"

"No."

"You sure?"

"I'm sure."

"Even to go to the bathroom?"

"They had porta-potties at the park. Pia never left."

"You mean you sat somewhere for five hours straight staring out the window at Pia without moving yourself?"

"Yeah."

"Did you go to the bathroom?"

"No."

"To the kitchen, get a drink? Anything?"

"No."

I waved my head from side to side in three slow motions. "That's a hard sell, Lance," I said.

"Listen," he said, and he was angry. "If you ever felt about anyone the way I feel about Pia, you wouldn't be questioning me."

That slammed me between the eyes. When I recovered, I said quietly, "I believe you."

"Thanks," he said with an edge of sarcasm. I didn't blame him. I was very much afraid I was experiencing the same rejection myself. I could even visualize myself spying on Joan. I was going to the Sunday matinee and, in essence, I'd be doing just that.

"Did you know Pia had a gun?"

He nodded.

"When did you find out?"

"When she got it."

"Ever see it?"

"No."

"Know where she kept it?"

He shook his head. "If she ever told me, I forgot. We broke up right after she got the gun."

"Know where she got it?"

"From Fab, where else? He was probably hoping she'd shoot *me* with it."

"How far do you live from Pia's place?"

"Next door, why?"

"Why? You know why. Fab is yelling at everyone he sees to find you. He's convinced you did it."

"He's wrong."

"So—can anybody testify you never left your post watching the party?"

"The only person I can think of is my friend Kyler Ziskind. He lives in the house I was sitting in. He hung out with me there for a while," Lance said. "People came and went. Being next to the party, it kind of became part of it."

"But can anyone verify you didn't leave there?"

"No."

"Did Pia talk to anyone while she was at the party?"

He looked at his feet—"Yeah."

"Who?"

"A couple guys."

"Know them?"

"Don't want to."

"See any of them leave the party?"

"No."

"Are we talking about two guys? Or six? Or ten?"

"Seemed like every guy at the party came on to her," he said, prompting sadness. "I don't blame them."

"So you're sure Pia was nowhere near her room around nine p.m.—say eight to ten?"

"Positive."

"Wasn't Fab just window dressing in your breakup?" I asked. "Fab, irascible as he might be, paled next to the randy landlord, no?"

He didn't answer. I didn't press because I needed him. I didn't discuss with him the brutal paradox—if he helped clear Pia, he would incriminate himself. I didn't have to tell him, I could tell by his expression he already knew.

"Thanks for your help," I said. "You might be able to save Pia by showing up in court. Any chance?"

His attention was still on the wall of the tent—away from me. "I'll think about it."

"While you're thinking, is there any way I can get in touch with you here? Any phones on the place?"

"No."

"Any computers? Anyone get e-mail?"

He shook his head. "Pretty isolated here," he said. "That's why I like it."

"So how can we get in touch?"

He didn't answer for an eternity. I weighed my options. I couldn't think of any benefit of walking out, save perhaps little things, like self-respect.

Finally, I turned to go. Lance had the nerve to say— "Give Pia my love."

That made me angry. "That's a copout," I said. "*You* give her your love. Go visit her in jail. Tell her you'll testify for her. You do and she'll be acquitted."

With my back to him, I heard a huge intake of breath. As I pushed the tent flap back for my exit, I heard him say to my back, "I'll think about it."

Riding my bike down the hill was a lot nicer than riding it up. I decided it was something I should think about—riding more often.

Back at our Victorian office building, Bomber was occupied at his desk, talking on the telephone. When he wanted to see me, I dropped everything and hustled into his office. When I wanted to see him, I cooled my heels until he was disposed to grant me audience.

You might think that after all the years I have been locked in indentured servitude with the great Bomber Hanson, I would have overcome my stutter in his presence. I didn't do it with anyone else. It wasn't only intimidation—a lot of people intimidated me. This was a special intimidation that went back to my childhood. Bomber was a fairly attentive father to Sis and me. I wouldn't say doting, that was not his style. He *was* authoritarian. We didn't dare say "Boo!" when he was working on a case in his study at home. He was often preoccupied, but when it suited him, he could be attentive, parental even. He taught me to play chess when I was five or six and pounded me mercilessly until I lost interest. I've come to look on that chess dominance as flattering. He didn't see any need to pander to my lesser skill— no reason to let me win a game or two to bolster my confidence. From the beginning, he treated me as an equal. I wasn't, of course, but the mere treating me as one gave me a peculiar kind of hope in my future. I was a reasonably secure child, free of any abnormalities. Sis had the corner on abnormality. She was born with a withered arm, and though she was a delightful, intelligent and personable young woman, she despaired of ever landing a man. So she drove herself off the Angelton pier in the middle of the night.

Bomber went to pieces. He was immobilized by his grief. I stepped into the breach—a kid taking over the family in the interim while Bomber pulled himself together. It never seemed right to me—I was uncomfortable about it, I just didn't see any other option.

After Bomber eased back into the driver's seat, I could no longer speak to him without this ridiculous stammer. It was as though that were my contribution to salve the embarrassment he must have felt for defaulting his position as head of the household to his young son—Bomber never said anything about that awkward period in my upbringing. Was I waiting for him to blow up—reprimand me for my audacity? Was my stammer a defense? A proclamation that I knew he was superior, and to prove it, I couldn't speak normally in his presence?

Or was it due to a morbid fear that Bomber might slip a gear again—my greatest fear being that it might happen in the courtroom?

Of course, with each day distancing us farther from the trauma, my fear should have diminished proportionally, and in a way, it did—but the germ remained. I may have been making progress, but it was slight.

We never discussed that either. There were subtle exchanges that signaled his understanding. He never pressed me to speak voluminously in his presence. He was satisfied with a nod, a shake of the head, or a parsimonious answer of one or two, sometimes three, words. That I could usually muster without a glitch in the flow.

I've tried to overcome it, so far without success. So, while I was awaiting being summoned to his august presence, I attempted to tame the butterflies that were running rampant in my stomach. It was no secret I was a happier man composing music. I even got some pleasure from investigating the cases.

The only thing that scared me more than an audience with Bomber where he sought my counsel, was having to wait for a meeting where I was in the position of trying to convince him to do something he didn't want to do. Like now.

Our resident poster girl for Beauty over Brains, Bonnie V. Doone, announced in her inimitable way, "Honcho wants to see you, sweet meat." Before I knew it, I was sitting in the great man's office.

"Well, you've had quite a few days," he said, starting the ball rolling.

I nodded.

"And the little lady is reposing in the slammer, where the pillars of the establishment have seen fit to place her for the protection of society?"

I nodded again.

"And you would like me to defend her?"

"It would be n-nice," I said.

"I suspect you're convinced of her innocence?"

I nodded.

"Well, so am I."

I beamed.

"So any lawyer worth his salt should be able to get her off. What evidence have you discovered?"

I told him about Lance.

"Very nice," he said, "but the lad will not come forward—I'll bet you dollars to doughnuts. He's the ideal suspect to take her place if the D.A. swallows her alibi. He was next door, torn apart with jealousy—just as Fab would have it. Lance was watching Pia, but no one was watching Lance."

"He still l-l-loves her," I said.

"Well and good, but the test will be, does he love her enough to trade places with her in the hoosegow?"

"Doubtful," I said.

"He says he didn't do it?"

I nodded.

"Believe him?"

My nod was slower this time.

Bomber stared at me, as though trying to read my real thoughts. We both knew statistically normal people didn't murder, and we were dealing with normal people. The murder class was brutal, unintelligent, animalistic—yet there were exceptions, and those exceptions were what was noticed, publicized, talked about.

Breaking his stare, Bomber jumped to his feet. "Come on," he said, and we headed for the Bentley, in which he drove me to the office of the district attorney of Weller County, the honorable Webster A. Grainger III.

Bomber didn't bother with Web's secretary, but barged right into his office, with me trailing behind.

Web looked up, startled as he always remarkably was when Bomber made a surprise visit—which was only when the big man wanted a favor. Not many of the favors were granted, but that was okay with Bomber. It was a psychological game with Bomber, and no one served as a better psychological target for him than Web.

"Sorry, Bomber, I didn't hear you knock," Web said sardonically.

"I didn't," Bomber said in his bully mode. "What? Should I be afraid of catching you in a compromising position or something?"

"Of course not!" Web exclaimed.

Unbidden, Bomber plopped himself in the chair facing the D.A. I knew Bomber would have preferred to be on the other side of the desk, but that would have entailed a rather awkward maneuver, so he made do. I slipped into a chair at the back wall.

"What do you want?" Web asked curtly. "And make it quick—I'm up to my eyeballs in work."

Bomber waved his hand at Web, indicating that was no concern of his. "You've got Pia Franceschi in the slammer. She doesn't belong there."

Web raised an eyebrow. "The evidence says otherwise," he said.

"No it doesn't," Bomber reposted. "She's in there as innocent as the day she was born—along with her father, who's guilty as sin."

"A somewhat lesser charge, however," Web muttered.

"That may very well be, but it is a serious and felonious charge, and there are broad daylight witnesses," Bomber said. "I don't need to remind you, I'm sure, that there are zero witnesses to the DeWitt Izuks murder."

"What's your point, Bomber?" Web asked, in just such an insulting fashion, Bomber felt compelled to answer in kind.

"Oh, sorry, I forgot, you *are* a little slow on the uptake," Bomber said. "I thought you'd realize if I came to see you— never the highlight of my day—I must, *ergo*, have a stake in the case."

"What's your stake?" Web asked through tight lips pressed white in his fuming red face.

"Both of them are clamoring for my representation in the courts of law."

Web shrugged as if to say, What else is new?

"My options are these: one, I take the girl's case—a slam dunk for the defense. Two, I take *both* cases."

"So?" Web said. "You're here to offer me a deal I can't refuse, is that it? What's the deal?"

"I thought you'd never ask," Bomber said with that supercilious smile he had honed to a fine art. "The deal is your choice. You keep him in the slammer and I take only her case— let him settle for a second-rater you can eat alive in the court-room. You release the fabulous Fab and I take *both* cases."

Web's smile was not without admiration. "Clever," he said, "I'll give you that—but unworkable. The statutes conspire against it. I know what a pain Franceschi is, but I can't hold him indefinitely and that's what you're asking me to do."

"Not indefinitely. Just till we can clear up the mistake you made arresting Pia."

"He'll post bail," Web said, shrugging his shoulders.

"Ah," Bomber said, " you know there are ways."

"It doesn't make any sense from a legal standpoint," Web said. "It isn't even logical. And I believe it smacks of illegal bribery."

"Oh, nonsense. First, I brought a witness to the conver-sation." Bomber looked around the room, "I don't notice you have any. Second, how could you go public with such a conver-sation? Who would believe that you cared a fig whom I repre-sented? Why, it would look like there was cause for you to harbor some fear of me—spoil the fearless defender of truth and justice image." Bomber shook his head and clicked his tongue.

"You think your offer and its rationale are more defensible? You want to keep your prospective client in jail so he won't get in your hair while you are defending his daughter. So methinks if I let him out of jail you will have less incentive to defend the girl."

Bomber seemed surprised at Web's perspicacity.

"Try me," Bomber said with the gesture of a grandstand poker bluff. "The girl is *innocent* and deserves the most vigorous, conscientious, and effective defense. I would be remiss in my duty to society to turn my back on her."

"And him?" Web asked, eyebrows askance. "Can you offer some similarly high-sounding rationale for defending him?"

"Certainly not. He's a miscreant and should by all means remain under lock and key for the duration. My offer is not for my sake, but for yours."

"How very thoughtful," the district attorney said, laying on the sarcasm.

"Think about it," Bomber said, rising.

"Wait," Web said—and that was a word Bomber loved to hear during an exit.

Though Bomber was shorter than Web, he was standing and the district attorney was sitting, giving him the psychological advantage. Web must have known Bomber wore elevator shoes, but if he ever mentioned it, it wasn't in my presence.

"Hypothetically, and off the record," Web said, "what would it take to get you to walk away from both cases?"

"That's a no-brainer, Web," Bomber said, looking his adversary hard in the eye. "Drop the bogus charges against Pia Franceschi."

Bomber turned and marched out of the D.A.'s office without waiting for an answer.

I followed.

15

Every time I entered my apartment over the garage near the ocean I looked at my telephone answer unit in the hope of seeing the telltale flashing red light telling me I had a message. The few times it flashed, it was not from Joan.

The violin and piano duo I had thought about for the case of Pia Franceschi was languishing in my subconscious. The way things were going I might have to write it for piano solo.

To lift my burden I sat at the piano and doodled some thematic ideas, but before I realized it, I was pounding away with the kind of gusto that sent the neighbors into hiding. This kind of abuse of the instrument gave me relief from the pressures, stress, anger and frustration that were unavoidable in life.

The next morning, with no sleep to speak of, I did my duty showing up at the office. Not that I was of much value to the shop. I closed my door and brooded, and not about the case. It was self-pity mostly.

I was only dimly aware of the ringing of the telephone. It was the whooping sound from Bomber's office that caught my attention. Torn between not wishing to appear too bold, and not ignoring the glad tidings, I opened my door in time to hear Bomber's penetrating voice:

"Bonnie—get the boy in here!"

I didn't wait for her inimitable summons and its attendant patronizing, diminutive "Cuddles", "Sweet meat", or "Stud". I marched directly to Bomber's office, passing Bonnie en route and holding my hand up to spare me the indignity of her harassment.

My perfectly modulated knock elicited the cry, "Come in." I entered and was careful to close the door behind me. I didn't want that airhead snoop privy to any more than absolutely necessary.

"Well, me boy," Bomber began, "that was our fearless district attorney Webster A. Grainger, three—on a scale of ten," he grinned. It wasn't new, but it always served its purpose. "He has apparently given due thought to what he yesterday referred to as 'an unseemly bribe' and has found a tiny corner of light in that dark heart of his. He allows as it would only be serving the noble cause of justice to keep the fabulous Fabrizio Franceschi locked up—to protect society from his abuses, you understand. Could it be better? We can serve the girl and be free of that meddling nut case."

I nodded. No use trying to follow that oration with words. Nor did I have to ask him what he wanted me to do. Bomber was in his nonstop mode.

"Pay the girl a visit—tell her the good news. Tell her also she doesn't have to worry about paying, we'll bill the old man."

Great! I thought. The guy who is so tight with his daughter she has to sleep with the landlord to pay the rent. Naturally, I didn't say anything.

"Then check out the scene. Talk to the witnesses—the roommates, the guy who lent Lance his place. The ex-boyfriend will be vital to the defense. See if you can tie him down somehow. Check?"

I nodded.

"What are you waiting for?"

With a rueful smile, I saluted and left. It is not often I have an audience with Bomber that I don't have to say a word—when he fills the air from start to finish—but it is gratifying when it occurs.

I drove out to the county jail where the powers that be were holding Pia Franceschi. In no time, the matron brought her into the visiting room. Her eyes were red, no doubt from a bout of crying.

When she sat down, facing me, I said, "Been a little rough?"

She nodded, then burst into tears.

"Now," I said. "I have good news. Bomber is taking your case."

She stopped crying for a moment, looked at me as though surprised, then burst again into tears.

I looked at her, perplexed. "That's not good news?"

In a few moments she got her sobbing under, more or less, control. "I'm sorry," she said. "It's just that the reality has sunk in. There *is* a case—how *can* there be? It's just, like, so *stupid!* I didn't kill that moron. I wouldn't know how. He was free rent. It was such a stupid mistake! Now I room with hookers and druggies—child abusers and thieves instead of college classmates," and the tears returned.

"Listen…Pia…the first thing Bomber is going to do is try to get you out of here—on bail." Then I realized bail for a murder charge was practically impossible to come by—and, in the event a miracle happened, where would she get the money to post the bail?

I couldn't tell if she knew what I was thinking, so I helped her. "In the event Bomber worked a miracle, do you know anyone who might come up with the money?"

"How much?" she asked, her eyes showing a new hope.

"Depends on the judge. If you get a bail bondsman to post it, it costs you ten percent of the amount. $50,000 bail would cost $5,000—$100,000 bail, 10,000 and so on."

"Maybe my mom could do it," Pia said uncertainly, "if it isn't too much."

That was encouraging. I made a mental note to call her mom.

"Has she been to see you?" I asked.

"Gosh no. I haven't told her. She'd just die!"

"She's not in touch with Fab?"

"I doubt it. He's in the habit of going off for days or weeks at a time—claims he's investigating cases."

"Does she believe him?"

"Who knows? I think she *wants* to believe him, but she's not that naïve."

I decided to drop my bomb. "Think Lance would help you?"

"Lance?" It shocked her. "I don't think Lance wants anything to do with me."

"Why not?"

"Isn't it obvious? I'm not guilty of murder, but I'm not exactly an innocent. That stupid deal with DeWitt—like, do you think Lance could ever forgive me for something like that?"

"Would it shock you if I told you Lance is still crazy about you?"

I could see from her expression that it had.

"You found Lance?" she asked.

"Yeah," I said. "Up where you told me."

"And?"

"And he is pining his heart out for you."

"No *way!*"

"Yes way."

"I can't believe it," she said, but it was easy to see she wanted to.

"Let me tell you what he told me, then you can decide," I said. "He was so shook up at your breakup he couldn't think of anything else. On the night of the murder—the night for which you could use a rock-solid alibi-—he wanted to go to the party to beg you to take him back."

"No *way!*"

I nodded. "Instead, he sat on the second floor of the house next to the park and watched you from when you got there to when you left."

Her eyes swelled. "He did *that?*"

"What time did you get to the park for the party?"

"I don't remember."

"Was the band playing?"

"No, they started after I got there."

So far so good, I thought. "Remember when you left?"

She shook her head. "The party was over, I guess. The band had packed up and gone home."

We stared at each other for a long minute.

"Are you thinking what I'm thinking?"

"I guess so," she said.

"Lance is your ticket out of here."

"Yeah," she said, luxuriating in the possibility.

"So if I sent him down here to see you, do you think you could patch things up with him?"

Pia frowned. "Yeah, well, like, that wasn't the only problem. There was Fab."

"Fab's in jail—"

"Well, but he won't always be."

"Okay, but your life *depends* on Lance, Pia. This is an opportunity I would recommend you didn't turn your back on."

Her mouth was moving as if to form words from her thoughts. "Yeah, well, like, how can you be sure you can get him to come? I mean, like, even if he gets *me* off the hook, what about him?"

"He's got the alibi," I said, "He was watching you all night. And I'm about to check with the person who can verify that." Of course *he* couldn't verify that for the *whole* evening, but I didn't want to bother her with those details just yet.

"Yeah, well, sure," she said. "Like, what have I got to lose?"

"And you will be able to give Lance some encouragement?"

"Yeah, I'll try."

"You'll have to do better than try. I'm sure it's not lost on him that if you have a solid alibi, he needs one too."

"I'll do my best."

"I hope so," I said, "Your life may well depend on it."

When the matron came back to take Pia back to the cell she shared with the hookers and druggies *etc.*, I saw a touch of hope in her eyes, and hope is what keeps the world going round.

16

In university housing, free enterprise ruled the day. There were not enough campus housing units to satisfy the demand of those who lusted for higher education. Most of these seekers after organized enlightenment were motivated by the hope of it giving them a leg up in the job market.

The most desirable houses and small multiple units were along the ocean. It helped if you had a high tolerance for the noise of the street parties or a hearing impairment. The noise levels on the street made studying in the houses virtually impossible at any time of the day or night. That made it difficult to find anyone home to question.

Saturday and Sunday mornings were most likely. The street was quiet, the natives were not restless, they were resting, sleeping off the intemperate behavior of the night before. If they weren't raising Cain in the streets, they weren't conscious, or as the denizens of the district would have it, they were zonked.

Sunday I planned to win Joan back. That left Saturday morning. Getting there before nine would have been a fool's errand, and I wasn't adverse to a little extra sleep myself. The police had cleared the house and allowed Pia's housemates to return.

DeWitt Izuks was more or less a typical landlord on the strip. Not a poor man, but not the big-time operator either. The big boys steered clear of these small, labor-intensive units. The nature of the tenancy was such that they could gouge, sure, but the transient residents were adroit at getting them back for it, and though they took horrendous deposits, they would often end up spending them to get the places back in shape.

At a little after nine, I drove slowly up and down the street trolling for signs of life. Zero. In spite of logic looking the other way, I looked for a place to park the car. I quickly deep-sixed the notion that someone would fortuitously move their car and I would ease into the space, unencumbered and unopposed. Cars were parked three and four deep in driveways and front yards. I found a place less than four blocks away and took my time moseying back to the student strip along the beach.

I headed for the pocket park—the width of two house lots and wondered at the largesse of the generous soul who donated land to the common weal, forgoing a sizeable chunk of change. Perhaps it was simply the pound of flesh extracted by the city to permit the building of one or more units.

The architecture leaned toward Motel 6, and no pains were taken to encumber the structures with any originality. The street actually brought shame to the word utilitarian.

I scoped out the park and the houses on the small lots on either side. I imagined the drill here was to build the maximum number of bedrooms on the tiny lot, then cram it as full of warm bodies as was humanly (if not humanely) possible.

The houses I was interested in at the moment were to the west of the park. The ocean was on the south, giving the climate the flair of the Mediterranean.

All was quiet on the western front. With trepidation I approached the house bordering the park—the one where Lance Ludlow said he watched Pia Franceschi for the duration of the party, giving her an alibi for the murder she was accused of.

I found the door, hidden behind a bevy of cars in the front and tapped on it ever-so-shyly so as not to wake anyone, but loud enough to be heard by anyone who might be awake.

No response.

I remember Pia saying her landlord locked the front door and didn't give them a key, forcing them to enter and exit via the sliding glass door in the back—I walked around the house to the beach in the back and was startled to see this gangly fellow strung out on a canvas hammock that sat him—or the sitting part of him—directly on the sand.

My first impression was of a strand of wet macaroni—but he wasn't that thin. More like one of those fat pretzels unraveled.

His head was covered with a shock of sun-blonded hair, and it was a shock. It looked like it had been combed with an eggbeater. He appeared to skimp on sunscreen, camouflaging what I speculated was a pale pallor in the wintertime.

"Oh, excuse me," I said when I turned the corner and was startled to see him sitting there. There was no activity on the beach, no other person in evidence.

He turned his head slowly to look up at me, then, not recognizing the face turned it back. I couldn't tell if the gesture meant to convey I was excused, or "Buzz off, bozo."

"I'm Tod Hanson," I said to the back of his head. "I'm looking for a friend of Lance Ludlow."

The head turned again, slower than before. "I know Lance," he said, sans gusto. "What's up?"

"Do you know Pia Franceschi?"

"Oh," he said, "that."

My sense of interpersonal dynamics told me I should be on his level, not towering over him as I was. There was no place to sit—chairs came and went with the sitters. A chair left out overnight would not be there in the morning. If our college students are the hope of the future, should we all dig bomb shelters?

I squatted next to him so I could look at him more or less eye-to-eye.

"Pia is in jail," I said, "for the murder of her landlord."

He shook his head with sadness. "Yeah," he said. "That guy was a piece of work." Then he mumbled something I heard as "the work of Satan."

I let it go for the moment. I thought if he wanted me to hear it, he would have said it louder.

"He your landlord?"

He shook his head.

"I'm sorry," I said, "I didn't get your name."

"I didn't give it," he said, concentrating on the ocean as though to make certain it wouldn't get away from him.

After a pause I said, "Will you?"

"Will I what?" he said, distracted. "Oh, name—Kyler—Kyler Ziskind—with a Z."

"Tod," I said, "Tod Hanson."

"Yeah, you said. So what do you want to know about Lance?"

"I met Lance in connection with Pia Franceschi," I said. "We are defending her in the murder case. Lance says he watched Pia the night of the party—the night the landlord was shot. Watched her from a window at your place—that true?"

Kyler nodded. "Yup—"

"Remember when he got here?"

"Sometime before the band started."

"And left?"

"After the band stopped."

"What hours approximately?"

"I don't know—eightish to twelveish—somewhere in there."

"Where were you during that time?"

"In and out," he said.

My heart sank. "Out? How much?"

"I don't remember—an hour or so—I checked out the party."

"Did you see Pia at the party?"

"I may have—I wasn't looking for her."

"Happen to drop in the house next door at all?"

He shot me a menacing glance.

"No, why would I do that?"

"I don't know. You know any of the girls that live there?"

He stared into space—"Seen 'em around is all," he said. "They all seem kind of slutty."

"How so?"

"The people are 'how so'—goings on not fit to talk

about among the righteous."

Uh-oh, I got the feeling he was one of the righteous, but I didn't know how to verify that without setting him off.

"Well," I said, as casually as I could, "in the righteous sweepstakes, I fear I fall short—you can tell me."

He didn't find that funny. "Fornication is no laughing matter," he said. "It's no secret there's girls up and down this street sleeping with that creep to pay the rent. It's an abomination in the eyes of the Lord."

"Well, there's one less abomination now."

Kyler nodded.

"You think the Lord had something to do with it?"

"I'm sure of it. Nothing escapes the eyes of the Lord."

"Vengeance is mine, saith the Lord?"

"Yeah, he did."

"And you think he—the Lord—took it—vengeance?"

"That's obvious, isn't it?"

"Perhaps," I said, "but there was a mortal involved. One who pulled the trigger."

Kyler Ziskind shrugged. "Maybe only an instrument of the Almighty—all we are are instruments of His will."

"So if the Lord told you to shoot DeWitt Izuks—or anyone else—would you do it?"

"Wouldn't have a choice," he said.

"Did he tell you to…shoot DeWitt Izuks?"

He paused and looked at that huge ocean for a long moment. Then shook his head. "Not me," he said, "but somebody."

"If the Lord told someone to do it, would it be the responsibility of the person who did it, or of the Lord?"

"The Lord, of course," he said. "But that doesn't satisfy man—we got to have our scapegoats."

"What about 'Thou shalt not kill'?"

"What about it?"

"Didn't the Lord say that?"

"Yeah," he said.

"How does that square with the Lord telling someone to kill someone?"

"Well, if the Lord said it, it must be true."

"Can they both be true?"

"No," he said. "The Lord speaking directly to you—that takes precedence."

Scary, I thought, but I kept it to myself. "See any action next door this morning?" I asked.

"No," he said, shaking his head again. "I don't expect any stirring in that congregation until 'round noon."

"Notice any effect the murder had on the girls?"

"Freaked out at first. Went home—stayed with friends—made themselves scarce. I guess the police cleaned up the place and they're all back now—except Pia, of course."

"Like to see her back?" I asked.

His look said, What possible difference could that make to me? "I don't care one way or the other."

I thanked him, and went to check out the girls' house. I peered in the uncurtained sliding glass door. No sign of life.

My gentle tapping went unanswered.

When I left the house, Kyler Ziskind was still staring at the ocean. "See ya," I said.

He didn't answer.

17

I returned to the park and roamed around the area, looking up at the window on the second floor of the house Lance Ludlow claimed he sat at the night of the party and never left Pia out of his sight. I tried to visualize the park packed with college kids and what the chances were Lance could keep Pia in his sight. If Pia had been alone in the park she would have been visible from the window. But if she had been surrounded by the mass of humanity or had taken it in her head to disappear behind the houses on the beach, she could have, theoretically, slipped back into her house, shot DeWitt and taken the gun back to the party, or deposited it in a dumpster and returned to the party in five minutes or so.

Could Lance *really* have sat or stood at that window for over four hours without flinching? Why would he have wanted to? It's a nice story now that his girlfriend has been accused of murder, but before there was knowledge of a murder, there would have seemed no compelling reason for such obsessive behavior. I suspect the district attorney would ridicule the story in short order.

I headed to the edge of the water where the tracking was better. A glance back at Kyler Ziskind sitting with his back to his house showed me no sign he recognized me.

I wanted to concentrate on the case, searching for the key that proved Pia's innocence, but thoughts of Joan kept crowding my head.

There was a soufflé of fog over the ocean, giving the water a gray cast to match my thoughts. Looking back at the houses sheltering sleeping students I was reminded of the teeth of a young whale. I tried to imagine all the secrets those teeth held. Was the secret key to the case locked in there somewhere?

By the time I got to the end of those whale teeth and turned around, my thoughts had wrapped themselves around Joan and my fateful surprise visit to her on the morrow for the Los Angeles Philharmonic Sunday matinee.

I marched up and down the beach numerous times without having any revelations or epiphanies, until I began to see signs of life.

Then I circumscribed my peregrination to focus on Pia's house, hoping for some activity to signal the girls were awake. Before I got to the beachside sliding glass door, I noted a shaggy male approaching between the houses. He wore ratty jeans with holes plugged with colorful bits of unrelated fabric. His long chestnut hair and struggling goatee reminded me of a horse. He seemed an uncool guy trying to look cool. I turned abruptly to change my course, then tried to appear I was on my way to the park, keeping the house and the male in a sidelong glance.

He turned the corner and let himself in the sliding glass door at the back of the girl's house, without any warning knock I could ascertain.

I hurried to the park, then went to the street and rounded the corner to Pia's house—I went down the setback until I came to a high window. It was open, and I ducked down to make sure I wasn't seen. There were voices coming from inside.

"What do you think you're doing in here?" from a female.

"This is my place now."

"Your uncle wasn't wanted either. You saw what happened to him."

"Is that a threat?"

"Why don't you just leave us alone?"

"Why don't you ask Suzy if she wants me to leave you alone?"

"Suzy?" she said. "What are you talking about?"

There was some mumbling from him that I couldn't hear. Had I been discovered?

"Suzy's sleeping," the woman said.

"I'll go up and wake her."

"No you won't."

"Hey—get real."

"I *am* real. You get real and get out of here."

"You don't want to talk to your new landlord like that."

"Now who's threatening? We have a lease, and believe me, we're leaving the day it runs out!"

"You obviously don't know Pia."

"Pia's in jail."

"She didn't mind a little help with *her* rent."

"Pia was strapped. DeWitt took advantage of her."

"I wouldn't call it that. It was a fair trade. I just came by to tell you other trades are possible—in case any of the rest of you get 'strapped'."

"You're sick, Gillian!"

"Just a suggestion—"

"Well, like, I suggest you get out of here. And while you're at it, how about a *key* to this back door—and front door?"

"Sorry, no can do."

"We'll get a lawyer," she said. "You can't push us around any more. There's such a thing as tenants' rights."

"Oh, really?"

"Yeah, really."

"Thanks for the tip," he said. "Now you don't worry your pretty head about keys or anything else till you talk to Suzy."

When I heard the door slide open I realized he was going to see me, and I would have to do some tall acting to pass my appearance there off as a coincidence.

I moved as fast as I could toward the back. That way I could see his face, and he wouldn't think I was running away from eavesdropping.

When he turned the corner I was there and almost bumped into him. "Yo, man," I said, "how's it going?" He was shorter than I thought. So much of his cosmetic stature could be attributed to his hair.

"Hey," he said, with a proprietary air, "Where do you think you're going?"

"I'm sorry," I said, feigning being startled by his audacity, "What did you say?"

"I asked you where you thought you were going."

"Well, to the beach obviously," I said, nodding my head toward the water. "Anything else out there?"

"Why are you coming this way?"

"Why not?"

"This is private property."

"Hey man, you some kind of cop or something?"

"I'm Gillian Izuks. I own this place," he said as though he were a famous man, then added to cement the impression, "and three more like it."

"So?" I said. "You think I'm going to vandalize the place? Paint graffiti or something?"

"You a wise guy?" he asked, and believe it or not, I was flattered.

"Thanks," I said.

He tensed, his hands balled into fists and his muscles twitched as though he were going to hit me. Through clenched teeth, he said, "This is *my* property and I don't want you on it."

"Yeah?" I said. "It's not access to the beach?"

"No. It's *private* property," he snarled. "Now get off it, and don't come back."

I looked him in the eye. *Would* he hit me? Did he want the kind of trouble that would bring him? I am speaking, of course, of a criminal charge of assault, not a counterpunch.

"Okay," I said, and sidestepped him until I was on the half of the passageway between the houses that must have belonged to the neighbors. I passed him without incident and kept walking to the water's edge, where I stayed until I sensed he was tired of staring at my back and had left *his* premises.

DeWitt Izuks had apparently bequeathed his property to a clone of himself. Was there, somewhere in Gillian's soul, a little pragmatic murderer? He had the motive (inheritance), opportunity (the open door, the distraction of the party in the park) and the method (Pia's available gun).

There was, I decided, no one I'd rather pin the murder on than Gillian Izuks.

18

When I was reasonably certain Gillian was gone, I turned back to the house, moved nonchalantly to the door, and knocked with the gentle precision I had learned at the knee of my father.

A blond girl came to the door, her hair unbridled, her eyes bleary. She was short and on her merry way to adding the allotted poundage charmingly referred to as the freshman fifteen.

Though I was a stranger, she seemed relieved to see me.

"Oh, thank God," she said, "I thought Gillian was coming back for another torture session."

"Oh," I said, with a conservative chuckle. "No, I'm Tod Hanson. I'm a lawyer and we are representing Pia Franceschi. How are you girls holding up?"

"Um, okay. I'm Veronica..."

"Hi," I said. "If that guy bothers you..."

"He bothers me."

"I can help you."

"Really?" she said with some hope. Then frowned. "How much will it cost?"

"Oh, nothing. Pro bono," I said.

"What's that?"

"Pro bono publico—Latin—for the good of the public. Every now and then the less greedy attorneys do charity work— for the public good."

"I like that," she said. "Come in. Sit down...anywhere."

There weren't many choices. The housekeeping was of the chaotic school: books, clothes, even potato chips seemed rooted to their particular locales.

98

The lots on the ocean were small and the setback restrictions confining and when you wanted to build a thousand bedrooms to maximize the take, it didn't leave much room for a living room and kitchen.

This postage stamp arrangement featured a counter dividing the, quote—unquote, kitchen, which was the size of the cockpit of a single engine airplane. There was a row of four stools pushed under the lip of the counter, one for each inhabitant. Since these housemates wanted a table in the living room for gracious dining, no doubt, it limited the number of seating units in the remainder of the living room. I found a card table chair and Veronica pulled a bar stool up and sat on it. She crossed her bare legs—the shorts she wore seemed a little tight—and swung the top leg back and forth while she twirled her hair between her fingers. It was like an absent minded what-do-you-want stance. It behooved me to start the ball rolling. "So, what's the problem?"

"Gillian is DeWitt's nephew. He's taken over all DeWitt's properties."

"Offering free rent?" I asked.

She seemed surprised at first, then nodded and said, "Yeah, same old shtick."

"Just walks in here—doesn't knock?"

She nodded.

"Well, I'll write him a letter on our legal letterhead—explain the facts of life to him."

Veronica grunted a short laugh—"He doesn't need any help with that."

"Landlord / tenant law," I clarified. "We'll get you a key to the front door and a lock for the back."

"No way," she said. "You could do that?"

"Absolutely."

"Wow—" the hair twirling continued at its leisurely pace.

"Veronica?"

"Hmm?"

"Do you remember the night DeWitt …died?"

"How could I forget it?"

"Know where everyone was?"

"Pretty much—" she said. "Like, we all talked about it."

"I imagine," I said. "So where were you all…between eight-thirty and ten-thirty p.m.?"

"Erin and I were at the party together. Pia was there but she wasn't with us."

"Did you see her there?"

"Sure. But we weren't like, hanging out with her the whole time."

"Where was Suzy?"

"She was…I think, gone for the weekend."

"Where?"

Veronica shrugged. "Said to her parents' house."

"Where do her parents live?"

"Fresno."

"You don't believe it?"

"It's…*possible* I guess."

"But…unlikely?"

"Well, she doesn't really get along with her mom. I don't know…"

"Were you here when DeWitt came into the house?"

"Yeah," she said. "That's why we cleared out so early."

"How early?"

"Before the party started. I don't know what time it was. He and Pia were doing their thing. It always disgusted me. I mean, like, I couldn't take it—that creep and poor Pia."

"*Poor* Pia?"

"Well, yeah," Veronica said. "He was totally taking advantage of her—her dad wouldn't give her any money, so she did what she could."

"I'm sorry to hear that. How do you feel about DeWitt being shot?"

"Not *that* bad—I only wish it had happened somewhere else."

"Any theories on who did it?"

"Well, the cops are like, pretty sure Pia did it. I guess they think she finally got sick of the whole thing."

"Did you ever see Pia's gun?"

She shook her head.

"Did you know she had one?"

"Yeah, like, fabulous Fab told all of us—gave me the creeps to know that it was in the house."

"Think she'd have told you about it if she had planned to use it?"

"I don't think she *planned* on it. I think she just freaked out and couldn't take DeWitt anymore."

"Hear any shots?"

Veronica shook her head. "We were all at the party. It was pretty loud."

"What time did you get back from the party?"

"Around twelve-thirty. A group of us hung out a while after the band packed up. When we got home Pia was crashed out on the couch. We went straight upstairs to bed."

"But you saw Pia at the party?"

"Yeah, like, my guess is DeWitt passed out when they were done—typical. She went to the party and when she got back, was surprised to find him still in her bed. They fought, she grabbed the gun, shot him—then I guess she dumped the gun somewhere."

"The police seem to be satisfied from talking to you that Pia is guilty. What do you think? Did you give them that idea?"

"Yeah, well, just between us, we all freaked out—the police were saying we were all suspects and that's pretty heavy, you know?"

"I imagine—"

"So when they finally arrested Pia, we were all, like, pretty relieved."

"Can you imagine any one of you having a motive strong enough to kill Izuks?"

"Not really. Pia maybe. He could have finally gotten to her. I don't know why she waited so long."

"Think she really did it?"

101

She shrugged. "I don't know what to think."

"Yet *someone* convinced the cops."

"They didn't need any convincing, and like I said, we were pretty relieved," she twirled her hair and kept the leg in motion. "You know what I wish?"

"What?"

"I wish there was some way to hang it on Gillian. He's just like his uncle, except at least DeWitt had some charm."

"He inherited the properties?"

"That's what *he* says."

"A reasonable motive."

Her eyes widened in hope. "You think so? Can you find out?" Her leg stopped moving.

"I can give it a try."

"Jeez, that would be cool."

I let the hope sink in, then said, "Your housemates still sleeping?"

"I guess," she said, giving me as close to an affirmative as she could muster.

"Any idea when they'll get up?"

"Oh, noonish," she said.

"What about Suzy?" I asked. "I confess I overheard you talking to Gillian, and he seemed to think she was an ally."

"Yeah, he does."

"Is she?"

"Why don't you ask her?" she asked me while nodding toward the stairs. I turned to look and saw a lithe but sleepy young woman flowing down the stairs in her pajamas with little Teddy Bears all over them. She seemed to be on her feet against her will.

19

Veronica got off her stool. "Suzy, this is Tod. I'm going to leave you alone—Tod is investigating the murder. He's Pia's lawyer," Veronica passed Suzy at the bottom of the stairs.

Suzy floated to the kitchen without looking at me. When she was in the kitchen, I said, "I just met Gillian. I understand he speaks highly of you."

"I gotta have my coffee," she said. "I can't think without my coffee."

I was patient while she brewed the coffee.

"Want some?" she asked.

"No thanks," I said.

Suzy poured her coffee and leaned on the counter behind the partition and drank it slowly as though she actually savored the flavor. From her body language people would say she was keeping a barrier between us.

"Gillian Izuks," I said, prodding being called for. "What's your impression?"

"Yeah, well, I guess he's the landlord now," she shrugged, "I don't think you get anywhere fighting the land-lord."

"A lot of landlords treat their tenants okay," I said. "You get along with DeWitt?"

"He seemed okay."

"Gillian any better?"

The second question seemed to surprise her. "Yeah, well, so far he's okay, I guess." She shrugged as though to emphasize how blasé she was about the whole thing.

"Think Pia could have killed DeWitt?"

"Yeah, I do," she said.

"How about Gillian. Could he have done it?"

"Oh, no," she answered, a mite quickly.

"Inherited a pot full of property, didn't he?"

"I guess. But he wasn't even around here till DeWitt was killed."

"You just met him?"

"Yeah."

"When?"

"He came around to introduce himself as soon as we all got back in the house."

I nodded. "Seem all right to you?"

"Yeah, well, like I said, I don't see the point of fighting the landlord."

"If he doesn't give you keys to a locked door? If he comes in your place without knocking?"

She shrugged. "Well, like, it is his place really."

I shook my head. "When you lease it, it becomes yours. He has no right to enter without your permission—only to save his property in an emergency."

"Whatever," she said, as though it didn't interest her.

"Where were you on the night of the murder?"

"I was home for the weekend."

"Where is home?"

"Fresno—"

"You have any siblings?"

"A brother—he doesn't come around much."

"Why not?"

"He lives in Santa Rosa—never got on too well with my dad."

"Did you?"

"Oh, he's okay."

"Mom?"

She wrinkled her nose. "We don't really get along."

"But you go to see her?"

"You got to once in a while."

"Did you go home for spring break?"

"Yeah, but I didn't hang around much."

"Did you this time?"

Her face flushed. "Quit with the twenty questions, will you?"

"Sorry," I said. "Just trying to get an idea where everybody was—"

"Well, I wasn't here," she said.

"You were in Fresno," I said, confirming but still questioning.

"I wasn't here," she said. I noticed the evasion but didn't press.

"Did you know about the gun?" I asked.

"Pia's gun? Sure, we all knew. Her crazy dad made sure we all knew there was a gun here in case we needed it to protect our honor—or whatever he called it."

"Did you ever see it?"

"See it? No, why would I?"

"I just thought you might," I said. "So how did you find out Gillian was the new landlord?"

"He came here and told us."

"Yeah, but did he show you any evidence?"

"What kind of evidence?"

"A copy of the will, or a letter to you from a lawyer or something."

"No, I…"

"Were you ever intimate with DeWitt?"

"No—gross! He was a creep."

"Is Gillian a creep?"

She stared at me as if to determine the real meaning of all these questions. She answered carefully: "Less."

As though on cue, the sliding glass door to the beach slid open, and the new landlord swung into the room, every inch the swashbuckling pirate.

"Suzy!" he exclaimed, "What's this guy doing here?"

"He's Pia's lawyer."

"Might I turn the question on you, sir?" I asked, "What are you doing here?"

"This is my house."

"Are you on the lease?"

"I will be."

"Oh? As a lessee, or lessor?"

"What's the difference?"

"Landlord or tenant?"

"Landlord."

"Lessor then. But if you think you can barge in here anytime without notice and without knocking even, you have a serious misunderstanding of landlord/tenant law."

"Oh, yeah? Well my uncle did it, and he knew what he was doing."

"Then he knew it was illegal."

"What are you doing here, anyway?" Without waiting for an answer, he turned to Suzy and said, "I caught this moron snooping around outside. Lied to me—said he was going to the beach."

"I went to the beach."

"You were snooping, weren't you? Trying to pick up evidence to clear that murderer who killed my uncle?"

"Guilty as charged," I said. "I am trying to pick up evidence in Pia's favor. Do you have any to give?"

"Not me," he said. "I think Pia is guilty as sin. Look at the evidence: my uncle was found in her bed—it's not exactly a secret they had a deal going on, and she wasn't happy about it. She had a gun—gimmee a break—good luck with getting her off."

"Seem like a person who could murder in cold blood?"

"I don't know her."

I made a quick check of Suzy's face. Her struggle to keep it impassive wasn't panning out. "Excuse me," I said, "didn't I just hear an impressive litany from a guy who 'doesn't know her'?"

"Suzy told me," he said, rather sheepishly.

"Oh, so you know Suzy?"

His head snapped in her direction. She turned her head to one side a tiny bit. It amused me that these adults were insensitive to their body language.

"No," he said, "she just told me."

"When?"

"After Pia shot my uncle!"

"When after?"

"After. Hey, listen, I don't have to answer anything to you. Don't you need a warrant to be in here?"

"I don't need a warrant to ask questions."

"Oh no?" It was belligerent.

I shook my head. "That's for searching the premises. Think that would be a good idea?"

His shoulders bounced up. "No skin off my rear," he said. "Now why don't you get out of here? You're not wanted."

"Is that your idea," I looked at Suzy, "or a universal truth?"

"I'm telling you, wise mouth, beat it!" he started to come toward me with his fists balled. I had a sudden fright, but I held my ground.

"You want to hit me?" I said. "We'll have good cause to lock you up. Maybe the cops can get to the bottom of your stories."

Gillian Izuks was fuming, there was no hiding it. He stowed a barrel of air, turned to Suzy and said, "I'll see you later," and stormed out.

"Knock first," I said to his back.

20

Suzy turned her head away when I looked at her for some explanation.

"Do you want to go after him?" I asked her back.

"No," she said.

The house was quiet. I cocked an ear toward the upstairs, hoping for some sounds of stirring. Nothing.

"Is your other housemate up?" I asked Suzy.

"Erin's gone home," she said, "for the weekend."

"Where do her parents live?"

"Down in L.A. somewhere."

"Does she have any special connection to DeWitt?"

"No more than the rest of us. He was here, he annoyed us," Suzy shrugged. "What else do you want to hear?"

"I'd like to hear more about your relationship to Gillian."

She froze, fixing a lethal stare on me. "There is no relationship," she said.

"Just a friend?"

"Not even that," she said. "He's just as presumptuous as his uncle."

I didn't argue, but I didn't buy it. After saying my goodbyes and giving the girls my number, in case one of them remembered anything else they might want to tell me that would help Pia, I took my leave. I left Suzy slurping coffee in their postage stamp kitchen.

That afternoon and evening I lost myself in writing music—doodling music would be more like it—my thoughts being on my impending surprise meeting with Joan.

The Walt Disney Concert Hall where the Los Angeles Philharmonic hung out was really something. Frank Gehry, the architect, had had a crowning success with the Guggenheim Museum in Bilbao, Spain—designed with irregular clumps of odd silver shapes. It was the toast of the architecture world. Then they began springing up all over the world. I exaggerate a bit—shameless hyperbole really. I wondered how many there had to be to render the design old-hat. It reminded me of the Parthenon theory. The Parthenon was beautiful. Someone did a composite rendering with dozens of Parthenons on a hillside. The point was made. We value originality, then can't wait to devalue it through imitation.

But I'd never been to Spain and the Walt Disney Concert Hall was spectacular, outside and in. It was original, innovative, dramatic. Just like the Guggenheim.

For my surprise visit I chose a seat away from the orchestra. The new hall had seats behind the stage where you could look into the conductor's face and down on the orchestra. I was afraid of being seen and perhaps unnerving Joan during the performance.

So I settled for a seat near the top of the hall where Joan would need telescopic vision to spot me.

The program was to open with a Sibelius Romance. I didn't care for Sibelius—Finnish schmaltz I called it. It didn't matter. I was mesmerized by Joan, I didn't even notice the music. Fortunately Stravinsky's Firebird was on the program and I was crazy about Stravinsky. Sandwiched in there was Maurizio Pollini playing Beethoven's "Emperor" Concerto. Pollini was one of the highest paid soloists, but I never could tell what the fuss was about.

The orchestra began filtering in, and my focus was on the left side of the stage where the violins sat. I thought Joan would never come in. Her fellows were in various states of agitation, with some practicing a difficult section assiduously, a few sitting calmly, doing nothing.

Virtually all the chairs were full, and I still didn't see

Joan. I was beginning to get paranoid, thinking something had happened to her—like she was so distraught about our misunderstanding that she quit the orchestra and returned to Chicago.

I would swear all the seats were occupied, when suddenly I saw her—my Joan—sauntering in in rapt conversation with a violinist of the male gender. My heart sank like a string bass descending glissando.

They took their places, side-by-side at the music stand they shared.

In the normal course of things, the concertmaster would come in and signal the oboist to sound his A while the sections tuned in turn. Then the conductor would come to the podium bowing to acknowledge the applause, turn to face the orchestra, give the down beat, and they would be off to the races.

I suppose that is what happened in my presence, but I couldn't swear to it—my presence not being present. I couldn't take my eyes off Joan—and I couldn't stop speculating about her stand mate—not a bad looking guy, if a little older. What was it about proximity and relationships?

Pollini did his bit with the Beethoven Fifth, and somehow I drifted through the intermission. I was back in my seat in plenty of time to watch the troops reassemble for the Firebird.

Joan came in earlier this time—alone—and sat at her stand and practiced some parts of the score. The Stravinsky offered more challenge than Sibelius and Beethoven.

She barely looked up when her stand mate sat down. Maybe they had a fight at intermission.

Somehow I got through the Firebird. Before I knew it, the conductor was signaling the wind and brass soloists to take bows—then the orchestra rose to their feet as one. I was so proud of Joan as she stood, her violin hanging indifferently from her hand. I thought at that moment—and I don't know why—about how much more money she made than I did and wondered if that would have an influence in the long run. If there was to be a long run.

Before the applause stopped, I made my way toward the

stage, bucking the crowd as the applause ceased and they rose together from their seats—just like the orchestra did before filing out.

Fortunately Joan didn't seem in a rush to leave. I made it to the stage as she was disappearing through the orchestra exit—I gave chase, passing a bassoonist, trumpeter and a gaggle of strings. When I pulled in behind Joan, I tapped her on the shoulder. When she turned around, I said, "Pardon me, you look familiar, do I know you from somewhere?"

It was a risk, I know. She could have bonked me with the violin—or at least the bow—she could have frowned and hurried away from me—she could have said, "No, I don't know you." She could have said, "I used to know someone who looks something like you, but I forgot his name."

She did none of that, God bless her. She let out a yelp of surprise, said, "Oh, you…" and threw her arms around my neck. How often we worry about the wrong things.

"Speaking of worrying about the wrong things," I said.

"Were we?"

"No—I was just thinking—I saw you come on stage with your stand mate…"

"Oh, Stan…"

"Yes. Anything to worry about?"

She laughed. I just loved her laugh—so musical it could have been played on her violin. "If I were a boy, you could worry. Girls are not Stan's thing."

"Whew!" I said. "Another wasted worry."

Arm in arm we made our way to a hamburger place down the street—Joan jealously clutching her violin. I should have been jealous of the fiddle, but the euphoria of my relief being back with Joan lifted me above it.

We settled into a booth and started jabbering about how foolish we both were.

"It was a wonderful concert," I said.

"Oh, thanks—"

"Can you tell me why the winds and brass get to bow if

they have eight bars and the strings are killing themselves through the whole piece?"

"Well, there are so many strings—the concertmaster gets his hand shaken for all of us. I don't know, it's just a tradition. How is that little bimbo that was in your apartment, anyway?"

"Pia? She's in jail."

"She really was going to jail?"

"Yeah, really. Everything I told you was true. I have never lied to you—"

She hung her head. "It was an emotional reaction. Can you understand it?"

"Sure, I can. I just wanted to explain."

"I didn't want to listen. What is it they say? 'Don't confuse me with facts, my mind is made up'."

We talked for two hours straight—in that time some food was consumed, but I don't remember what.

I told her the story of the case. She listened patiently. When I finished she shook her head.

"It doesn't sound like something a woman would do," she said. "A man might but not a woman. We just aren't wired that way."

"It does happen," I suggested.

"Not often. Big in the papers when it does. That doesn't mean you should get complacent."

"You know how to shoot?"

"I could learn," she said. "What about her boyfriend?"

"I talked to him," I said. "I'm not a flawless judge of character, but I want to believe him."

"Alibi?"

"Not iron clad. He was in the vicinity. He's the alibi for Pia. It will be interesting to see, if the suspicion starts to focus on him, will he stand by his alibi for Pia?"

"You say there are other girls who make the trade for rent?"

I nodded.

"Any of them have boyfriends who might be less than happy with that arrangement?"

"Not that I know of."

I suggested I drive her to Angleton with the promise I would return her Tuesday for her rehearsals for next week's concerts.

I didn't have to twist her arm.

21

Suffice it to say, the reunion between Joan and me was magnificent. No details; just take my word for it.

On Monday while Joan slept in, I slugged to the office where I brought Bomber up to date, then suggested I hunt down Izuk's other tenants, who might have bartered bodies for rent.

"Nah," he said. "Hold off. Let's see what Web comes up with. I don't think he has a case. Shouldn't get by the preliminary hearing. Can we get the boyfriend to testify at the prelim?"

"I h-hope so."

"Check it out—as your generation is wont to say."

Wow, I thought, And your generation is wont to say wont—but of course I didn't say it.

"But if W-Web knows he d-doesn't have a c-case, won't he go g-grand jury?"

"Very likely," Bomber said. "There's the rub. Grand juries will indict a ham sandwich if the D.A. tells them to."

I laughed as expected, though that old saw had gray whiskers. It was probably as old as the grand jury institution itself. That didn't make it any less true.

No one was surprised when, later that day, a rumor reached us that the district attorney might be opting for the grand jury. I was dispatched to explain the procedures to Pia and tell her what it would mean to her and her case.

Though I called ahead, Pia was not waiting for me when I arrived at the lockup. The jailers were not waiting for the Bentley to pull into the parking lot. What was that about rank and privileges?

Pia did not seem to be adjusting too well to her environment. Not that I expected to find a happy camper—not many were in these circumstances—but the change in Pia was noticeable and distressing.

I smiled a cheesy smile as the guard left, and Pia sat across the table from me. I thought how fascinating it might be if the table could talk—and, of course, had a memory. But then I realized it could be tedious stuff.

"What's happening?" Pia asked before I could trot out the small talk.

"Good and bad," I said. "A mixed bag."

"What's good?"

"We're getting a hearing."

"Don't tell me," she said, "that's bad, too." It wasn't so much a question as an acceptance of the inevitable.

"Well, the district attorney might go to the grand jury instead of a preliminary hearing before a judge. If it's true, it could be an encouraging choice for us—it shows the district attorney recognizes he has a weak case. Indictments are easier to come by from a grand jury. They usually do whatever the district attorney asks." I didn't go into the bit about the ham sandwich. I'd leave that for Bomber at a later date.

"Do you mean, if we did it the other way—the hearing in court—I'd have a better chance of getting out of here?"

"I don't have a crystal ball, but from experience, yeah, you'd have a slightly better chance."

"Can we request that?"

"No," I said with a sad tone. "It's the district attorney's call."

"Oh," she said, and she was, understandably, sadder than I was. "Do I go to a grand jury?"

"You could go to a court hearing, but not to the grand jury."

"What do they do at a grand jury?"

"It's like the hearing in secret. The district attorney brings witnesses to establish he has a reasonable basis for a trial.

The evidence doesn't have to be overwhelming, just enough to give a jury something to chew on."

"If it is a court hearing will I have to, like, testify?"

"Usually Bomber doesn't want to show his hand at these things. He doesn't want to forfeit the element of surprise. He has never let the accused testify. In an effort to nip this in the bud, he might have Lance testify as to your alibi. Think you can get him to do it?"

"I don't know," she frowned.

"It may be worth a try. Bomber will weigh the risk."

"What risk?"

"Showing the district attorney what we have. Give him time to find someone to refute it. In this case he could establish that Lance *wasn't* there all night, or that no one saw him there all night. And anyway, the district attorney can create enough doubt and tell the judge there is a difference of opinion, and it really is a matter for the jury to decide."

"So what are my chances?"

"Never too great at this juncture. Just in case Bomber wants to use him now I'm going to try to get Lance to see you. We'll definitely need him for the trial, if not before."

She let the information sink in. It was sinking fast and deep. I promised to do my best to get Lance here to see her, in the hope that would perk her up.

If her spirits got any spike from that hope, her face didn't show it. We said goodbye, and the matron took her back to her cell.

I went right home, dumbed down my clothes, threw my bike in the trunk of my car and headed up the mountain. Joan was grocery shopping, so I left her a note telling her where I was going.

I thought about parking farther down the hill than last time to get more exercise. I chickened out, reasoning that, like it says in those legal contracts, time was of the essence.

When I arrived at the flats on my bike, I saw no one. So I made tracks for Lance's tent in the rear of the compound.

When I found Lance taking the air outside his tent, but with no apparent purpose, I thought I saw him look at me with a flicker of interest. But then, as though he had already relegated my visit to the dustbin of good intentions, he turned morose. I didn't let the feeling linger.

With my most triumphant, upbeat exclamation I said, "Good news. Pia wants to see you."

He looked at me with a suspicious look on his face that let me know he didn't find that believable—or worse, he didn't care.

He said nothing.

"Well," I encouraged him, "isn't that great? Want to go back with me now?"

He looked at my bicycle. "On that?"

"I have a car down the road."

He nodded as though I had told him I was in the process of growing a third eye.

"Did you talk to Ziskind?" he asked.

"I did."

"What did he say?"

"He corroborates what you told me."

"Really?"

I nodded energetically.

"He says he was there with me all night?"

"Well, he was either with you or down at the party with Pia."

"Hmm," Lance turned pensive.

"What's the matter?"

"Isn't it obvious? 'While he was down with Pia' that gives Pia a good alibi, but what about me? He doesn't know if I left my post to shoot that creep."

"Did you?"

"Of course not."

"Then what's to worry about?"

"Hah! Pia didn't shoot him either, and look where she is."

It was a point I had difficulty contradicting. I didn't try.

"I mean, who else besides Pia would be suspect? *Me!*"

"Perhaps, Lance, there is *less* connection between you and the victim than between Pia and him. If you had been her boyfriend I'd say, yeah – but you were an *ex!*"

"So they'll think I was so outraged by my jealousy that I popped him so I could get Pia back."

"Did you?"

"No."

"Exactly," I said. "Pia *needs* your help. She is desperate for it—but don't take my word for it—go to see her. Tell her how you feel. Run all these doubts by her. She's liable to *beg* you not to take any chances. She's liable to say she loves you so much she'd rather go to the gallows than have you inconvenienced."

He looked at me funny-like, as though he were probing my seriousness quotient.

"I have heard of people so much in love they would give up their life for their loved one." I didn't see the reaction I'd hoped for on Lance's face.

"But," I added, "I suppose that is fairy story stuff. Who could be *that* much in love?"

He didn't look as though he was going to answer, so I charged on. "Don't put yourself out. I see your point. You would be suspect. I'm not sure you'd be more suspect if you showed yourself in the cause of truth and justice or if you hid out here and refused to tell what you know—that knowledge which might turn her loose to love you again—Ah," I sighed at the hopelessness of it all—"but we all have to look out for number one, don't we?"

I reached in my pocket for my card. I handed it to him. "Anyone here have a phone?"

He looked at the card. "Why?" he asked.

"Just wondered. If you find it in your heart to do some random acts of kindness like the bumper sticker says, give me a call. I'll set it up. Otherwise just drop by the jail—women's detention out at the dump. But hey, I understand. Doing the right thing can be an annoying inconvenience. You're a lot safer moping around here."

As I turned away from him I said, "Take it easy."

I walked out of there so slowly. I was hoping he would any minute summon me back.

He didn't.

22

Joan and I played violin and piano duets to our heart's content. There was simply nothing like it for cleansing the soul. We even tried out a few fragment sketches I was able to make for my piece commemorating the case.

Everything ends, and so did her visit. Early that morning, I drove her back to Los Angeles for the next series of rehearsals and concerts with the Philharmonic and returned to Angleton. It was time to refocus on work. If all work and no play makes Jack a dull boy, all play and no work makes him a poor one.

Perhaps the most difficult aspect of my job was talking to my father. It was the cause and effect of the stutter I exhibited in his presence alone. I usually dreaded that I was not living up to his expectations—though I didn't have a good grasp of what those expectations were.

Bomber has a load of work—much of which I am not privy to. If it doesn't require investigation, I usually don't know about it. As time creeps on, Bomber micromanages me less, leaving me pretty much to my own devices while he is preoccupied with some weighty matter I refer to, secretly, as sidelines. The Pia Franceschi case seemed to have slipped through the cracks. Then, as soon as I got back from L.A., I got the summons.

As I sat facing him, breathing deeply, in the testimonial-laden walls of his baronial office, he said, "So, what do you have on Pia Franceschi?"

I brought him up to date. When I finished and my stutter subsided, he said, "Anything from the D.A.?"

I shook my head.

"Natch," he said. "He *has* nothing. Grand jury for sure. Any day now, his time is almost up. Perfect venue for Web," he said. "No darling schoolgirl to sway the hearts and minds of judge or grand juror; no defense advocate blasting his witnesses to smithereens. Just old Webster A. Grainger III, leading them by the hand down the primrose path to indictment."

"Sinister," I contributed.

"Ah, yes, indubitably," he said, "but it's the system. You have any theories, say for a SODDI defense?"

SODDI was an acronym for Some Other Dude Did It.

"Her ex-b-boyfriend, Lance. Franceschi is p-pushing Lance."

"Franceschi! I'd repressed that idiot. He's still safely under lock and key, I trust?"

"Far as I know."

"Why not drop in on him—see if you can worm any info out of him? Has he had a change of heart, stewing in the slammer? What's his next gig? Grand jury? Get chummy if you can stand him. Better to have him on our side than the prosecution's."

I nodded. "You think he'd g-go against his d-daughter?"

"That turkey would go against God himself if he could see some profit in it."

I didn't ask what profit Franceschi would reap.

"How do you assess this Lance?"

"Decent g-guy," I said. "T-troubled by his r-relationship with Pia."

"Murderer?"

I shrugged. It was difficult for me to visualize any functioning member of society as a murderer. Psychotics, yes, but not the Lances and Pias of the world.

"Okay—I expect the next surprise we suffer at the hands of Web Grainger will be the ham sandwich blue plate special. And Web will be so pleased with himself, he'll think I've had the surprise of my life. Look like I fell off the turnip truck. Well, there's no reason to disabuse him of these notions. I love to be underestimated."

I doubted Web would underestimate Bomber, but I held my counsel.

So I was off to the lockup to see Fab Franceschi. While I was out, I thought I would check in with Pia—keep her spirits from lagging too badly.

I'd hoped his incarceration had taken some of the edge off Fab's bristling persona. It was not to be. He was brought into the visiting room in handcuffs, and before they were unlocked, he started in.

"When are you going to *do* something? I hope this is a visit to spring me from this trap. I'm a private detective for God's sake. This is a *travesty*. The greatest miscarriage of justice in the history of mankind—"

Good old Fab. You couldn't ever say he was a stranger to hyperbole.

"What is happening? When am I going to get out of here?"

"Do you have a lawyer?"

"Bomber is my lawyer."

I looked hard at his face. He didn't flinch. "Bomber doesn't think so," I said, quietly.

"What does he know? I am *entitled* to counsel."

"Yes, but not necessarily of your choice. Have you asked for a court appointed lawyer?"

"Why would I do that? Settling for some kid wet-behind-the-ears, so inexperienced he sits panting at the door of the courthouse waiting for some judge to throw him a bone?" Fab gave me the I-just-sucked-a-lemon face.

"It could be better than nothing."

"It could *not!*" he boomed. "Don't let Bomber hear you refer to him as *nothing!*"

"Would you like me to help you find a lawyer?"

"*No!*" Fab fairly yelled. "I *found* one."

How could he be so stubborn and self-defeating?

"Tell me, Mr. Big Investigator," he mocked me, "have you been able to get the evidence that her boyfriend is guilty?"

"He has an alibi," I exaggerated to see his reaction.

"It's a *lie!*" he said, looking me hard in the face. "I'm telling you, that you are getting this from one of the top private investigators in the United States. Lance What's-His-Name is guilty as sin. You prove that, and Pia will be free as a bird."

"You know Fab, I met Lance Ludlow. I spoke to him. I must confess I don't see any justification for your suspicion. Can you tell me what it's based on?"

"Listen, whippersnapper, I'm not going to investigate your case for you. Just take it from a P.I. with twenty-some years experience under his belt. I *feel* it in my gut."

"Why?" I asked, and got him good and angry.

"You don't? When you've had my experience and my unerring instincts, you come back and we'll talk."

"Okay," I said. "I just thought if you wanted to get this guy, you might be able to share some insights that might help out. But I guess you don't have any. It's all just instinct. That's okay, I'll keep digging. Have you testified before a grand jury yet?" I asked.

A better reaction I couldn't have hoped for. His lips tightened and his eyes narrowed. He looked for an instant like he had drawn his last breath.

"That," he said, "is none of your business!"

I had my answer. I bid him good day and turned away from his farewell vituperation.

I heard, at my back, amid Fab's ceaseless chattering, the clicking of the metallic handcuffs on his wrist. I speculated that the guard would have been grateful for a similar device to lock Fab's mouth shut.

The dump was especially redolent as I drove past it to my visit with Pia.

And what a contrast she was to her father. She was smiling broadly, riding the shoulders of the world. I knew right away why—Lance had been to see her.

"He's been here, hasn't he?"

She nodded with great enthusiasm. "Oh yes," she said, "I'm in love again."

"Good!" I said, then added on a crest of emotion. "Will he testify?"

The smile didn't leave her pretty lips. "He said he would do anything for me. Anything in the world."

Including, I wondered, giving up his freedom? But I didn't say anything.

23

I made another trip to the ocean house of Pia and her room-mates in the hope of finding Erin at home.
I didn't. Nobody answered my knock on the rear sliding glass so I opened it. I heard muffled voices upstairs that bespoke some activity of a private nature; principals of which would likely not appreciate my presence. I slid the door shut quietly and went for another stroll on the beach, keeping my eye on the house. Then I worried that the front door might have been unlocked, and I might miss the characters should they egress that way.

It took a bit of doing, watching both doors. Anyone who could have seen me would have had to conclude I was nuts. I stayed as close to the two doors as I thought reasonable. I developed a routine walking back and forth between the back and the front street through the park. The windows in the house were in the back for the ocean view, so I stayed as clear of them as I thought I could without missing any action.

I was in the park looking toward the house when I saw them come out perhaps half an hour after I began my vigil. They were both carrying surfboards. I didn't have to squint to recognize Suzy and the inimitable Gillian Izuks.

A confrontation, I decided, was not in the cards. The knowledge of their deception, which Suzy at least thought was necessary, was fodder for thought. I returned to the office.

Bomber seemed detached from this case. I sat before him after delivering the news and watched him toy with his fountain pen. "Obviously has to be more here than meets the eye," he said. "That's the conclusion I am inexorably drawn to by your investigation. It could also explain why the district attorney felt compelled to use the secret grand jury venue."

"Hmm," I muttered to let him know I was still alive.

"Well, two things," Bomber said. "We'll have to hammer Web for a complete discovery on the case and push for an early trial. Web's method may be to indict Pia, then sit around until some real evidence comes down the pike to support it. We don't want to wait. The defense is entitled to a speedy trial, and we shall press for it."

'We' turned out to be me, and I was dispatched to the office of the district attorney of Weller County.

I waited only twenty-five minutes for my audience with his highness. Not too bad in the scheme of things. I wasn't exactly a legal heavyweight in the county bar. It wasn't like keeping Bomber waiting, so Web took full advantage of the snub by proxy. After all, the D.A. always felt snubbed when I showed up to do Bomber's bidding.

"What can I do for you, son?" Web asked. Had he *ever* called me 'Son' before? Perhaps it was a cut more respectful than 'Boy', so I wasn't complaining.

"Bomber would like to have your discovery list as soon as possible. I'm willing to take it back with me today. Whatever you have so far, and if you need another day or so to refine it, that's no problem."

"Oh," he said, cocking an eyebrow with what he would have liked me to believe was a gesture of surprise, but I knew better. "What's the hurry?"

"Speedy trial," I said. "Bomber and the defendant want a speedy trial, which, if I'm not mistaken, is her right."

He nodded slowly with a somber turn of his features. On paper that looks a little smart-alecky, but all my dealings with Web are humble pie. "Well," he said, fishing around his desk for something, "I've got a full calendar…"

"Oh, I'm sure," I said. "The wheels of justice can sometimes grind exceedingly slow, but Bomber didn't think this was a matter that would engage your full attention. Probably fob it off on one of your ace prosecutors."

Now Web's head moved with a seesaw motion, as if to say maybe so.

"I imagine Bomber would like that," he said, then added, a mite immodestly, I thought, "give him an easier time of it." He rocked back in his chair, to give me the impression he was one confident puppy. "I'll have my secretary give you my witness list. If, after you see that, you still want a speedy trial, you shall have it."

His tone implied we would be scared to death of his case and would want all the time in the world to prepare a defense.

I thanked him for his help—he spread his arms as magnanimously as all outdoors and said, "That's what I'm here for."

Yeah, right, I thought, but as I noted before, I kept my counsel.

In less than an hour and a half I was out of there with a half-baked list of witnesses. I suspected something was missing.

I dutifully delivered the goods to Bomber, told him I had made the pitch for the speedy trial, even suggested Web would probably not want to bother himself with such an insignificant case. Bomber smiled. We all knew better. You didn't get much more significant cases than sex and murder, and when the accused was unusually young and pretty, the papers couldn't run her picture often enough, and every time they ran her picture a presumption of guilt was fortified, and the name of our fearless District Attorney Webster A. Grainger III was inevitably mentioned.

Bomber looked over the list. "What've we got here?"

"No surprises," I said. "The housemates, th-three of them. C-coroner, cops, Fab t-to tell us he bought the g-gun."

Bomber shook his head. "Something's wrong. This is no case. Why is Web so cocky?"

I shook my head in response. "M-maybe one of the roommates is g-going to say she *saw* her d-do it?"

"Wouldn't *that* be something? You talked to them all. What's your sense?"

"Didn't. The third g-girl, Erin, I couldn't get a hold of."

"Think this Suzy could be our nemesis?"

I nodded.

"How can we find out?" he asked. It was obviously a question directed at me which I didn't have a good answer for, but I knew from experience he didn't expect an immediate answer, though he did expect me to find one.

I laid out my housemate theory, that they were all frightened they would be blamed and so lined up in a solid phalanx against Pia, who, on the surface would have the greatest motive. Then there was Suzy and creepy Gillian who could easily be in cahoots to get Gillian the inheritance which he might share with Suzy for her role in throwing the suspicion on Pia.

"An accomplice?" Bomber asked.

"Maybe."

"And the elusive girl? Could there be a connection there?"

"Could be," I admitted, though I didn't know what.

"Ah, well," Bomber said, lacing his hands behind his head and tilting back on his chair, much as the district attorney had done earlier that day. "Doesn't get us anywhere speculating unless we can pin it on someone. All four of the girls could have *wanted* to kill him for different reasons, but that doesn't cut a lot of ice down at the courthouse. You gotta find the missing pieces here," he said; he seemed so satisfied with himself, as though he had discovered a cure for cancer by fobbing the solution off on little me, that I didn't have the heart to respond. I didn't have to tell him that if someone had something to hide they were unlikely to blurt their secret out to me. Witness the odd relationship between Suzy and Gillian.

24

Erin Winterbottom was a *femme fatale*, and she was avoiding me with some creative ruses. I'd left several messages on her cell phone and had yet to receive a return call.

"Oh man, not you," she said when I trapped her in the University library. "This is *such* a drag."

Erin's attire sent a message: I don't care about clothes. I wouldn't dress up to save my life. At the same time her 'casual' and uninteresting attire unmistakably called attention to all the places on her well-formed body deemed worthy of attention, which was to say, just about everywhere.

Tight, low-rise jeans, a bare midriff to put you in mind of Connecticut, and an off-white (we wouldn't want anything *too* clean looking) stretch halter top which did its job but not much else.

I sat next to her at the long table, surrounded by earnest students looking at books and thinking about their boy/girl-friends. The move made Erin uncomfortable. I tried small talk, it didn't take. She finally said, "Like, don't you get it? I don't want to talk to you about Pia or anything else. So leave me alone. I already told the police everything I know."

"You don't seem too forthcoming, Erin. Is there a reason for it?"

"Yeah, well, like I said, it's a drag. I don't want to be involved."

"Do you think *anyone* wants to be involved? Don't we owe a fair shake to those in trouble?"

"Yeah, well, Pia made her bed and now I guess she's got to lie in it."

"If you were in her shoes, wouldn't you want honesty and decency from your friends?"

"I wouldn't call her a friend, actually," she said. "We lived in the same house is all."

"All right, that's a bond, isn't it?"

"Hey, look, what do you want from me?"

"Just tell me what you know."

"I don't know anything. I *swear!*"

"Then why do you suppose the district attorney wants you to testify?"

She was silent for a moment—brooding. She rubbed the eraser end of her pencil back and forth on the table in front of her. Finally, she shrugged. "Like, he told me I don't have to talk to you if you ask."

I nodded. "Did he also tell you you *could* talk to me if you wanted to?"

She nodded. "I don't want to," she said.

"Why not?"

"It's just really...a drag."

"Think how it is for Pia."

"Yeah, well, that's like, her problem," Erin said. "I got problems of my own."

"Oh yeah?" I said, my interest perked. "What are they?"

"You don't want to know."

"Oh, but I do," I said, trotting out my store of earnestness.

She stared at me for a long moment, as if trying to decide. Then she shook her head with resolution. "No," she said, "I'm not going there."

"Why not?" (Last gasp.)

"It's none of your business."

There was something about the futility of trying to get honey from lemons. I couldn't even get lemon juice.

Soundly beaten, I stood and left her with, "If you have a change of heart, here's my card." I put the card on the table in front of her. She didn't look at it.

On my way out of the front door of the library, I thought I saw a familiar face approaching in the distance. Just in case it was who I thought it was, I ducked behind the nearest kiosk, which was crammed with flyers, announcements, ads for roommates. After I dodged Gillian Izuks moving in haste as though with a mission toward the library door, (I'd managed to keep out of his sight,) my eye landed on a simple announcement:

Want to make a lot of money?
Women call 555-5505!
NO WIMPS!

Curious, I thought. I called the inimitable Bonnie V. Doone on my "celery" phone and asked her to call the number. Then I headed back to the library reading room with its long tables and Erin Winterbottom.

As I half expected, Gillian Izuks was occupying the same chair I had just left, his head bent in earnest conversation with Erin. From my vantage point, hidden by a shelf of newspapers, it looked to me as though Erin was no happier talking to him than she had been listening to me.

Neither of them seemed too happy with the encounter actually. Gillian, I'd say, was downright angry—Erin more sullen.

Suddenly Gillian grabbed her wrist and yanked her to her feet, releasing a muffled scream from her mouth. He froze in place long enough for her to collect her books and belongings and then pulled her from the room. If anyone noticed, no one moved a muscle.

I kept a safe distance between us as I followed Gillian and Erin out to the parking lot, where I had luckily parked. It was a big lot, and I could imagine him throwing her in a car and driving off without me being able to track them.

Gillian opened the doors of what must have been his uncle DeWitt's Lexus with the electronic signal from his key, then he threw her in the back seat and locked the doors, opening his door without unlocking hers. He must have had it set on kiddy control because I thought I saw her trying to get out and being unable to open the door.

I hustled to my car and barely kept him in my sights until I saw him turn onto the freeway. I gave chase, and though he was fairly far ahead of me, I was able, by changing lanes like a drunken sailor, to keep an eye on him.

He got off at the exit just before Albert Avenue where our office was. He made one turn onto Vine Street—a bit seedy—then drove a few blocks before pulling into a driveway.

He popped his door open, jumped out, clicked the back door open with his key, then grabbed Erin by her wrist again and pulled her out of the car and toward the house in the back of the lot. From where I was, it looked like it could have been a converted garage.

When I heard a door slam, I left my car, hoping to quickly search the belongings Erin had left behind in the car, and if they yielded no hints, I might approach the house, check it out, and maybe knock on the door to see what kind of response I'd get. I wasn't sure how I'd explain my presence there—I don't think they'd have believed a Fuller Brush Man pitch. I could say, Oh, it's you—I thought I was witness to a kidnapping, but if it's you, I'm sure it's just a misunderstanding—right Erin?

Oh well, it was an idea. I won't say a good one, but *something*.

I approached the car stealthily, and then, as I touched the back door handle, a horrendous alarm went off.

I quickly dashed for the nearest bush, but too late. I felt a thud on the back of my head, then all was silent.

The alarm had miraculously stopped.

25

Flash bulbs were popping behind my eyeballs. I was afraid to open my eyes.

If they called this "coming-to" it wasn't all it was cracked up to be.

My head felt cracked...up. I gingerly lifted a hand to feel around my skull in case I had to push my brains back in.

I heard a roaring sound in my ears.

I don't know how long I lay there or how long I was aware I was lying there or when I caught on to my surroundings while I searched for a memory of what happened.

My first indication that I was rational occurred when my hands sent a message to my scrambled brain that the surface underneath me was sand and the roar I heard in my head was the ocean. I heard no other sounds of civilization and speculated for a while where I could be. I was still afraid to open my eyes.

Then an odor hit me: alcohol. Was I near a barroom? I heard no noise. Another mystery.

Civilization began to thin up the coast from Angleton. I was probably somewhere up the coast, but how far and how would I get back? A quick feel of my pockets confirmed my suspicion. I had been robbed. The question was, had I been robbed by someone who wanted to rob me, or was I the victim of someone whose motive was not robbery, who robbed me to obliterate my identity, and throw me off the scent?

My head was throbbing, but since I was more or less conscious I began planning to find my way out of there. The easiest idea might be to go down the beach. I just didn't feel in any shape to go anywhere, and following the coastline could result in a long a hazardous schlep—so long, I doubted if I could complete it. I had to find the nearest road. Depending how far north I was, that could be a far piece.

When, at last, I felt able to brave opening my eyes a crack, everything was black and I thought I had gone blind. I snapped my eyes shut in fear, as though leaving them open might exacerbate the blindness.

Finding civilization, if I were blind, might be a challenge.

Did I fall asleep again? It must have been some time before I was conscious again and dared to open my eyes—just a slit at first then more bravely. It was dark, but for the first time I had a sense that it was a different darkness than when my eyes were closed. I saw a pinpoint of light which soon came into focus with the black ocean; a roaring of the waves rising and falling.

My next goal was to get on my feet. It didn't happen. The pain in my head was too great and it knocked me back down before I'd managed to get the second foot under me. I did a lot of deep breaths and stretching in place as a tribute to the yoga gods. It was a painfully slow process.

Somehow I managed to drag myself in the direction away from the ocean to the place where the sound of the waves began to intermingle with the sounds of a freeway. The traffic sounded intermittent, and I realized it must either have been the wee hours of the morning or I must have been pretty far from any population density.

I must tell you, already at that early stage of my pain-wracked odyssey, I was beginning to rethink my chosen profession. "Chosen" may be a stretch. I could say I was hounded into it by my father, who bided his time while I was pursuing my dream of being a composer. A more income-parched livelihood I can't imagine. That was intelligence Bomber had at his command, and when he felt the time was right he proffered law school, books, tuition, room and board and all the spending money I needed. He had let me sink or swim as a composer, and

I wasn't swimming.

It went okay at first after I graduated and came to work for Bomber—starting the payback which was not mentioned initially. Of course I could have sought employment elsewhere, but Angleton was not fertile ground for advocates. Everyone wanted to live here including you, me and every lawyer on the face of the earth.

What do you have when you have five thousand lawyers buried to their necks in the sand?

Not enough sand.

With my head pounding like a jackhammer, I was contemplating reducing the pool of Angleton lawyers by one. Then I realized I didn't really practice law, I did investigation for a guy who did—the guy who suckered me into this death trap in the first place.

I got to the freeway—don't ask me how—but I was exhausted, and I found I couldn't take another step. I vaguely remember thinking it would be foolish to lie down by the side of the road, where the cars whiz by at eighty-five miles-per-hour, but by that time there wasn't really any choice.

The next thing I remember is staring up into the soothing face of a policeman, who was speaking to me kindly in a high voice. I didn't expect any cop, under the circumstances, to be kind to me, then I noticed the face was finely featured and as I closed my eyes again I realized it was a woman and a very attractive one. My natural thought was, "Oh, no, don't let Joan see me with her."

My next memory was of being loaded into an ambulance. Then I lost consciousness until I awoke in a hospital bed with the gorgeous officer of the law standing over me, smiling like an angel of mercy, not to mention justice.

"That must have been *some* party," she said.

"Party?" I said, "What party?" Speech was coming somewhat easier to me, though it was still no piece of cake.

"Don't tell me you put on that roaring drunk alone?"

"Drunk? What drunk?"

"You were sleeping it off by the freeway. You smelled like a still."

It was coming back to me—that foreign alcohol smell that I couldn't understand. It didn't take me long to speculate I had been doused with booze to make it seem like I was drunk. The grievous assault on my person had been by amateurs.

I forced my eyes open to focus on the officer of the law standing over me. She was not stable, but parts of her were drifting one way and other parts the other—like one of those desert mirages aided and altered by intense heat.

"Don't drink," I said, the words barely clearing my teeth.

"That's good advice," she said. "Why didn't you take it?"

Then suddenly I was back where I started, and everything went black.

26

I had visitors in the hospital—sometimes before I realized it. There were flashes of consciousness, but they didn't last. The ceilings of the room swam by, or a face beside the bed and over me drifted into fuzzy focus and drifted out again. I heard voices, but not what they were saying.

In time, the images prolonged their visits to my brain, until I could recognize my mother by my bed. I felt her caring warmth, her concern, her anxiety—real but not overt.

Then there was Bomber. I don't know if he came before I realized it and if so, how often. I never had the nerve to ask him. Then one day there he was, larger than life, and I remember thinking he must have traded his elevator shoes for stepladders he was so high above me.

"Jesus Jenny, boy! What the Sam Hill's going on here? You want some down time? Say so. You don't have to go to this extreme. Get back on your feet. We need you," and he was gone. But that "we need you" stuck with me till my next memory.

Joan. I felt her lean over and put her cheek next to mine, and when I began to feel a familiar yearning, I knew I was getting better.

Then there was the police officer hovering by my bed as though to see that no one spirited me off to oblivion. There was something peculiar about her. I don't mean to seem ungrateful, for a strong case could be made that she saved my life. But I got the weird vibe that she thought I was hiding something. I was hit on the head and dumped—what did she expect me to remember that I didn't?

As I draw on these memories for this report, I am

suddenly struck by doubt. Had my loved ones really been there in my hospital room as I remembered, or was it my imagination based on my subconscious recollections?—that bizarre arrangement of atoms and quarks, or what have you, that was lodged in my subconscious—or had their voices triggered memories of them? They had each acted just as I remembered them, as I would have expected them to act.

Would, for instance, my father bawl me out while I was semiconscious (or un-) in a hospital bed? Would he do it just for fun? I wonder, but I wasn't going to ask him, because I wouldn't be able to trust his answer.

But as I said, it was my yearning for Joan that put me back on the road to conscious recovery. That just seemed indisputably real.

And this nagging cop seemed as much a part of the room as that gizmo that dripped something into my arm. I should have felt good about her—been reassured—after all she must have had a stake in keeping me alive, and how can you look that gift horse in the mouth? But something about her annoyed me, and I don't mean to be ungrateful.

It turned out my original impression she was a looker was a wishful hallucination. Her name was Nellie Rucker. She was a big-boned woman, who must have challenged the weight limits of the police department. She was shaped like a top and always seemed to be hiking her pants up, the weight of the firepower on her belt and gravity acting at counter purposes to her shape. I wanted to suggest suspenders, but I didn't think it was my place.

"Hi, Big Guy," she said when I opened my eyes, seeming to think all men would be flattered to be called Big Guy. "You up to a chat?"

I groaned.

"Good. My name's Nellie Rucker, but you can call me anything but late for dinner."

This lame old joke seemed to amuse her—giving her a sense of accomplishment in remembering it (I wish I could forget it), not to mention her flawless delivery.

"I work vice," she said, hiking her pants. "I'm not a hooker or a pimp, I work the other side of the street—and I don't mean vice president."

If there was some relevance to my condition she was holding it back.

"So let's talk about the party, Sport," she said. At first I thought she was talking about some unrecognizable party-sport that I couldn't get my fuzzy mind hunkered down around the idea of. Then I realized she was calling *me* Sport—but what the heck?—as long as she didn't call me late for dinner.

"I don't know anything about a party," I said. "I don't remember any party. What are you talking about?"

"You a solitary drinker?" she asked, "Out there in the wilderness, just you and your bottle?"

I shook my head, and that was not a good idea. There was something loose in there—rattling around. It was probably my organ of good sense, which had become detached in the festivities. "Don't drink," I said, and I had some dim memory of imparting this intelligence to her before.

"That's good advice," she said, hiking her pants. "Pity you didn't take it."

"I don't know what…"

"You smelled strong of the sauce, Sport," she said as though lecturing a nincompoop. And she was at no pains to disguise the fact that she didn't suffer nincompoops gladly. When I said nothing—what was the point?—she said, "How would *you* account for the horrendous smell?"

"Well, I suppose someone could have poured the booze on me to make it look like I was drunk."

"And tsetse flies give milk," she said, nodding her ridicule of the thought—but I could sense she was considering the possibility.

"Okay," she said, "what's the last thing you remember before you came-to in no-man's land?"

"I followed this guy—the murdered guy's nephew…" I

was embarrassed I couldn't think of the name of either of them, "…to a house on…" now I couldn't think of the street name. Was I rendered senile before my time by the untimely blow on my head? "…then I went up the driveway to investigate his car, and that's it."

"Lights out?" she said, completing my thought.

"Yeah."

"Did you see where this person went? The nephew, was it?"

"Yeah—into a building in back—a garage, a second house, I don't know."

"Was he alone?"

"No," I said, reaching for a clearer picture of this past trauma, "…a girl."

"Woman," Nellie corrected me. "How old was this *woman?*"

"College girl."

"Woman."

"Of course," I didn't want to fight political correction with the politically correct, though I expect Bomber would have ridiculed her had he been there. That thought gave me a thought. Perhaps I should have Bomber here as my attorney while Officer Rucker was grilling me.

"You catch the address of the property where you got hit?"

"No. I wasn't looking for street numbers, I was trying to protect the girl."

"Woman."

"Yes."

"Protect her from what?"

"I don't know—harm, I suppose."

"What did you think was going to happen to her?"

I frowned. "I don't know."

The pants were elevated again for emphasis. "Tell that to the Marines, Sport," she said. "I'm from Missouri—the show-me state."

"You really from…" then I realized it was just a figure of speech.

"Why were you looking in the car?"

"For clues," I said, before I realized I was saying too much.

"Clues for what? You playing cops and robbers again?"

It was the "again" that threw me. When had I played before to her knowledge? What *was* her knowledge, and where did she get it? I didn't give her an answer because I didn't have one.

"Okay, Sport, I'm going to show you some pictures. See if you recognize any of these places."

She showed me a bunch of pictures. There were some similarities, but I picked one out I thought was the place at which I was hit over the head. I handed it to her.

She looked at it and nodded.

"You know the place?" I asked, when it became apparent she wasn't volunteering anything.

"You might say that, Sport," she said. "We have it under surveillance."

"For what?"

"Ah," she said, "divulging that information would be against department regulations." She smiled with self-satisfaction as she hiked her pants. "Sometimes the less you know, Sport, the safer you will be."

She took that enigma with her as she slogged her odd shape out of my hospital room. The need, or the desire to protect my person seemed to have gone out with her.

Recuperating took me longer than it seems to in those hard-boiled crime novels where everyone is hit over the head and charges ahead full bore almost as soon as they come to.

One of my later visitors was Bonnie V. Doone, "Cuddles" to the cognoscenti.

"How's it goin', Sweet Meat?" she greeted me with her studied irreverence.

"Did you call that number?" I asked Bonnie Doone who was in rapt concentration on her newest chartreuse fingernails. My memory must have been on its way back.

"Ugh," she said, then shuddered. "A man answered. Not a voice you wanted to talk to a second more than you had to."

"What was the job?" I prodded, lest Bonnie Doone forget the question.

"Entertaining men, he said, and he obviously thought he was being coy and mysterious. Then after a couple of moments for his nefarious scheme to sink in, he said, 'The money is very good. If you *have* no problem with that, I'll set up an…interview' and there was something about the way he pronounced the word 'interview' that gave me the creeps. I *had* a problem with it, so I hung up on him."

By the time I felt reasonably steady on my feet, and the hospital was willing to release me to my own care, it was time to investigate the pool of jurors from which our panel would be chosen.

The profiles of favorable jurors for Pia Franceschi's case were not as simple in concept as some cases were. For instance, it would seem that young women who might have found themselves in similar abusive relationships would side with Pia emotionally, but there was the risk that some women who were, or had been, in abusive relationships were in them by choice and might be cowed by the man or the idea of the man rather than sympathetic to her fellow female. This may seem far-fetched, because we thought our client was innocent, but decisions are often made and jury verdicts are often obscured by emotions. It has been said that, in an election, about ten percent of the voters understand the issues, which causes you to wonder how the other ninety percent make up their minds.

In my early days of working for Bomber, I advanced a notion or two similar to the reasoning that what he was telling me to look for was not really connected to the issue at the bar. For example, in a case like Pia's, I might have expressed the thought that a prospect's past life was far removed from how he or she would consider hard evidence presented in court.

Bomber scoffed. "Far removed," he said, "is often the difference between victory and defeat. It only takes one rotten apple to spoil a barrel of jurors—and that contrary vote is too often grounded in emotions, prejudices, biases, irrationality not admitted to or discovered in the initial questioning of jurors. Sometimes the jurors don't understand their hang-ups themselves. So don't be intimidated by far removed. Dig for it— bring it to me. We want to know *everything.*"

Since those early days I have achieved a hard-won perspective on Bomber's high-sounding pronouncements. It is so much easier to talk about what we want in an ideal world than it is to get it in the real world. I do my best. When we have an inkling of some unsympathetic thought or trait in a prospective juror, Bomber will challenge, then failing that, which he usually does except in egregious circumstances, he will use a peremptory challenge. When the peremptories have run out, it becomes a crapshoot. My job is to minimize the risk. We all acknowledge it would be so much better if you could rely on people to be always rational, but that is too far removed from reality to even consider. Bomber has become a master of the emotional appeal to the irrational.

Would men be more sympathetic, generally, to Pia than women? She is accused of killing a man, after all—not something you would expect the males to sympathize with.

Generally a defense attorney in a murder case is not eager to have law and order types on his jury.

The bad news was the list for this trial was loaded with law and order conservatives—and this was a liberal town. The mayor and one hundred percent of the city council were liberals. The university and city college faculties kept the politics sympathetic to liberal causes, and that included opposition to the death penalty, sympathy for the accused, and a wary eye for the police, suspecting authority figures of being rogues. That *had* to include our district attorney. Oh, where were these sympathetic jurors when we needed them?

There were some, of course, but I didn't see how we could mathematically expect to get even seven of the twelve of that favorable stripe.

When I handed Bomber my sheets of findings, he studied it and shook his head.

"We have to solve this thing before it goes to the jury room."

"Like Perry Mason?" I offered, and shouldn't have.

He shot me one of his unmistakable disgusted glares. "That's fiction," he said, "this is real."

I knew he didn't like to be compared to Earle Stanley Gardner's fictional defense attorney. People did it all the time—but it wasn't okay for me to do it. I knew it; I did it anyway, because I knew what was coming next.

"So the onus is on you, me boy," he said, with a bright, cheerful, dare I say supercilious, smile? "Get us the killer before the jury speeches."

"But I c-can't, I m-mean, I d-didn't …yet."

He waved me and my sentiment off. "Start with the bozo who hit you over the head."

"B-but I d-didn't see him—"

Another wave from the all-knowing Bomber. "The cops are, or were, watching the place. They owe you that much."

"Don't want t-to t-tell."

"Naturally," he said. "Never do. But I think you are entitled to know who tried to kill you. Attempted murder is, the last time I looked, still taken seriously in these parts."

I started to talk—well, I opened my mouth anyway—but Bomber cut me off again. "I know," he said. "They don't want to jeopardize their investigation and all that blarney. Well, you tell them for me they've had plenty of time and a free hand to nail the culprits. The trail is already colder than a naked Eskimo, so there's no jeopardy involved. Go to Web if you have to."

Not, I didn't add, an appetizing prospect. Bomber knew, and I knew, Web was not disposed to muddy the waters of his case by taking the spotlight off Pia Franceschi and directing it on someone else. He considered that a Bomber tactic of subterfuge—which he had come to expect. That Bomber expected it was one thing; aiding and abetting the defense was quite another.

So I went to see Officer Nellie Rucker—what were my options?

She didn't look so peculiar seated behind the desk she had been provided, or commandeered, for the occasion. I told her my story—so sympathetically any hardboiled cop would have had tears in his eyes.

Not Nellie—"My heart cries out for you," she said, "*plus* I *feel* your pain."

She *didn't* feel my pain—couldn't, wouldn't. We both knew that.

"My hands are tied," she said, holding up two hands that were decidedly *not* tied.

"Untie them," I said. "Someone tried to kill me. I don't think asking you what you know about it is asking too much."

"I see you're in a jar."

"What's that?"

"You're in the pickle jar—in a pickle, get it?"

I groaned. Nellie was not dissuaded. "You want help with your case. Everyone understands that. I can tell you, the information you want has no bearing on your case, but giving you our suppositions would not only jeopardize our investigation, it could open up a can of worms, leading to an unpleasant lawsuit."

There it was again—the old shibboleth, the canard that was stymieing institutions everywhere: fear of lawsuits. Unfortunately, the fear was not unfounded.

"Okay," I said, "let me ask you just a couple of questions—shake your head for no. Don't say anything for yes. Okay?"

She shook her head.

"Okay," I said, "I'm going to ask them anyway. I don't know about you, but I'd sure rather answer *my* questions than have Bomber ask me them on the stand. You know his reputation for reducing witnesses to blithering idiots?"

"I don't intimidate," she said, with an edgy bravado that made me suspect she *did* intimidate, that is *could be* intimidated, just like the rest of us.

"Okay," I said, "Your investigation involves the property on which I was assaulted—let's say with intent to kill, or at least do grievous bodily harm. That last was eminently successful."

She said nothing.

"Is one of the subjects of your investigation the victim in the case of California vs. Pia Franceschi? One DeWitt Izuks?"

No answer.

"Or his nephew Gillian Izuks?"

Nothing.

"Was Pia Franceschi associated in any way with that property and whatever went on there?"

She didn't respond to that either, so I said with more hope than reason, "The answer to all of my questions is affirmative?"

She continued to stare me down. "I told you, Sport, no can do."

"You mean you'd sooner send this innocent Pia Franceschi to the gas chamber than 'jeopardize' your investigation?"

"I don't make the rules, Sport."

"Who does?"

She wouldn't tell me that either. My option was to work my way up the chain of command in hopes—of what? Someone would slip up? I decided to get directions from Bomber.

When I told him my tale in his office, I was dispirited.

Bomber wasn't. He was delighted. "*Wonderful!*" he crowed. "Good work...Sport? Not a bad nickname for you. If we get no more out of Nellie Bly—"

"Rucker," I corrected him.

"Yes, yes, whatever, but here's the beauty of the thing. Don't go any farther."

"Why n-not?" I asked, confounded. "D-don't you think it's im-important?"

"Sure it is, but we'll put her on the stand. Let the jury get a gander at her hiking up her pants and sitting there like a deaf and dumb dodo bird. She won't answer and that'll be *great!* That's got reasonable doubt written all over it. I can't wait. Good work...*Sport!*"

28

We got our jurors—though calling them *our* jurors was a stretch. Four of them, at most, could be counted as favorable, or at least disposed to our point of view. The rest were dead serious about the "Thou shalt not kill" commandment, and that "An eye for an eye" was a philosophy to live by. You could argue that "An eye for an eye", if strictly adhered to, would eventually cause universal blindness, but "Thou shalt not kill" was pretty much unassailable in polite society.

"Not to worry," Bomber said expansively at the defense table in the big courtroom after we were settled with this motley crew that was to hold in their vengeful hands the fate of our innocent Pia. "You are going to find the *real* culprit before we have to make any appeal to these vigilantes."

"Thanks," I muttered.

The judge we had drawn, Damien Fairly, was a straight arrow who had gone as far as possible to remove his personality and personal biases from his conduct of his cases. Bland, perhaps, but a refreshing change in cases involving the volatile, histrionic, polarizing Bomber, who too often had difficulty subordinating his intellect and knowledge of the law to a judge he was convinced was his inferior.

Bomber didn't seem to be in any hurry to leave the courtroom after the jury selection had been completed. While we watched the back of District Attorney Webster A. Grainger III saunter out of the courtroom without a care in the world, and Pia being taken back to her cell, Bomber leaned back on the hind two legs of his chair. It reminded me of how in my impressionable youth Bomber would growl, "The chair has *four* legs for a reason. Sit on them all!" whenever I attempted the same trick.

"Web is so blessed confident," Bomber said, shaking his head in wonder. "I've never known him to have a *weaker* case, and yet to look at him, you'd think he had a slam dunk."

There was no arguing that proposition.

"I wonder what he has," Bomber mused. "Are we going to see some bozo on the stand say he *saw* Pia pull the trigger, or another tell how he saw her discard the gun in the ocean only to have the gun introduced into testimony with a foolproof ballistics match-up?"

"Don't see anyb-body on the witness l-list…"

"Oh, you know. Some trick at the last minute. Remember the guy who came in with the gun in that Chicago matron murder—in her estate on the ocean here?"

He was referring to the case I wrote up as *She Died For Her Sins*. The gun appeared during the trial and there was a legitimate question about how long the district attorney had had it.

You'd think our public servants like the district attorney would always be above board—only wishing to serve truth and justice, but sometimes they want to win, the same as everyone else, and can easily fall into the temptation of shortcuts.

But the next morning when the trial began in earnest, Web's opening statement held no surprises. Nor was there any indication he had anything up his sleeve.

Bomber made no opening statement, and after Web paraded the boilerplate witnesses, that only succeeded in establishing there had been a murder by gunshot, the victim being found in Pia Franceschi's bed without any evidence of whodunit.

Bomber was playing it real cool, hardly asking any questions, giving the impression of a man who was confident in his case. The most confident trophy was going to be hard fought between the two advocates.

That afternoon Bomber got what he considered a brutal shock, and in typical fashion he overreacted.

After spying the visitor in the audience, he interrupted Web's case to ask for a conference at the judge's bench.

At first I didn't know what he was so worked up about. Then I turned to the audience and saw.

"Your Honor," Bomber began before the judge, "the district attorney and I had an agreement which he has apparently broken. It was an agreement my taking the case was contingent on. I took the case, he broke the agreement."

The judge looked perplexed and I didn't blame him.

"Why are you telling me this? It sounds like this is between you and the district attorney."

"I'm telling you because the district attorney has broken an agreement affecting my very participation in this case."

"What exactly was the agreement?"

"There is a man in the audience who Web had in custody for attempted murder—a charge I hope you will agree is serious. The man in question is, I am convinced, certifiably insane. He also happens to be my client's father. His presence will make defending his daughter impossible. I have neither the stomach, nor the stamina for it. The whole concept is quite simply out of the question."

"Well," the judge said, "that's your decision." Bomber wasn't getting any sympathy or action.

"And Web waited until the case started to spring this surprise on me."

"Your Honor, if I may," Web said, the soul of patient forbearance, "Mr. Franceschi has been incarcerated from when he was booked for aggravated assault. Attempted murder is a charge our office has not made, judging it might be difficult to get a favorable verdict on. As Your Honor well knows, and as I expect Bomber well knows also, we live in the United States of America and cannot hold a suspect indefinitely. Mr. Franceschi is a key witness in this trial. He, quite frankly, refused to give his testimony unless he was released from jail." Web shrugged. "My hands are tied."

"What do you mean?" Bomber demanded. "You told

him the consequences of refusing to testify—was he going to take the fifth?"

Web shook his head. "He wasn't going to testify," he said, "even if we electrocuted him." Then Web put on his Cheshire cat smile. "You want to get off the case, I'm sure the court will indulge your wish, in spite of the unfortunate timing."

I didn't often feel sorry for Bomber, but this argument wasn't going his way and he appeared a petulant teenager in the bargain. He wasn't on very firm ground and I expect he knew it.

"Well, Bomber," the judge said, "if you are quitting the case let's not go any further. What do you say?"

There, the judge had put the great Bomber on the spot. No anger, no recrimination—you want out?—get out. I wonder if the judge, knowing what a handful Bomber can be in court, really wanted him to bow out—doubtless it would save the judge a lot of aggravation. Then, as an afterthought, the judge turned to Web, "What is the nature of this man's testimony?"

"He's the one who gave his daughter the gun."

"Used in this crime?"

"We are assuming that, yes."

"*Assuming?* You have no evidence?"

"Not yet."

The judge settled back on his high back swivel chair.

"So what is all the fuss about? You aren't expecting the father to implicate his daughter, are you?"

"Merely establishing the chain, Your Honor. Fabrizio Franceschi gave Pia Franceschi a gun. The victim is shot with a gun of a similar caliber. The gun is missing. Our duty," Web said, and shrugged lifting his upturned palms to the level of the judge's bench.

Why, I wondered, was Bomber leading us into this quagmire? But I have wondered about his unorthodox actions before and been rewarded with the embarrassment of the unseeing.

But what was it this time? Points with the judge for staying on the case against his will? The judge had preempted that

151

by leaving it up to Bomber—with no emotion whatsoever in his question. Putting the district attorney on the defensive? I saw no evidence of anything of the sort taking hold. Positioning himself as a bargain chip for later redemption? I didn't see it.

Perhaps time would tell—though it could very well tell nothing.

Bomber stood silently before the judge as though he expected someone to solve his dilemma.

"What is it you want, Bomber?" the judge asked.

"I want the interests of my client to be served, as the district attorney vouchsafed they would be. The defendant can in no way get a fair trial with her father on the loose. He was in jail for trying to kill her—now he's out."

Web broke in, "Bomber, as is his wont, exaggerates. It was a vehicular accident. He wasn't trying to kill anybody. I can't keep him in jail indefinitely as the defendant's attorney wants."

"Then why did you promise?" Bomber asked.

"You must have misunderstood. I *kept* him in jail until the trial. He can't testify from jail."

"Put him back."

Web shrugged and looked at the judge for guidance.

The conferences at the bar were intended to be out of hearing range of the jury, but Bomber had a way of letting key words drift through. Of course he would be admonished to keep his voice down and he would duck his head and say, "I stand corrected."

Then, too, Bomber's body language was a giveaway. The glances at the audience, the gestures—he never looked at the jury, he didn't want them thinking he had any designs on influencing them unethically. I watched the jury. They weren't deaf, dumb and blind and I suspect by the time Bomber was finished most of the jurors had in their minds there was something suspicious about the witness who was about to be called to testify.

"Cases are not always won with facts, kid," he'd said to me more than once. "Psychology. That's what we've got to know.

Psychology rules the day."

"Call your next witness, Mr. District Attorney," the judge said.

"The prosecution calls Fabrizio Franceschi."

29

No doubt about it, this was Fab's big moment. His approach to the witness stand was positively Shakespearian: his arms swung like a raw recruit of the French Foreign Legion, his head tilted up like Iago spinning a tale.

He took his seat and surveyed the audience to check that all eyes were on him, then jumped up when the clerk reminded him he had to take an oath. It gave him an early opportunity to show his wares.

"Truth, truth? You bet. Nothing but," was his response. The clerk was befuddled and looked to the judge for direction.

"Mr. Franceschi," the judge said patiently, "the response is 'I do'—if you promise to tell the truth and nothing but the truth, say 'I do'."

"I do, yes, you bet. I'm not going to lie to you."

Judge Fairly inhaled and sank back in his chair. "Very well," he said, "you may begin."

"State your full name for the record, please," the clerk said.

"Fabrizio Fruta Franceschi."

"Fruta?" Bomber whispered to me—the whisper breached the distance to the jury. "Fruit? Three F's—I'll be damned."

Web stood up to distract the attention from Bomber's indiscretion. By now we knew there was no point in calling attention to all of Bomber's outrageous actions.

"Mr. Franceschi, what is your occupation?"

"I'm a private detective," he said, puffing out his chest.

"Are you related to the defendant?"

154

"The defendant?" he asked as though surprised at the question. "Well, yes, I'm her father."

"Do you know her occupation?"

"Her occupation? Well, she was a student before all this mess."

"What mess are you referring to, Mr. Franceschi?" Web asked.

"Why this trumped up murder charge," he said. "She's as innocent as the day she was born."

Bomber was smiling. So far, Fab wasn't hurting us at all.

The judge stepped in. "Mr. Franceschi, please don't offer us your opinion on anything, just answer the questions."

"I did answer it," Fab said, more innocently than defiantly.

"Your daughter's guilt or innocence is a matter for the jury to decide—after they've heard all the evidence."

Fab shrugged as though that were of little moment to him.

"How long has your daughter been a student at the university?"

"This is her first year."

"And how long has she lived at her present address... near the university?" Web added, so as not to confuse his question with jail.

"Since January."

"About four months?"

"That's right."

"Where did she live before January?"

"In student housing."

"Did you approve of the move?"

"Approve? Yes. Well, I want her to be responsible. I don't want to second-guess everything. The way she presented it, it sounded okay."

"How did she present it?"

"Moving to a house on the ocean with three other girls—a three bedroom—no men involved. She was excited about having her own room. She didn't say anything about the landlord."

"Who was the landlord?"

"Izuks, or something like that. DeWitt, I believe—"

"As far as you know, is he the victim in this case?"

"Yeah—you could say that—but I think the *real* victim is Pia."

"Your Honor?" Web pleaded.

"Yes, Mr. Franceschi, no editorializing."

"Yeah, okay."

"Did you have reason to change your mind about Pia's living arrangements—after she moved in?"

"Well, yes I did," Fab said. "Indeed!"

"What caused you to change your mind?"

"I was hearing scuttlebutt about this so-called landlord. How he was coming to the house at all hours, letting himself in without knocking. I heard he tried to sleep with the girls."

"Did you recommend any action to your daughter?"

"Well, yes, I did. I told her to get out of there as fast as she could."

"What did she say?"

"She said she had a year's lease and couldn't get out of it. She'd lose her deposit, the landlord would take her to court, she could lose all the rent."

"How did you respond?"

"Well, I told her in no uncertain terms, I would use the full force of my well-regarded reputation in law and order to see that she got a fair shake. No judge on earth would rule against a daughter of mine."

"Her response?"

"She wouldn't hear of it. She wanted to be grownup, you know, *independent.*" He pronounced the word as though it was poison on his tongue.

"Did you accept it?"

"Well," he shrugged as though asking for understanding, "what was I going to do? The law says she's an adult."

"Were you fearful...for her safety?"

"Indeed I was."

"Did you do anything about it?"

"Hell yes, I did."

"Please, Mr. Franceschi—no profanity," Judge Fairly said.

"Well, I bought her a gun," Fab said.

"Did you give it to her?" the district attorney asked.

"Yes, I did."

"Did you show her how to use it?"

"I tried to, but she wasn't interested. Said she'd never use it anyway, so I could save my breath."

"What did you do with the gun?"

"I put it in her dresser drawer."

"Did you show her where?"

"I told her."

"When did you see the gun last?"

"That was it. I was going to show her how to shoot it..."

"Did you have cause to look for it anytime after you put it in her dresser drawer?"

"After I heard about the murder, I made a beeline for that drawer, you better believe it."

"Did you find the gun?"

"No—nothing. I went through all the drawers and though the entire house with a fine-toothed comb. Believe me, I'm a detective, I know my business. If it was there, I'd have found it."

"Did you find it?"

"No," he said.

"No further questions."

Bomber stood up, buttoned his jacket and approached the witness. "Mr. Franceschi," he began, "how would you characterize your relationship with your daughter?"

"I'm her father..."

"Yes, that's implied in the question," Bomber said. "If

157

she's your daughter, that would make you her father."

"Your Honor," Web said, without standing, "I must object to Bomber lecturing the witness."

"Sustained."

"I stand corrected," Bomber said, without his usual humble-pie bow. "Can you answer the question, Mr. Franceschi?"

"What was it?"

"How would you characterize your relationship with your daughter?"

"Characterize? I just told you. Father / daughter."

"Do you get along, Mr. Franceschi?"

"Good as any father with his college-age daughter."

"Know that for a fact, do you? Can you cite any specific scientific studies on the matter?"

"Objection, Your Honor, this is all argumentative and outside the scope of the direct..."

"All right," Judge Fairly said, turning to Fab. "Are we to understand you think your relationship with your daughter is a good one?"

"Yes, I do."

"You may continue, Mr. Hanson."

"A good one?" Bomber said, letting his skepticism get a good airing. "Then why did you try to kill her with your automobile?"

"That's a *lie!*" Fab said, while Web jumped to his feet.

"Objection! Bomber knows better—that comment was inflammatory, without foundation and outside the scope of the direct examination."

"I'm trying to lay the foundation," Bomber protested.

"The objection is sustained. Mr. Hanson, you *do* know better."

"Mr. Franceschi," Bomber turned to Fab, "where have you been residing these last few months?"

"Objection!" Web shouted. "Immaterial—prejudicial."

"His residence is prejudicial?" Bomber asked, all innocent—like he didn't *know* Fab was in jail. "That's news to me."

We were called up to the bench and Web was hot under the collar, so Bomber dropped everything a couple of notches so he was cool as a cucumber in sight of the jury, and it was the district attorney who was agitated. Bomber argued, with quiet dispassion, that his client was on trial for murder and entitled to a vigorous defense and that forestalled any niceties about protecting Fab's good name. "The fact is, Your Honor," Bomber said, "Fabrizio Fruta Franceschi rammed his car into a car driven by my son, with Pia Franceschi as his only passenger. I'm surprised they both weren't killed. I intend to question Franceschi on this *and* introduce the accident report as evidence for the jury to ponder."

"And I will just as strongly object!" Web cried.

"We'll see about that at the proper moment," the judge said. "As for the objection to the question about the witness's 'residence' in jail—it will be my ruling it is not proper at this time, but may be gone into if you decide to call him as a defense witness, Mr. Hanson."

"Fine," Bomber said. "But the district attorney can waive the restriction in the interest of saving time."

"No way," Web said.

"After all," Bomber added, "he broke an agreement with me. He owes us this one."

Web shook his head, "No way," he repeated.

"Very well," the Judge Fairly said, "you may continue, Mr. Hanson." When we were back at our tables, the judge said, "The objection by the district attorney has been sustained at this time. Mr. Hanson will proceed with his questioning."

Mr. Hanson? This is one of the first local judges who was such a stickler for propriety—he didn't call dad, Bomber— "Mr. Hanson" this, and "Mr. Hanson" that. I rather liked it. On the one hand, "Mr. Hanson" was more respectable, on the other, the easy familiarity of "Bomber" was seen by Bomber as a message to the jury he was one of the judge's pals, and this association with the prime authority figure in the trial was bound to rub off on Bomber. This was Bomber's general take on being called Bomber. I'm not sure it had any validity.

Since Bomber had fairly committed to re-calling Fab as a defense witness, he wound down his cross-examination.

"Mr. Franceschi, or should I call you *Detective* Franceschi?"

"That would be fine," Fab said, puffing up.

"All right, Detective, did you tell your daughter the gun you gave her was missing from her dresser?"

"I did."

"How did she respond?"

"She said she didn't know anything about it. She had never touched it, never even looked at it after I put it in there."

"And did you tell her three roommates where the gun was?"

"Yes."

"In case they needed it for *their* protection?"

"Yes."

"Very good," Bomber said, "no further questions."

The police, coroner and ballistics expert did little to lift the case from the realm of circumstantial. If Web had something up his sleeve it wasn't evident.

When we were packing up for the day, after Pia had been taken out of the courtroom to return to her cell, he said in that maddeningly casual manner, "You know we've missed something…"

"What?" I fell for it. I should have kept my mouth shut.

"The wife. The mother, where is she? Does she exist? Why isn't she here? Are they still married?"

"Far's I know—"

"Get the goods from Pia, check her out, as your generation so quaintly puts it. Maybe there's something there we can use."

"Like Fab—Fab did it and confessed to h-her?"

"Nothing would make me happier," he said. "Has she ever even come to see Pia in the slammer?"

"No. Pia said she hasn't even told her what happened."

"That's got to mean something."

"But what?"

"That's what you're going to find out. Maybe she's off balance enough to murder," he said. "I don't know, but anyone who would marry Fab has got to have some screws loose. You'll solve it, I feel it in my bones."

Pia looked better in court than in the meeting room of the jail. I guess that's not surprising, but my heart sank, nonetheless. It had been a while since I'd seen her in this environment, and I'd forgotten how forlorn she looked here. Perhaps it was my projection of her sad circumstances.

We sat facing each other in the secure visiting room. The guard stood outside—lawyer-client privilege.

After Pia reassured me she was surviving her ordeal I asked, "What about your mother, Pia? You haven't told me much about her."

Pia shrugged. "There's not much to tell. She works three jobs to support us."

"*Three?*"

She nodded. "Fab has never been known for his money making. He talks big, but that's all it is—talk. I wouldn't be in college if Yvonne weren't killing herself a hundred hours a week. It's a big stretch as it is."

"What are her jobs?"

"She checks at the supermarket seven to three. Then she waits tables at a restaurant at night. She has Monday night off. Weekends, she's a cashier at a car wash."

"So she hasn't been to see you...down here?"

"When would she have time?" Pia said with a far-off look. "She doesn't have time to get sick."

"Why does she...?" I couldn't finish the question. I realized too late it was insensitive.

"What?"

"No."

"It's okay—you should know everything..."

"Why does she kill herself for Fab?" I asked. "I mean, couldn't she get him to take one of those shifts?"

She shook her head. "Ask her. She'll tell you he's an important man—a *private detective*. Earning a living is beneath him."

"It must be difficult," I said, "to keep you in college."

"A real stretch," she agreed.

She gave me the particulars of her mother's whereabouts. "You might get to talk to her between the market and the restaurant," she said. "If you're lucky."

30

You might say we were blindsided. Erin Winterbottom was District Attorney Webster A. Grainger III's secret weapon, and I'd failed to discover it. You might also say I was on my way to discovering it on Vine Street, before someone so unceremoniously hit me over the head from behind. A hit on the head can play tricks on your reasoning.

Erin Winterbottom looked good on the stand—young, but not naïve. She'd been around the block, but you couldn't say she looked hard. Whatever she was up to wasn't taking a toll on her conscience.

Web started with puffball questions to put her at ease. Though he was on her side, testifying in court could be intimidating.

After he was satisfied Erin was comfortable, Web got to the meat.

"What is your relationship with the defendant, Pia Franceschi?"

"We were housemates."

"How long were you housemates?"

"Since January."

"Of this year?"

"Yes."

"Would you describe your relationship as close, or distant—"

"Oh, close, I'd say close. When you live together like that you get to know each other pretty good."

I looked at Bomber, and he looked back—thin smiles were exchanged. Erin Winterbottom was trying too hard.

"During your acquaintance with Pia Franceschi, was she, to your knowledge, dating anyone?"

"Yes."

"Do you know the name of that person?"

"Yes, it was DeWitt Izuks, our landlord."

"Your landlord?"

"Yes."

"And did that relationship end?"

"Well, yes, it did."

"*How* did it end?"

"She shot him."

"Oh, Your Honor," Bomber said, rising, "that is so outrageous. I must object to it being without foundation, inflammatory, speculative—unless she *saw* it with her own eyes. The response is grossly out of order."

"Sustained," the judge said.

"What is the basis of your response that Pia Franceschi shot DeWitt Izuks in her bed?"

"She told me."

There was a gasp in the courtroom. Both Bomber and I resisted the temptation to look at Pia.

"She told you she had done it?"

"She told me she was going to do it."

"Tell us about that conversation. Where did it take place?"

"At the table. We were having dinner together. I guess she'd had a bad day."

"Objection," Bomber said, "speculative."

"Sustained."

"All right, just tell us what Pia said."

"She said she was fed up. She felt dirty, and she couldn't get away from him. She had to kill him or she would go insane."

"That's a lie!" was shouted from the audience—male, Italian-accented voice. Bomber looked at Web. Dare I say Bomber was crowing? Pia, on the other hand, seemed calm at the testimony.

The judge banged his gavel. "Order in the court," he said. "One more outburst and you will be removed from my courtroom, Mr. Franceschi."

In spite of himself, Web looked at Bomber, who was smiling broadly.

"May we approach, Your Honor?" Bomber asked.

"You may." We went.

"Your Honor," Bomber began, "this man who is interrupting the proceedings and will again if not stopped is the subject of the controversy between the district attorney and myself. He should have been charged with attempted murder and kept locked up. That was our agreement. The district attorney reneged on that agreement mid-trial and now we will all pay the price."

"Your Honor, what Bomber calls attempted murder was really an auto accident. The man's daughter was in the car he hit. He was merely trying to stop the car. He had irrational fears, I admit, but he certainly wasn't trying to kill his own daughter. Now his shouting 'That's a lie' at my witness's testimony certainly isn't helping my case. I wouldn't object to barring him from the courtroom."

"You should lock him up," Bomber said.

"Oh, Bomber," Web said wearily, "you know better. You can't keep a man in jail indefinitely for reckless driving."

"Well, okay," Bomber said. "I'll settle for a restraining order."

"I don't know if we have to be that dramatic," offered Judge Fairly. "Why don't we bar him from the courtroom? We can tell him we don't want him to hear the testimony as he may be called again. I suppose *I* might call him if neither of you want to. If he doesn't obey, we might have firmer ground to lock him up, at least until the trial is over."

"Great solution, Your Honor," Bomber said.

"Agreed," Web said, perhaps chagrined he couldn't have been first with the encomium to the judge.

Judge Fairly announced his decision from the bench,

and Fab rose to express his outrage. "I must protest this, Your Honor. I am a *professional*. I can't be influenced by testimony. My daughter is on trial for her life. I must stand by her."

Bomber whispered to me, "Stand by her in the hall."

With some more commotion, the bailiff escorted Fab to the hall. The judge was reminding the jury that Fab's outburst was emotional; it was not testimony subject to examination. It was from a highly prejudiced father of the defendant.

Web wound down, and it was Bomber's turn.

Bomber rose with a broad smile, as though the opportunity to question Erin Winterbottom was a lifelong dream come true.

"I noticed the prosecutor didn't use your name in his examination. May we remind the jury what your name is?"

"Well...sure...Erin."

"Erin what?"

She paused before answering; I've no doubt she'd had plenty of fun made of her name in the schoolyard. "Winterbottom," she said. I could hear it, but it was a little faint, giving Bomber the opportunity to say, "I'm sorry, could you repeat that a little louder for the jury?"

"*Winterbottom,*" she said, overdoing it in her anger. Bomber had succeeded.

"Very well, Miss Winterbottom. Now, have you, in your lifetime, ever been angry with someone?"

"Well, sure."

"All right, Miss *Winter*bottom—" Bomber was starting to play with inflections of her name. "Did you ever—say in a fantasy—say something like, 'Oh, I'm going to kill that person'?"

"I don't think so—"

"Well, think—did you or didn't you?" Bomber goaded. "Take your time."

"No, then, no. I'd have to say I never wanted to kill anybody."

"Never used it as a figure of speech, say?"

"No."

"Now, please be careful Miss Winter*bottom*, there is a rule of evidentiary law, *falsus in uno falsus in omnibus*. Do you know what that means?"

"No."

"It's Latin—'False in one thing, false in all things.' In other words, if a witness is caught in a lie, the jury may consider all her testimony to be false. So if we bring in a witness who heard you say—'Oh, I'm going to kill so-and-so,' you will have been caught in a lie, and all your testimony will be for naught, so think about it, Miss Winterbottom. Could you ever in your life have said anything that could be construed to be a threat to kill someone—no matter how you meant it—whether to be taken literally or just as a display of anger?"

Erin Winterbottom pondered. She took her lower lip between her teeth—Bomber had put a different slant on her testimony, and she was taking more care. "Well, I *could* have, I suppose," she said, "Though I don't remember any specific instance."

"If we gave you time to think, perhaps if the judge would grant a recess so you could recall…"

Web stood, leisurely, as a man worn down with inanities. "Your Honor, I must rise in objection. Bomber is beating a dead horse. He's badgering, and I object to that. He's trying to intimidate with his '*falsus in uno*' talk, he's lecturing the witness, and it has gone nowhere. I object to continuing this line of questioning, and I would respectfully ask the court to strike the entire exchange from the record."

"That's a little excessive, Your Honor," Bomber said, provoking a flash of anger in the judge.

"Mr. Hanson, don't interrupt while I am considering an objection."

"I stand corrected," Bomber said and let it drop.

"The objection is sustained, but the testimony will remain in the record."

"Okay, Miss Winterbottom, what did the police say

when you told them of this conversation, this threat of Pia's to kill your landlord?"

"Objection," Web said, "without foundation."

"Sustained."

"Did you tell the police, Miss Winterbottom, that Pia Franceschi threatened to kill your landlord?"

"No."

"*No?* Why not?"

She shrugged.

"Can you make an audible answer for the record, Miss Winterbottom? The recorder can't hear your shrug."

"I guess I didn't think about it."

"Well," Bomber honed in, "when *did* you think about it?"

"I don't know."

"The police interviewed you, didn't they? After the murder in *your* house?"

"Yes."

"Did you mention this to them at that time?"

"I don't remember."

"You don't *remember?* Something this important—life or death for my client—your housemate—and you *don't remember?*"

Web rose. "Your Honor, I would respectfully object and ask the court to remind Bomber to eliminate his histrionics and stop badgering the witness with his irrelevant comments."

"Objection is sustained."

"All right, Miss Winterbottom, one more question on the subject. When did you remember this purported conversation with the defendant?"

"Remember it? I always remembered it. I said I didn't remember if I said anything about it to the police when they came to the house—"

Bomber had that half smile-half smirk on his face. The one that said, A likely story, to the jury.

"Now, Miss Winterbottom, are you familiar with Vine Street in town?"

The blush rose to her cheeks. "Yes."

"Have you had occasion to visit a house on the fourteen hundred block?"

"The fourteen hundred block?" She was stalling. Obviously this had not been discussed with Web, and she didn't know how to handle it. "I don't really know," she said, "I may have."

"And what would have been the occasion of your visit?"

"Occasion? No special occasion."

"Nice, Miss Winterbottom—why did you go there?"

"I'm not sure I did," she squirmed in her chair and shifted her eyes, hoping to evade the question. "If I went there, it was to visit a friend."

"What friend?"

"What friend?"

"Yes—does he or she have a name?"

"Well, I'm sure all my friends have names," she said, "but I just can't recall a specific person on Vine Street."

"Were there *many* people you visited?"

"No-o-o-o…"

Web stood. "Your Honor, may I please object to this line of questioning? It is outside the scope of the direct and irrelevant to this case."

The judge looked at Bomber. "Mr. Hanson, is there going to be a connection to this case?"

"That is my goal in pursuing this line."

"It's not just a fishing expedition?"

"No, Your Honor."

But with a few more parries and thrusts, Bomber failed to convince Judge Fairly he was on solid ground—that he had some evidence that would exculpate his client and/or incriminate the witness. Web finally won his point that Erin Winterbottom was not on trial, and Bomber was well known for smokescreen productions. We adjourned for the day without having made up the ground we lost.

"There's something here," Bomber said to me as we

were packing up. "I can smell it. Go back to that fateful house—do some first-class surveillance. Get to the bottom of this thing. Drugs, prostitution, white slavery, porno movies, there's got to be something there. And that kid—what's his name? Gillian. What's his connection?"

That didn't mean any of it connected to our case, I thought, but I knew there was no arguing with him this time. Pia's mother would have to wait.

"Oh," he said, as we walked out of the courtroom, "be careful this time. Don't get hit over the head."

31

Pia told me where I could find pictures of her housemates and I proceeded with caution. I'd hoped to bring the retrieval from her bedroom off with a minimum of fuss. That meant not seeing any of her housemates and having them ask me what I wanted with their pictures.

I was met at the front door by Veronica, on her way out with a backpack full, no doubt, of books. I told her I wanted to collect some things for Pia for the trial.

"Whatever," she said. "She did us all an enormous favor, take anything that will help you."

"I see the front door is in service," I said.

"Yes," she said, "thanks to that letter you sent Gillian, so we opened the front door and locked the back."

As happy as I was to get in without difficulty, I was saddened to hear Veronica, and by extension all of them, assumed Pia was guilty.

In Pia's room I found the box in the bottom drawer of the dresser, as promised. It was a smallish box, not large enough for a pair of shoes, but large enough to hold a passel of pictures thrown in without benefit of organization.

A quick look at the contents and a cursory glance at the rest of the drawers convinced me to take the whole cache without pausing to separate the wheat from the chaff.

I took the box back to the office and repaired to my cubicle, where I went through the photos, separating those I thought had any visible sign of a housemate. I stashed the reasonable collection in my inside jacket pocket and headed up the street in my car, though the destination was walking distance from the office. Under different circumstances I would have hoofed it, but I figured I needed the car in case a quick getaway was called for.

I drove by the house at 1410 Vine Street and around the block twice, casing the joint, as they say in the finer detective novels. I didn't see any sign of activity, so I parked the car across the street, only a few doors down. I sat still for a few minutes, watching the front door of the infamous rear building. When I was satisfied there was no activity there, I approached the house next door at 1412 Vine Street, watching my back all the time. I noticed side windows looked out on the building in question. A rather nice view of the comings and goings, should anyone be interested.

I ascended to a small porch and rang the doorbell. No one answered. Perhaps the bell wasn't working. I opened the screen door and knocked on the door—a knock that Bomber might have found too aggressive had I hit the same decibel level on his office door.

The sounds of reluctance stirred inside the house, shuffling and shifting, but no approaching footsteps. So I tried my caressing knock—the one Bomber would criticize as too pussy-footing, in the hope of appealing to the mysterious denizen.

In a few more painful minutes I heard footsteps approaching, then a voice through the door. "What do you want?" It was the voice of a woman, not too spry, probably comfortably past her biblical allotment and more than a little scared of unsolicited intruders.

"I'm Tod Hanson," I said through the door, "I work down the street for Bomber Hanson, attorney, who is counsel for Pia Franceschi, a student at the university accused of murder."

"I don't know anything about it," the voice came back.

"It will only take a few minutes," I said. "We are convinced the girl is innocent. You could help save her."

"Why should I?"

So she was going to play the curmudgeon.

"The golden rule?" I asked.

"I didn't murder anyone."

"Neither did she."

"It don't matter," she said. "I don't open my door to strange men."

"I'm not that strange," I said.

I thought I heard chuckling from inside—or was it guttural disdain? But the door opened and there she stood, or more accurately, slouched. She was thin to the point of anorexia, her lips were pursed in disapproval, and her eyes were slits to keep out the light and evil spirits.

"Bomber Hanson, huh?" she said. "You work for that rabble rouser?"

"You know him?"

"I can read," she said.

Did I also confess to being his son? Not yet. If she indeed could and did read the papers, she'd probably figure it out. My dilemma was, would it help or hinder my chances if she knew I was related to the great Bomber?

I tried to look behind her to get a sense of her house. I couldn't get any—just an average living room in a small house on Vine Street.

"Well," I said, forking out my hand to shake hers, "I'm Tod Hanson." She graced me with a sidelong disdainful glance at my hand. "What's your name?"

"What you want to know that for?"

"Well…I…I mean…I like to know who I'm talking to."

"Talking is right. But that don't mean I'm listening."

I gave her my most engaging smile. She wasn't engaged. "Look," I said, "I'm a little cold out here—could I come inside for a minute?"

She raised an eyebrow without opening her eye. "What for?"

"To show you some pictures—in pursuit of truth and justice."

"Hah!" she exclaimed. "No such thing."

"Maybe not," I said, "but shouldn't we keep trying?"

"Fool's errand," she said.

"Please," I pleaded like a grandson begging for a cookie.

"Well, you're nothing if not persistent," she said. "Okay—just a minute?"

"Yes."

She stepped back to admit me into her humble abode. I was startled however, to see it wasn't that humble: Expensive furnishings, a huge plasma screen television, and porcelain figurines of the larger variety. This stooped-shouldered mamma must have been a trust fund baby. There was an Aubusson rug on the floor that must have set her back a couple of years of my salary.

"Well," she said, "I guess you'll be wanting to set down."

"Oh, thank you," I said, looking for a chair with the best view of next door. I found one oddly placed, as though my hostess perched there on occasion with the express purpose of checking the comings and goings of the neighbors.

"You have a nice place here," I said. "You have exquisite taste, Mrs....."

"Miss Howser," she said, the flattery finding its mark. "Gladys Howser if you must know."

I sat in the view chair and had the odd impression she wanted that for herself, but she said nothing and moved to the sofa also facing the side window.

"Can you tell me anything about what goes on next door—in that building behind the house?"

Gladys Howser stiffened. "Why should I know anything about that? You think I'm a busybody? I'll have you know I mind my own business. I couldn't care less about what my neighbors are up to."

"Oh, of course," I said. "I just thought maybe you'd inadvertently seen something—like a lot of people coming and going?"

"No," she said, clipping the word like a two-dollar haircut.

I reached for the cache of photos in my inside jacket pocket. "You didn't happen to see any of these girls coming or going next door?"

She waved the pictures away. "I don't pay any attention to the goings on over there."

"There are some goings on, though?"

"I wouldn't know," she said, smug in her defiance. "I mind my own business."

"Didn't happen to see me get hit over the head some weeks back?"

"No," she said, but I noticed a glaring look of surprise or concern.

"Have any idea who might have hit me over the head, or why?"

"No idea whatsoever."

Just then I noticed a hulk of a man exiting the rear building next door. Instead of going into the house or walking down the driveway to the street, he let himself in the back door of Gladys's house and came through the kitchen to the living room where he seemed surprised to see me.

"Oh," he said, "I see you have company. I'll come back. Everything's all right?"

"Yes," she said, though his statement sounded more like a declaration than a question.

I stood up. "I'm Tod Hanson," I said, "are you familiar with the property next door?"

"Not at all," he said.

"Didn't you just come out of there?"

"I'm just a handyman."

"Fix something over there?"

"Yeah, that's it," he said, giving me his toughest guy eye. He turned to Gladys, "Who is this guy?"

"Oh, he's working on the case of the student who murdered her landlord."

"Maybe you would recognize some of these girls," I said, showing my pack of pictures to him. He took them and paged impassively through them, then shook his head.

"Nice looking bunch of girls," he said. "Never seen any of them before."

"I saw one of them go into the building behind the house you just came from. Any idea why?"

He shrugged.

"Went in with a guy named Gillian Izuks."

"None of my business."

Another guy with fastidious reserve.

"You wouldn't happen to know why I was hit over the head in the driveway, would you?"

"No—" then he added, "sometimes when guys poke their noses in other people's business, they have to take the consequences."

I had the feeling he was trying to be mysterious rather than transparent, but a schoolboy could have seen through him.

"Well, if it's any consolation, you…or whoever thought I was getting too nosey, almost killed me."

He shrugged again, like it was no skin off his anywhere. He looked at Gladys. "Want me to escort this guy out?"

She waved a hand of dismissal at him—he checked me again, as if for cooties, turned on his heel and was gone—out the back door from whence he came.

"Must be handy to have a handyman like that around the house."

"Oh, yes," she said, "he's very handy. So many things I can't do. He works the whole neighborhood."

"I see," I said, and looked over at the house next door. The hulking handyman was the only traffic I'd seen. I was about to give it up as a bad job when I saw the first traffic coming from the mysterious building in back. I saw a familiar figure exit. It was male.

Fabrizio F. Franceschi.

"Miss Howser," I said, jumping up. "Come here. Do you recognize that man?"

She looked disinterested, but faced the window and said, "Oh, no, I never pay any attention."

I thanked her for her time and ran out the door to

confront Fab. When he saw me, he ran to his car, jumped in and drove off before I could reach him.

I drove back to the office a little ashamed I hadn't walked the short distance. Easy enough to say after an uneventful exit.

I let myself into the empty office with my key. I didn't want to call Bomber, but I knew I had to. I made the call from Bomber's commodious reception room—too many times the size of my closet to mention.

"Yo ho," he answered the phone on the second ring. He was expecting me, and experience showed that expectations were ripe for disappointment.

Bad news, he wanted to hear all about it. Worse news, he wanted me to drive to his house up the hill to make the recitation in person.

Mom always seemed so delighted to see me, it made me sorry I didn't visit more often.

The door was barely open before she enquired, "How's my Joan?"

First of all, it wasn't her Joan, but mine, but I suppose the proprietarial declaration was flattering.

"Hunky Dory," I responded without editorial fanfare.

"He's waiting in his library," she said with a smile of coconspirality. Any time we could gang up on Bomber, if only in fantasy, made me feel grownup.

His door was cracked open, so I took the liberty of giving it a gradual push. He was at his desk, and he seemed uncharacteristically delighted to see me.

"Well, well," he said. "It looks like you made it without companion lumps to the noggin." He pointed to the chair facing him. "Tell me all about it."

I sat and did. Instead of his prevalent pose, where he gave the awareness of knowing everything I was telling him, he seemed rapt and engaged in my narrative.

"So," he said, sitting back when I'd come to a stuttering halt, "a fine kettle of fish. Fabrizio Fruta Franceschi, I'll be— should have kept him locked up. But what was he doing there?

He can't claim to have been there for Pia, she's engaged elsewhere. What do you make of it, boy?"

I shrugged. "You're the m-master."

The flattery was obvious, but he went for it. People do.

"Yeah, well," he smiled, leaning forward, his forearms resting on his desk, "you might say that." He put his hands together to make a little tent with his fingers, then raised the construction to his lips preparatory to relieving himself of some weighty wisdom. "Here's my take, for what it's worth," he said, leaving no doubt he thought his take was definitive and worth quite a lot.

"Check the Assessor's office—maybe the little lady has title to both properties. Is she sophisticated enough to hide under the name of a dummy corporation? Probably. The trade she is in throws off enough disposable income to hire a passel of lawyers. Her handyman keeps the customers in line. I expect the tap you got on your head was administered by the self-same handyman. She's running girls there, that goes without saying. College girls—the University is very expensive," he said by way of explanation. "Fruty's presence there is a touch more mysterious. He will say he was investigating—got the jump on you."

"Think so?"

Bomber pressed his tent-fingers to his lips. "No. Either he's involved in the operation, or he was simply a customer. I suspect the latter."

"Brilliant," I said.

"Yeah," he said, "brilliant, but useless."

"Why?"

"How are we going to get any of it in court? All irrelevant. Let's say DeWitt or his nephew half-wit—or both—were operators, and the hag was simply a den mother. It may open up more people to motives, but unless we can pinpoint one and hire Perry Mason to break her down in court, we come up empty. What's Fruty's part in the scheme? Partner with Izuks? Killed him over a partnership squabble?" Bomber shook his head, "Delicious, but unlikely. How long did you spend with the madam?"

"Twenty m-minutes—half-hour…"

"And you didn't see Fruty go in?"

"No."

"Patron," Bomber said. "Patron of the arts."

I must have looked disappointed.

"Prove me wrong," Bomber said. "I'd be delighted. Check the deeds. Has Pia said anything to you about the house?"

"No."

"She has to know something about it. Why is she holding out on us? This could even implicate one of her housemates. Talk to her. And what about her boyfriend? Any word on him testifying?"

"Not yet."

"Get them together. He's probably a sucker for a skirt, like most men. Soon as you get back from San Jose. We don't have any time to waste. Feel out Pia, and see if she knows what Fruty was doing there. Has he been to see her? What did they talk about? And why didn't she tell us about this house?"

"Maybe Pia w-wouldn't see him."

"Maybe," he said, pursing his lips. "But it gets lonely in the tank. I wouldn't bet on it."

In the interest of saving time, I turned down Mom's invitation to break bread at the homestead. She was disappointed and so was I.

32

On Saturday I left in my unpretentious product of a great American auto industry. I hoped the sunny day and light traffic would be an omen for my visit with Yvonne Franceschi.

It would have been fun to borrow Bomber's Bentley for the trip, but I don't have to tell you I didn't have the nerve to ask. I knew what the answer would be—"What?" he would croon with the eyes big as battleships. "Keep your nose to the grindstone, Boy, and buy your own."

If I kept my nose to the grindstone at what *he* paid me, it would be ground clean off before I could make a down payment on a Bentley.

I made the jaunt to San Jose in just under six hours. I found the Quality Market behind a massive parking lot with a line of strip stores off to the side.

As soon as I walked in the door, I spotted her. It had to be her. In case I had any doubts, I got close enough to read the plastic nametag that was affixed to her chest.

Hi. I'm
YVONNE

In that flash of recognition, I felt a stab of sympathy for Yvonne and all the other women who had to advertise their names to strangers. It seemed like an invasion of privacy—a mild form of prostitution even. I have let you into my private world, and I know nothing of you.

The market was medium scale—the aisles were not that wide. You could pass another cart, but that was about it. The light was artificial and the clientele working stiffs. Since it was the lunch hour, the deli department was getting a good workout, and Yvonne was busy. It gave me the opportunity to observe her—always a plus if you wanted to understand someone.

She looked tired. Not like anyone for whom life had been all kisses. She had a solid body, a good bone structure, but the sculptural quality of the flesh had seeped out some years before.

Her uniform of the corps was clean, starched and tidy, and I wondered when she found the time to bring off those requisite chores.

I joined the troops in the deli line, and when it was my turn I got a pastrami sandwich on rye and a bottle of water.

I stood in Yvonne's checkout line to pay.

When I got close to her, I heard her unfailing good cheer with the customers, "How are you today?" as though they were special and she really cared. Her voice was husky, with a notable Italian accent. I tried to work up some response in case she laid some of that sunshine on me.

After she sang, "Have a nice day," to my predecessor in line, I stepped up, dropped my wrapped pastrami on rye on the counter—

"And how are you today?" she said and made honest-to-God eye contact.

"I'm terrific," I said. "How about yourself?"

"Fabulous," she said, and I almost lost it.

"Is that like Fabrizio?" I asked.

She looked startled.

I came to her rescue. "I'm Tod Hanson—we are representing your daughter Pia…" I stopped, realizing this would not be news her customers or employers would relish. "I'd like an opportunity to talk to you," I said.

"And so would I," she said. "I'm on break in forty-five minutes. Could you come back?"

"Certainly. I'll eat my sandwich outside. Meet you there?"

"Perfect!" she said.

I paid, and she said, "Have a nice day."

I said, "Thank you, but I have other plans."

She laughed uproariously. I didn't understand how she could be so cheerful.

I went outside and sat at a small metal table in front of the Quality Market, where I could glance at Yvonne Franceschi doing her bit, and wondered what she must be like at her waitress job about ten hours from now. Could she possibly be as cheerful? Six days a week? Mondays she had only one job—that must be a piece of cake.

When Yvonne finally joined me at the small table, I could detect the relief in her eyes at the opportunity to take her weight off her feet.

"Thanks for giving me time to think," she said. "And for coming."

"You can think with all that going on?"

"You'd be surprised what you can do when you have to," she said. "There's so much more automation than when I started this job—just sweep the items across the electronic sensor—don't have to think."

"Pia told me about all your jobs. How do you do it?"

She shrugged. "You do what you have to do."

I nodded more in sympathy than understanding. "Maybe a better question is why do you have to do it?"

She laughed, in camaraderie, with an almost masculine laugh. "To live!" she said. "I'm not getting rich, that's for sure—we're just getting by."

"On four paychecks?" I said, though I knew better.

"Four? Where do you get four?"

"Your three and Fab's...well, I'm assuming he gets at least one..."

"You think I'd be working three jobs if that deadbeat made any money?"

"Deadbeat? He doesn't have any income?"

"Are you kidding? It goes out from that quarter—it

182

doesn't come in."

"So the obvious question is why? Why do you do it?"

"Ah, that's the sixty-four thousand dollar question," she said, looking into the sea of cars in the parking lot.

"What's the sixty-four thousand dollar answer?"

She looked at me with a question mark across her face, then back at the parking lot. Then she gave a sigh as though her thinking about her husband, her daughter, the case had all congealed in that moment and was looking for an opportunity to burst forth.

"Yeah," she said, "the answer. Yeah...well, see, I'm not sure there is an answer. It's all so complex..."

"I'm sure," I said. "Have you had any communication with Pia?"

She nodded. "We write. That's about all I can do. The telephone is tough. Getting us both near one when we can both talk."

Yvonne didn't seem any closer to answering my original question, so I changed my line of inquiry as they sometimes say at the courthouse.

"Is there any possibility Pia is guilty of this murder?"

She didn't answer right away—not the obvious "Lord no!" She was more thoughtful. "I've wondered," she admitted. "Deep down, every part of me shouts 'No way!'—but then I think about what kind of kid she was. Rebellious, she was. Pia wasn't a docile child who happily did everything we asked. No, we had some rough spots, she and I."

"What about Pia and Fab?"

"Oh, Fab is in his own world. He's only interested in power, and every time Pia crosses him he blows up. And that was not seldom. But Fab's involvement in her upbringing was off and on—off more than on if you want the truth. We're both old country—where the parent's word is law." She shook her head. "Not here. Kids have endless ways to get around authority. Pia wasn't old world. Isn't. The more independent she tried to be, the more Fab clamped down on her. Like locking her in her room after school. When she didn't come home after school, he went to get her."

"Did she ever run away from home?"

She shook her head. "I was so afraid she would," Yvonne said. "But she didn't. Maybe each person has his own limit to rebellion."

"The question I can't answer is, why didn't you run away from home—with or without Pia?"

She stared at me as though to understand where such a question was coming from.

"Guess I'm not made that way," she said at last. "Like I said, old world."

"Well," I said, "I guess that's admirable."

"Oh, I wouldn't be so sure about that," she said. "There are things you don't know," she said, and faded as if bodily from a scene.

"Can you tell me?"

"Can I? Of course. Will I? I don't think so."

"But I come as a friend of Pia. We are trying to save her life, but we know so little. Do you want our knowledge to be the exclusive province of Fab?"

"No," she said. "That wouldn't be fair."

"Then let's have your view."

"Oh, yes," she said, "my view. For twenty years my view hasn't mattered. The Lord and Master of the household was what mattered."

"Then why did you marry him?"

She gave a low chuckle. "I suspect for the usual reasons," she eyed me intently. "You ever been in love?"

"I daresay."

She shrugged.

"Did you have any idea what living with Fab would be like?"

"He was gentle in the beginning. Attentive. He couldn't stop telling me how much he loved me. Flowers, candy, jewels, the whole bit. Oh, I know what your thinking. But he worked in those days."

"Doing what?"

"Security guard mostly. He'd just come over. We foreigners have to start at the bottom. Fab just didn't have a taste for staying at the bottom. But he changed."

"When did he change?"

"When Pia was born."

"He didn't want children?" I guessed.

She shook her head. "It was the opposite. He was delighted. He was full of himself with plans for doing this and that—for making Pia into a model child—best student, best athlete. Best everything. It was actually charming for a while. Then she developed a mind of her own. She had her own ideas, not plans really—nothing long range. She wanted to have a good time. He wanted her to excel. She wanted to fit in. They were polar opposites. The more he forced her to conform, the more she rebelled." The breath came heavily from her lungs, as though her life were coming with it.

"Well, I hope you had a good marriage before Pia was born."

"Oh, I expect we did."

"How long were you married before Pia came along?"

She looked at me as though I had hit her in the face. "Why do you want to know?"

"No reason, I guess," I said. "Just to get an idea of when the trouble started."

"Not long," she said. "We weren't married long."

"A year or two?"

She studied my face, didn't answer. Looked off over the parking lot at nothing in particular. With every passing minute I became more uncomfortable. So what if it were a shotgun? It wouldn't be the first—or the last. Only now marriage seemed a nicety, a fringe benefit to a relationship. No disgrace any longer. Just is. But she seemed sensitive about it, so I didn't pry any further.

Finally, when her break must have been almost over, she fixed my eyes in a scary stare. "If I bare my soul to you, will you take a message to Pia for me?"

"Sure," I said, much relieved to have her participating in the interview again.

"Fab married me when I was pregnant with Pia," she said.

I nodded. "That was the right thing to do," I ventured.

"Right?" she said. "Yes. Wrong too. Wrong or right—in the old country having a child without a father on the scene is still a disgrace. In my little village especially so. Fab saved me the disgrace."

Well, bravo, I thought, and why shouldn't he? "He was, after all, the father," I said.

She kept her eyes steady on me. At length she said, "No, he wasn't."

"Oh...oh my...does he know?"

"Of course he knows," she said. "It's Pia who doesn't."

"You didn't want to tell her?"

"Of course I wanted to tell her. Fab didn't. I can understand it. Can't you?"

"I suppose."

"Let me finish," she said. "Can you understand now why I am supporting the family? Why I have three jobs to send Pia to college?"

"Yes," I said simply, a bit embarrassed at her shared confidence.

"I always meant to tell Pia—I just kept putting it off, thinking the perfect opportunity would present itself. If it did, I never recognized it," she paused. "Now, it's not only the right time, I can't put it off any longer. Not with all this going on down there. She needs to know."

"I agree," I said.

"Her father—and we always lived by that—he was her father. Oh, he didn't plant the seed, but he nurtured the plant—in his own clumsy way. I always thought, no matter how bad it got, that he was better than nothing." Her eyes dropped to focus on the fingers she was knotting into one another.

"So you want me to take a letter back to her?"

She ignored the question. "There is no time like now for her to cut herself off from Fab. He's become obsessed with her innocence—which is good in its way, but not in the way Fab goes about it; ramming into your car? Going to jail? What can be next? I just want Pia to know there is none of Fab in her, so she can at least stand on her own two feet without feeling guilty about it. She's a good girl. In answer to your question, I don't think Pia killed anyone. No matter what the evidence, and it seems to be heavy, I'll always know she's innocent."

"I believe you."

"Well," she said, pushing her chair back from the table, "I've got to go back to work."

"Were you going to give me a letter?"

"What letter?" she seemed perplexed.

"For Pia—telling her about all this—about Fab," I put it as delicately as I could.

"No," she said. "Don't you remember our deal?"

"Deal? No, I…" then I remembered.

"You agreed to take a message to Pia, if I bared my soul to you. Now you keep your part of the bargain. You explain everything to her. I don't have the nerve."

Before I could catch my breath, I was watching her back disappear into the market.

33

Fab, to whom Bomber so charmingly referred as Fruty, in tribute to his middle name, Fruta, made it easy for me. The next morning he was driving out of the jail parking lot while I was driving in. I made believe I didn't see him, but he saw me.

I waited longer than usual in the visitor's room. Was it significant? Deliberate? Was Pia so shaken up by Fab she didn't want to face me? Had Fab brought something to her she couldn't cope with?

I had a lot of time to think the darkest of thoughts.

When Pia was finally brought in she looked as though the cat had dragged her.

"You okay?" I asked as she sat down.

She nodded noncommitally. "Fab was just here. He takes a lot out of me."

"What did he want?"

"To keep his nose in my business is all I can imagine."

"Did he say anything about his visit to the house on Vine Street?"

"Vine Street? What house on Vine Street?"

I watched her closely for signs of deception. I couldn't discern any other than a suspicious turn of her lips.

"Fourteen-ten Vine Street. That's where I followed Erin and Gillian to, when I got hit over the head by someone who thought I had no business there. Mean anything to you?"

She shook her head. Her lips were acting up again.

"I saw your father come out of there yesterday."

Now I had her attention. "My father..."

"Any idea what he was doing there?"

"Investigating," she said. It was half a question. "He

says he's hot on the trail of DeWitt's killer. I begged him to lay off, but there's no talking to Fab."

"Why would the killer be in that house?"

She shrugged.

"Would someone there know something about the murder?"

She shrugged again. Suddenly, I brought my palm down hard on the table. "Pia!" I shouted, startling her. "You aren't leveling with me. I am sure of only one thing. If you don't play ball with us, you are going away for a long time."

Pia bit her lower lip. "I don't really *know* anything," she said.

"Speculate," I said. "You had a relationship with DeWitt Izuks—is that not so?"

She nodded.

"Was he involved in whatever is going on at 1410 Vine Street?"

"I don't know."

"Speculate. Have you heard any rumors?"

"Sure, rumors. I hear all kinds of rumors. I don't put any stock in rumors."

"Good for you," I said. "Why don't you tell me what you've heard, and I'll decide on how much stock to put in them."

"Well," she said, wilting before my eyes. "The rumor is girls work there."

"Doing what?"

"You know, hooking up with guys…for money."

"Do your housemates work there?"

"Maybe."

"Which ones?"

"Does it matter?"

"Yes, it could," I said. "Let's not be coy. I followed Erin and Gillian there when I got hit on the head—almost killed. Pia, I'd hope that would qualify for your cooperation. We are working for *you*—and who else?"

"Maybe—"

"You?"

"No!"

"Was an offer made?"

"Of course. DeWitt made offers to everyone he saw."

"Have you ever been there?"

"No."

"But DeWitt was involved?"

"That's the rumor."

"Do you know who was in charge?"

"No."

"What about Gillian? Was he part of it before DeWitt was killed?"

"I really don't know," she said.

"It is rather important, Pia. If someone there had a motive to kill DeWitt—and make it look like you did it—"

"I know," she said, deflating like a pricked balloon. "I just don't know who, or why. I wasn't in on any of that stuff."

"Okay," I said, disappointed in her favor. "What did you and Fab talk about today?"

"Lance."

"Lance? What about him?"

"Fab wants me to lure Lance into some kind of trap so he can confront him. Fab went to see him at the Flats but Lance wouldn't give him the time of day. That only made Fab more suspicious."

"Did you tell him we were trying to get Lance to testify?"

"Yes."

"Has Lance been to see you again?"

"No," she said sadly.

"What did Fab say when you told him about Lance testifying?"

"He said it was a terrible idea. He said Lance is the murderer, and if we give him a forum we are helping him escape his just punishment and sinking me at the same time."

"What do you think?" I asked.

"I don't know what to think."

"Okay," I said, satisfied I wasn't going to get more from her today. "I'm going to see Lance. See if I can get him to come and see you again. If he does, I think he'll testify. He's our best hope now."

"You think he will?"

"If Fab hasn't ruined it for us."

This time I took my car up the mountain, because I wanted to bring something back with me. By now I was an old hand at Lopez Flats, and I didn't expect the strange car would scare anyone off because *I* was familiar.

But I found the Flats just like I like to find them: devoid of humanoids. It was so quiet I had the feeling I was visiting a distant planet. I drove the car in as far as I could, then made my way by foot the distance to Lance's tent. I didn't expect to find him, the place was so quiet, but I was pleasantly surprised.

"Hey, how's it going?" he asked without enthusiasm, or any expectation of an answer that I could discern.

"Well, it's going," I said, matching his lack of enthusiasm. "But it's not going in the right direction."

"Oh?"

I shook my head, trying to convey the worst. "Pia's getting more discouraged every day. They've built a case against her out of thin air, and we now have our chance to rebut it, but we find ourselves dangerously low on ammunition."

He was watching me with big eyes.

"Which, of course, brings me here. You, Lance, are our last hope."

"Yeah, really?" he said, still without enthusiasm. "You think the jury would convict her? They don't have much, do they?"

"Without you, I wouldn't give a nickel for her chances."

"Me?" he said, looking off in the distance through the opening in the tent, as though he were trying to make some connection between Pia's chances and his personal involvement.

"What could I do to change anything?"

"Are you serious? You have the alibi for her. You *saw* her at the party when DeWitt was killed."

"You think the jurors would believe that?"

"Why wouldn't they? It's true, isn't it?"

"Yeah," he said, without conviction.

"You aren't having second thoughts, are you?" I asked him.

"Yeah, no, I don't know," he said, giving me an array of answers to choose from.

We sat in silence for a long minute before he said what was on both our minds: "You know, if I testify, they're going to think I did it.

"Your dad will probably rip me apart on the stand. If he can make the jury think I did it, Pia's got a chance. I mean, that's his job right? I'm not his client—Pia is."

I nodded. "But you make it sound like she really did it, and we are resorting to trickery to get a guilty person free. You don't believe she's guilty, do you?"

"No, but you don't think I killed him, do you?"

"No."

"But you know Bomber might make it look that way."

"No," I said, with some conviction. "Why should he? He isn't the prosecutor. He is only interested in getting Pia free, not in solving the crime. That's the district attorney's purview."

I watched Lance's expression. Unfortunately, he didn't seem convinced. "Well, okay," he said. "But I know if I testify, I know my choice comes down to, do I stick my neck out to have it cut off to save the woman I love, or do I mind my own business, save myself and hope Pia gets off?"

"That's a tough one," I said. "Who was it said, 'Better to keep your mouth shut and be thought a fool than to open it and prove it'?" I laughed, but it was a reserved sort of laughter. "You know, Lance, that fine specimen of manhood, Fabrizio Fruta Franceschi, is telling everyone you are the guilty party. So I don't think your telling the truth about Pia is going to suddenly throw suspicion on you. Fab is already trying to do just that."

"That idiot," he said. "If it weren't for him, Pia and I would still be together."

"I can hardly fault you for that," I said. "That turkey would be an obstacle to any relationship." I didn't bring up Pia's relationship with the landlord. Why shoot myself in the foot?

"Not only that…"

"What else?"

"Genetics."

"Genetics?"

"Yeah—I got to thinking, if Pia and I ever had kids, they might be like him."

I looked at Lance with renewed admiration. "Kind of unusual for a fellow your age to think about that, isn't it? I mean, to even look beyond infatuation for anything extraneous?"

"Maybe—but Fab is a special case."

I was on the spot. I wanted to tell him what I knew about Fab not being Pia's biological father, but the timing vis-à-vis Pia did not seem auspicious. "So what do you say we talk it over with Pia before you make up your mind?"

He considered the proposition, blushing.

"At the moment I am automotively deficient. I don't have any wheels. But I haven't forgotten. I'd like to see her. I feel for her predicament."

"Come on," I said. "I'll drive you down there."

"And bring me back?" he was legitimately startled at the suggestion.

"And bring you back."

He was out of excuses, but I still didn't detect any sense of mission for the task on his part. He followed me out of the tent all right, but I had the feeling he would rather have been doing anything else at that moment, including vegetating in his cocoon as he had become so adroit at doing.

For a while we drove down the hill without conversation. I didn't want to say anything that might rock the boat.

Lance spoke first.

"Man, don't you feel helpless sometimes?" he asked. "Life is so hopeless."

I shook my head. "Feeling helpless is a luxury. I don't have time for luxuries. Maybe later."

We did the rest of the trip in silence. I was speculating on what he was thinking, and he was thinking about what he would say to Pia, what she would say to him, and what his final decision would be.

When we pulled into the jail parking lot, Lance made no move to get out of the car.

"Well," I said, "this is it. I'm going to let you talk to her alone. I'd be a fifth wheel in there. Go to it, man, do your best."

"Yeah," he said, and I thought the way he said it translated to mean, Let's get out of here.

He took a deep breath, put his hand on the door handle and pulled it with a flourish. "Wish me luck," he said.

"Good luck," I said, and he was out of the car making his way through the parking lot to the jail like a man who had lost his last friend.

I waited an eternity for him to return. During that chasm of bottomless time, I speculated on what was going on inside. I thought initially that the longer he took, the better things boded for our side. But then my reasoning veered off the path to fits of negativity. She wouldn't see him. She had another visitor—her father—and Lance had to wait. They were having a heated and prolonged argument, and Lance would be irretrievably lost to our cause.

And so in that endless interval of time between what you hope for and what you fear, I sat immobile behind the wheel of my car, afraid to make a move lest that action, no matter how simple, would adversely affect the outcome.

When at last I saw my passenger and companion on this journey of truth and justice bounding toward me with a jaunty step, heretofore unseen, my spirits soared.

I sat expectantly frozen in hope as he opened the door

and started spilling his feelings before his bottom hit the seat.

"I'm in *love*," he shouted. "I'll do it. I'll do anything for her; give her my freedom—my life, if I have to. Anything!"

34

It was a happy drive back up the mountain to Lopez Flats with Lance. I'd never seen a happier man.

When I left him, we arranged for me to pick him up Monday morning at eight for court.

Bomber was delighted with the result. I called him as soon as I got home. There could even have been buried somewhere in his reaction a scintilla of praise for my success.

I called Joan in L.A. to share my euphoria, and she did her usual good job of praising me extravagantly.

I was so excited. I spent Sunday working on my composition for the case, which I thought of giving the title Love Conquers All.

Too hokey, though it would serve double duty—Lance and Pia, Joan and I.

I could hardly contain my excitement on my way up the mountain on Monday morning. I had only a fleeting doubt that we were overemphasizing the effect Lance's testimony would have. But coupled with Pia's innocent demeanor and good looks and our hope that the jury wanted to believe in her innocence, given half a chance, I pushed all doubt out of my mind.

I was so stoked, I arrived at Lance's tent fifteen minutes early. It was so quiet while I approached the tent I thought he must have been oversleeping. I was glad I was early. I rustled the flap to no response. I pushed it back and found an empty tent. I searched for a note, but found nothing. My vital organs suddenly felt unmoored. Where was he? Why? Perhaps, I thought hopefully, he had gone for a walk and would be back by our appointed eight.

I roamed the vicinity, knocking gingerly on trailer doors, and sundry unapproved housing. No one had seen Lance, and too many of them seemed to resent the early intrusion.

Where could he have gone and why? Was he really guilty? Did he have a terminal change of heart? Fearful that, though innocent, suspicion and possible conviction could befall him?

I jumped in the car, drove slowly out of the flats and at the entrance turned right to continue up the hill, in the hope he had gone for a hike and lost track of the time. I drove three miles to the summit, then gave it up, returning to the flats to make one more effort. Nothing. There was no sign of him being back, and no one I asked had seen him.

The morning session had begun, and since Lance was to be the first witness, my entry from the rear of the courtroom was met with some disdainful stares.

Pia was smiling broadly. I'd never seen her so happy. Both she and Bomber craned to look around me for the hero of the day. It didn't take them long to realize I had not succeeded in my mission.

I hurried to Bomber at the defense table and whispered in his ear. "Lance is gone." Pia overheard, and her face changed from joy to shock in an instant. Bomber took a deep breath and asked, "May we approach the bench, Your Honor?"

"You may."

Bomber, the district attorney and I trudged to the Judge's lair—his perch above the mortals. Bomber made his pitch.

"Our eyewitness has disappeared. Tod went to pick him up this morning at his temporary residence in Lopez Flats, and there was no sign of him."

"Did he know you were coming?" Judge Fairly asked me.

"Oh yes," I said.

"They had an appointment," Bomber added. "I respectfully ask a recess until we can locate him."

"A recess? You mean fifteen minutes?" the judge asked.

"Well, that would be fine with me if we could find him in that time. I'm just afraid it will require longer."

"How long?"

"I can't predict specifically," Bomber said. "Could we have a few days?"

"A few days?" Web didn't like the idea. "We can't hold this jury twiddling their thumbs waiting for your witness who apparently doesn't want to appear."

"He wants to appear," Bomber said. "He is our defense, period. You can't keep us from putting on a defense."

"All right, Mr. Hanson. Don't you have another witness you could put on in the mean time?"

"No, Your Honor."

"All right, have you any idea where your witness is?"

"No, Your Honor."

"Then I'll give you twenty-four hours," the judge said. "We can't wait indefinitely."

Bomber frowned, but he knew there wasn't much he could do. He could renew the argument tomorrow, but he wasn't optimistic.

"May I confer with my client before she is taken back to jail?" Bomber asked.

"You may," the judge then instructed the sheriff to see her to the conference room.

When we were inside with the door closed, Bomber asked Pia, "Any idea where he might be?"

She shook her head. Tears were welling up and spilling down her cheeks. I could tell she felt abandoned. To go from the pinnacle of joy one moment to abject sorrow the next was harrowing and dispiriting.

"Okay," Bomber said. "We have a day. Tod will do all he can. If we can't find him, I may have to put you on the stand."

That news didn't seem to sink in. The tears kept flowing but they were the old tears.

"I didn't think it necessary. Web hasn't put on that strong a case, but if we put no defense on it could tip the scales. We can say all we want about not needing to put on a case because the district attorney proved nothing, but the psychology is not right. So I'm going to prepare you now in case we can't find Lance—while Tod continues to look for him, can you tell us anything that might help?"

She shook her head.

"Good luck," Bomber said to me as I left the room, I knew not for where.

35

There won't be a lot of ink spilled on my subsequent search for Lance Ludlow. It was a complete bust. I fear I knew it would be, and I hope that didn't contribute psychologically to the failure.

I went back to the flats, talked to everyone I could find. When I was challenged, "Are you a pig?" I said no without lecturing them on using more respect for those who devote their working lives to our protection.

I returned to his former abode on the beach and asked if anyone had seen Lance.

Nothing.

Bomber seemed to accept the fait accompli without rancor. "We'll see what we can do with Pia on the stand," he said.

Tuesday morning I showed up in court to find Bomber had dressed Pia as though she were a child-molestation victim. A severely tailored gingham dress, and her hair in pigtails—yes, pig, not pony, and each one braided!

Bomber was all smiles as he stood before the jury, off to the side so they could focus on Pia and her testimony. When Bomber had a sympathetic witness he wanted the jury to focus on the witness. If the opposite were true, he would position himself so the focus was on him.

After years of practice, Bomber was at home in his elevator shoes. I remember in my youth his prancing around the house to get used to them. "Practice makes perfect," he would say with a grim smile. But direct reference to the stature-boosting shoes was *verboten*.

Bomber was nothing if not a consummate actor. His stance and demeanor were carefully calculated and well rehearsed. His role was now that of the friendly, laid-back savior of our damsel in distress. No anger, no edge, just soothing, mellifluous questions that came out more like a friendly tête-à-tête than a courtroom interrogation.

"Now, Pia," he began. "Have you ever had your testimony taken in court?"

"No."

"I've told you to try to relax, and just tell the truth, have I not?"

"Yes."

"Did you kill DeWitt Izuks?"

"No."

"Have you ever fired a gun?"

"No."

"Do you know how to fire a gun?"

"No."

"Have you ever touched a gun?"

"No."

"Thank you," Bomber said, with evident satisfaction at the brevity of his accomplishment. "You heard your father testify he gave you a gun, is that correct?"

"Yes."

"Can you tell the jury how that transpired?"

Pia looked at the jury—she was so natural about it—a super witness. I just wasn't sure how she would hold up when the district attorney got to her. Truth, beauty and goodness were often not a pretty sight when flustered. But I noted another of Bomber's subtle set ups: Pia was not calling him sir. Why should she? They were just pals. Would she call the district attorney sir? I'd give good odds.

"My father told me he was concerned for my safety, so he bought me a gun."

"Did he give it to you?"

"I told him I didn't want it. He brought it to my house

and said I had to have it for my own protection."

"Did he hand it to you?"

"No. I refused to take it."

"Why?"

"I told him I was afraid of guns. If I tried to shoot someone with a gun I'd only shoot myself."

"What did he do with the gun?"

"He put it in my dresser drawer."

"Which drawer?"

"The bottom one."

"Did you open the drawer from time to time?"

"No. I had summer clothes in there, things I couldn't wear until it got hot, and a box of pictures."

"Did anyone else—besides you and your father—know the gun was there?"

"Oh, yes," she said. "He told all my housemates just in case they needed protection."

"Did you feel you needed this protection?"

"No."

"Did you have any fears for your safety?"

"No…"

"For your life?"

"No."

"Now, Pia, does the name Lance Ludlow mean anything to you?"

Pia burst into tears.

Oh, man, I thought, you couldn't buy that performance. Bomber let her cry for a while, watching the jury out of the corner of his eye. Was he looking to gauge their sympathy, or to see when they'd had enough. Pia brought herself under control. "My boyfriend," she choked out.

"When was the last time you saw him?"

"Two days ago—" she sniffed.

"Where was that?"

"In jail. He came to see me," she said. "We made up…"

"Made up?"

She nodded. "We broke up a while ago," and she cried again.

"Why did you break up?"

"Lance couldn't take Fab—"

"Fab? Your father?"

"Yes."

"When was that break up?" Bomber asked.

"In January."

"What conversations did you have two days ago about getting back together?"

"Oh…oh—he was so nice—"

"What did he say?"

"He said he loved me—he couldn't get me out of his mind—my father was hopeless, but he realized he loved me more than anything," and here she burst into tears again.

"Have you heard from him since that—was it Sunday?"

"Sunday," she said. "No, I…"

"Was there another stated purpose of Lance's Sunday visit?"

"Yes," she said, reining in her tears. "He told me he would come to court to testify for me."

"What did he say he was he going to testify to?"

"That on the night of the murder, he was watching me at a party in the park. He was trying to get up the nerve to reconcile, but he just stared at me all night. He knew I didn't leave the party and couldn't have killed DeWitt."

"Did you see Lance on that night?"

"No. He was watching me from the house next to the park—an upstairs window. I didn't know he was there."

"What were your feelings about Lance at that time?"

"I still loved him."

"And if he had come down to the party to ask you to take him back, would you have?"

"Definitely," she said.

"Do you have any idea where Lance is now?"

"No."

"Or why he didn't show up in court yesterday?"

"No."

"Do you think it's because he changed his mind? Got cold feet?"

"Oh, no," she said. "I know him better than that. I'm just afraid…" she said and trailed off.

"Afraid of what?"

She began crying again, slowly—"I'm afraid…something happened to him." She made little effort to control the tears that flowed freely now.

Bomber paused to maximize the effect on the jury. Pia was struggling to regain her composure, and time was on her side.

"Now, Pia, what kind of relationship did you have with DeWitt Izuks, the victim?"

"Not a good one—"

"Were you friends?"

"No."

"Lovers?"

She paused, drew in a breath, staunched her tears and said, "There wasn't any love about it."

"What was it?" Bomber asked gently, "a business relationship?"

"Yes, that was it. He would exchange my rent for…certain favors…"

"Of a personal nature?"

"Yes," she dropped her eyes.

"Now, Pia, on the night of DeWitt's murder, he was in your room before the party, is that correct?"

"Yes."

"Had you been in there with him?"

"Yes."

"What was he doing there?"

"The rent was due…and he had…expectations."

"Expectations you were able to fulfill?"

"No."

"No?"

"No. He was there waiting for me when I came back from the library. I'd decided I wanted nothing more to do with him. I'd rather live on the street than let that scumbag touch me again."

"Didn't your father give you money for rent?"

"My mom gave me money for tuition and books, but that was a stretch for her. My dad didn't contribute anything. Mom works three jobs as it is."

"Your father doesn't work?"

"Oh, he claims he's a private investigator, but I don't know what he investigates. I don't think he has done much to support us financially."

"When did you get back to your room that night?"

"After the party. I don't know—around midnight, I guess."

"What did you find?"

"I found DeWitt still passed out in my bed. As soon as I turned the light on, I turned it off again. I was too tired to yell at him so I just went downstairs and fell asleep on the couch."

"You didn't know he was dead?"

"No. I thought he was asleep. I didn't get a good look at him."

"When did you discover he was dead?"

"The next morning. I went to my room, thinking—hoping— he would be gone. It's really bright in my room in the morning and as soon as I walked in I could see he had been shot. There was blood on my pillow."

"Did you see any weapon?"

"No, but I thought of my gun. I opened the drawer, and it was gone. I opened all the drawers in a panic."

"Did you find the gun anywhere?"

"No."

"Then or later?"

"No."

"Pia, did you kill DeWitt Izuks?"

She was shaking her head when Web jumped up and said, "Objection—asked and answered."

The judge nodded slowly and with a thin smile said, "Sustained."

Bomber's smile was broader. "Just so," he said. "You may cross-examine."

It was more a challenge than a question.

36

The courtroom was full for Web's cross-examination of Pia Franceschi. It was generally standing room only for Bomber's cases, and when a young, pretty girl was on trial it was guaranteed.

The larger the audience, the more audacious Web became. It began with his sartorial armor; his fifteen hundred dollar suit of clothes—deep navy pinstripe that would have made him at home in any Fortune 500 boardroom. He wasn't buying suits like that out of his paycheck. He had a modest trust fund for those niceties that a regular working stiff could only dream of affording.

Bomber could have afforded fine clothes, custom tailored suits and shirts—hand-made shoes. But Bomber thought clothes were silly. "They are meant to attract the opposite sex—keeping warm can be accomplished much more simply," he said. "In my time I attracted one of the complementary sex, and I have my hands full with her." "Her" being Mom, who had to catch him going out of the house or he would look sillier than he did, with mismatched everything. I've even seen him with unmatched socks, so extreme was his fashion malaise. The exception was, of course, his elevator shoes—they cost a pretty penny. Vanity, you know, all is vanity.

Webster A. Grainger III, the district attorney of Weller County, California stood to check not the witness, not the judge, not the accused or the defenders—but to see how the jury reacted to his fine suit. He placed his left hand on his right breast and slid it unconsciously down the goods. Look at me, his movement said. A man in a fifteen hundred dollar suit won't steer you wrong. Why would he have to?

But the demands of the ego cannot be sated by worldly goods. Web repeated the gesture. Was he checking that he had remembered to bring his wallet? Was he drawing attention to the fine cut and fabric of his suit? Was he checking to see that his mortal body was still there? Or was he unconsciously trying to tame the belly that was rising up at the extravagance of the costume, pressing against the goods in ever-increasing protest? My hope at the moment was that the tailor had left a generous amount of goods at the seams so Web would live to button it, jacket and pants, another day.

Satisfied the jury were as impressed as they were going to be with his lavish suit, Web turned to Pia, who had watched the charade with detachment. I expect Bomber had prepared her to expect anything from the district attorney and admonished her to go with the flow. Bomber probably also warned her to stay on her guard and not to let it down no matter how odd the circumstances.

"Miss Franceschi?" he asked, looking down at his notes as though he didn't remember her name. "Pia Franceschi, is it?"

"Yes, sir." There you go—"Yes, sir," on the first question, loading Web down with respect and formality.

"Your attorney asked you a lot of friendly questions. That's as it should be. I am on the other side, and you may find some of my questions a little rougher. Do you understand that?"

"Yes, sir."

"There's nothing personal in it, it is my way of getting at the truth, as the great state of California has deputized me to do. So unless you want to confess at the outset that you murdered DeWitt Izuks as you are charged with, the questions could get a little rough."

Bomber rose slowly to his feet. "Your Honor, the prosecutor appears to be speechifying with the intent of intimidating the witness before he even asks a germane evidentiary question. May I object to this laborious indulgence?"

"Yes. Sustained."

"You didn't like DeWitt Izuks very much, did you?" Web asked, slicing forward without acknowledging the small setback.

"No, sir."

"Might I even say you hated him?"

"No, sir."

"Wanted him dead?"

"No, sir."

"Where did you discard the gun?"

"Objection," Bomber said. "He's badgering. No foundation. She testified she never touched the gun, or any gun, and doesn't know where the gun her father put in her drawer is."

"Now he's testifying," Web bleated. "Giving a speech to the jury with his objections."

"Objection sustained."

"All right, Miss Franceschi, did you ever tell anyone you wanted to kill DeWitt Izuks?"

"No, sir."

"No? Didn't you hear your housemate testify that you told her you were going to kill the landlord?"

"I heard that," Pia said. "Yes, sir."

"So are you saying now that your friend is a liar?"

"Objection to the form of the question," Bomber said.

"Sustained."

"Are you saying her statement is untrue?"

"Yes, sir."

"Why would she lie about that?"

"Objection, calls for speculation."

The judge looked from Bomber to Web, to Pia on the stand as though the face of one would hold his answer. "I'll let her answer. She can always say she doesn't know."

"Miss Franceschi?" Web prodded, "Why would your friend lie about you?"

"I guess if she was a friend, she wouldn't lie about me," Pia said to an audible sigh of approval in the courtroom as well as unconscious smiles from the jury.

"All right, Miss Franceschi. She was a housemate, was she not?"

"Yes, sir."

"Lived in the same house near the university?"

"Yes, sir."

"Did you ever hang out together—outside of the house?"

"A few times," then she added as though she had forgotten something important, "Yes, sir."

"Any idea why she would make up something like that?"

"I honestly don't know, sir. Maybe…"

"Go ahead," he said.

"Maybe she has a reason for wanting me to take the blame."

"Oh?" Web got bug-eyed. "You think she could have killed DeWitt Izuks?"

"More than I could have," she said.

"Yet the police thoroughly investigated the crime and arrested you, not her. Or any of your other housemates, is that correct?"

"Yes, sir."

Web seemed about to press the matter further, then abruptly changed course, a ploy that seemed to give Bomber satisfaction. The district attorney tried to shake Pia's testimony about never touching the gun—leaving it in her drawer in her bedroom without ever looking at it. He tried to imply she had taken shooting lessons, had been at a shooting gallery, but Pia held her ground, answering "No, sir" to every thrust and parry.

District Attorney Grainger was reduced to making his points in the form of innuendos in his questions. He turned to what he thought was the ace.

"Miss Franceschi, you had an intimate relationship with DeWitt Izuks, did you not?"

"Briefly."

"That's a yes?"

"Yes, sir."

"You tired of him?"

"I never liked him—"

"Why did you do it?"

"Objection," Bomber said. "We've been over this ground. Nothing can be gained by rehashing it."

Judge Fairly appeared to be having a difficult time deciding, but finally said, "Sustained."

"Yes, well, Your Honor. Now Miss Franceschi, to your knowledge, did any of your housemates ever sleep with the landlord?"

"Objection."

"Well, she spoke of free rent. I just want to point out that the same charity was available to others."

"Well, I'm going to sustain the objection as to form."

"Okay, Miss Franceschi, did you have any conversations with your housemates, or anyone else, about DeWitt's offer to exchange their favors for rent?"

"Yes, sir."

"Can you tell us the substance of those conversations?"

"Everyone hated him."

"Except you?"

"Including me."

"And yet you gave him your body in exchange for free rent?"

Pia hung her head, blushed, and tears began to flow. Web brought his heavy hand down on the poor naive girl; her response could not have been scripted better. The scene was so effective, Web didn't wait for an answer before he said, "No further questions."

Bomber rose, poured a glass of water from the pitcher on the defense table, took three tissues from the box on the table—each stroke deliberate and dramatic—and approached the witness with them. She drank the water thirstily, gratefully, then blew her nose with the first tissue, balled it up, dried her eyes with the second, then put the third on her lap for future emergencies.

"Do you feel able to proceed, Pia?" he asked with his kindest, friendly-witness manner.

"Yes," she said, and caught herself before adding 'sir'.

"Now, Pia, the district attorney went to some lengths to question you about your housemates involvement with DeWitt Izuks, your landlord. Did he, to your knowledge, have another source of income besides the rent you and others paid to him?"

"He had a business at 1410 Vine Street."

"Another rental property?"

"No. It's a place where young women…entertain men."

"Do you know any of these young women?"

"Yes."

"Do one or more of your housemates work there?"

"Yes."

"Were you asked to 'work' there?"

"Yes."

"What did you respond?"

"I couldn't do it. Strange men?" she shuddered.

"How was DeWitt different?"

"I knew him. He sweet-talked me. I couldn't pay my rent and he told me I was 'to die for'. I was so stupid."

"Could you have made a lot more money at 1410 Vine Street?"

"Oh, yes."

"But you chose not to?"

"That's correct."

"What happened to DeWitt's property after he died?"

"His nephew, Gillian Izuks, claims to have inherited all his uncle's property."

"Does Gillian Izuks work at 1410 Vine Street?"

"To my knowledge, yes."

"And do some of your housemates work there for him?"

"Yes."

"Did my associate Tod Hanson tell you he had gone there, following one of your housemates to that same house on Vine Street?"

"Yes."

"What did he tell you happened to him there?"

"Someone knocked him unconscious and dumped him on the beach somewhere outside of town. He was in the hospital for a few days."

"Someone didn't want him to know what was going on there?"

"Objection," called an agitated Web.

"Sustained."

"No more questions."

The judge nodded. Web stood. "A few more, Miss Franceschi."

Pia looked at the district attorney and resolved to keep her composure.

"Where was DeWitt Izuks killed?"

"I don't know, sir."

"You don't know?" Web was incredulous, then he caught on. "Okay, where was he found?"

"In my bed, sir."

"Who found him?"

"I did, sir."

"You had a gun, did you not?"

"I never had it. My dad put it in my dresser. I never touched it."

"After you found DeWitt's dead body in your bed, did you look for the gun?"

"Yes."

"Did you find it?"

"No, sir."

"Now, your boyfriend Lance Ludlow was going to come to court to give you an alibi?"

"Yes, sir."

"He came to see you to tell you this two days ago, is that correct?"

"Yes, sir."

"Very well. He didn't come, did he?"

"No, sir." She was beginning to tear but was fighting it.

"Have you heard from him?"

"No, sir."

"Any idea where he is?"

"No, sir."

Web stared at Pia in a manner I thought unduly malicious. He was rigid of body for a moment, then relaxed. "No further questions," he said.

The judge looked at Bomber, "Will that conclude your case?"

"Your Honor, I would like the evening to decide. I may want to put on another witness or two before my character witnesses."

"Very well," the judge said. "It's almost four o'clock. We'll adjourn until tomorrow."

We went out in the hall behind the district attorney and found Fab jumping to talk to him.

"Listen," Bomber whispered and walked on leaving me to fend for myself, to look like I had some purpose in staying behind. I needn't have bothered. Fab was too preoccupied to notice me, and Web was so weary of Fab he didn't care.

"She didn't do this, Mr. District Attorney. With all due respect, you're prosecuting the wrong party. It was her ex-boyfriend Lance, and now he's disappeared. Was going to give Pia an alibi and disappeared instead. You have to find him."

Web looked at Fab blankly. I'm sure he wasn't charmed to have the father of the accused giving him orders. "How do you know what's going on? You've been barred from the courtroom."

"Hey," Fab said, straightening and leaning back to give himself what he must have thought was gravitas. "I'm a detective. I got sources in there."

"Then maybe you should find your daughter's boyfriend."

"I'm looking," he said, "don't you worry. But I'm running out of time. The state has so many more resources."

"Well, thanks for your concern. We have zero evidence against the boyfriend. Our case is against Pia Franceschi, and that is what I shall pursue. Good day."

Fab watched the district attorney hurry down the hall as if to outpace the defendant's father.

Fab seemed to see me for the first time. "Tod Hanson!" he exclaimed, almost joyous at his sighting what must have seemed to him as his best friend. "I don't think it's looking too good. We have to find Lance."

"I couldn't agree more," I said, "not because I think he's the murderer—for the alibi, for Pia. But tell me something, Fab. I saw you coming out of that back house in the 1400 block of Vine Street. What were you doing in there?"

"Investigating—what else? You know, it's a *house*—and a house is not a home. Young college girls. The housemate, Suzy, she wasn't with her mom and dad up north somewhere when the landlord was murdered. She was on duty—working in the house. But I checked. My Pia didn't go in there. *Never!* At least she didn't sink that low."

"You know about the old woman next door?"

"Never took her eyes off the operation. Izuks had a percentage lease with her and she just sat there counting the customers to see that she got every penny was coming to her. She owns the place, you know—I checked the assessor's records. Made a pretty penny on the deal.

"The husky handyman was her enforcer—keeping things under wraps. People got too nosey—wham!" He punched the air with his fist.

How well I knew.

"Anyway, Lance is your man. I doped it all out. We find him, Pia goes free. Otherwise...?" he raised his arms in a gesture of hopelessness. I left him in that position.

37

Apoplexy! That's what I thought Bomber would suffer the next morning when on arrival in the courtroom the bailiff greeted us and asked us to come into the judge's chambers. It would have been justified.

Since the district attorney was not at his table, we assumed he was already in the judge's chambers. What we didn't expect was to see, on entry, Fabrizio Fruta Franceschi sitting there, obviously pleased with himself and looking like the cat who swallowed the canary, cage and all.

Bomber shot a withering glare at Web, who put a hand out, palm up in a gesture of innocence.

"Sit down, Bomber, Tod," Judge Fairly said. "We have some bad news."

We sat, the defense team and the prosecution flanking Fabrizio Fruta Franceschi and facing the judge. I tried to take the seat next to Fab. Bomber couldn't get far enough from his nemesis and he made no pretense of hiding his feelings.

"I'm afraid I have some bad news for you, Bomber," (out of the courtroom the judge used the familiar Bomber rather than his formal Mr. Hanson). "Your alibi witness has been found…by Mr. Franceschi here—" he nodded toward Fab— "dead. He was apparently shot in the head."

"It was suicide," Fab piped up. "I'll stake my reputation on it."

"What makes you think so?" Bomber asked, with a not-too-friendly tone.

"I'm an investigator. I know my trade. The gun was the one I gave Pia. I'd recognize it anywhere. I'll bet you anything

216

his prints are on it. I told you he was the murderer. He was afraid to testify. He saw Pia the night of the murder all right, but no one saw *him!*"

"How did you happen to find him?" Bomber asked.

"I was looking for him. I *knew* he was the murderer. It's my trade and I'm good at it. The cops won't go after missing persons if they're adults. I had no choice. I didn't want this thing hung on my precious Pia. So I went to work. It's what I do best."

"And how did you find him?"

Fab gave a curt, affirmative nod, "Pia told me where he had retreated to—up in the mountains here." Fab tossed his head toward an imaginary mountain though I think he indicated the ocean instead. "I knew he wouldn't testify—he's the guilty party after all—he couldn't take the chance Bomber would tie him in knots on the stand. I knew that—so I went up there. Nobody knew anything, hadn't seen Lance. So I started snooping around. I did my detective dance; fanned out in ever widening circles. Impossible terrain up there, but that made it easier for the old pro," he tapped his head. "He obviously wouldn't be on these steep cliffs, even if he was a mountain climber he'd have to rest sometime. I thought I'd find him hiding out living off the land. I didn't expect he'd kill himself. Well, far as I'm concerned that's proof he's the murderer. You should let Pia go, forthwith."

"Not so fast," District Attorney Grainger said. "Let's see what the police find first. They're up there now."

"We ought to go up there now," Bomber said.

"Good idea," the judge said. "Web, you want to go?"

Web hesitated. "We're in the middle of a trial. I don't see how this affects us. A witness kills himself—"

"—With the gun used in the murder," Fab interjected.

"We don't know that," Web said. "Tests have to be run. A lot more has to be gone into."

"Don't tell me you don't think it's worth a day to check it out?" Bomber asked Web.

Web was pouting. "Well…a day maybe, but I'm not

willing to put this off indefinitely."

"Okay," Judge Fairly said. "Let's go. Why don't we let Bomber drive? I've always wanted to have a ride in that fancy car of his. A Rolls Royce, isn't it?"

"Bentley," Bomber muttered. I could tell he was less than keen on having Fab ride in his car.

Did Fab catch the vibe? He said, "Will you excuse me? I've seen the scene first hand. I've been up all night, I'm bushed. I need some sleep."

"Of course," the judge said. "No need...I expect you'll check with the court—make yourself available for questioning?"

"Of course," Fab said, relishing the thought of the lime-light.

We walked out together, Fab splitting off from the rest of us when we hit the sidewalk.

The judge sat up front with Bomber in the Bentley. The district attorney climbed in back with me.

"Nice car," the judge said.

"Yeah," Web grumbled. "I could buy one of these with three or four years salary—if I didn't spend a dime on anything else."

"Think of the security you have, Web," Bomber said.

"Yeah."

We wound up the mountain with ease in horsepower heaven.

"Does anyone know where we are going?" the judge asked.

"Just below the flats," Web answered. "You'll see the police cars. One road up, same road down."

It was a sparsely traveled road with a few turnouts for parking. Not nearly enough for all the police cars which were forced to park out in the road with a uniformed officer to control traffic if there was any and discourage any nosey-rosies.

The officer on the road peered into the Bentley. His respect for Bomber's car increased when he saw the occupants. He saluted and froze. "Where can we put this boat?" the judge asked from the inside of the open window.

"Right here, sir," the officer pointed to a sliver of road which might have been commodious for a VW Bug. Bomber cocked an eyebrow. "You guys get out, I'll find a more reasonable space."

My inclination was to go along with Bomber, but I thought I'd better stand by the district attorney and judge to keep conversation honest. You never knew what devious effort Web might make at transparent influence.

Bomber parked up the road and joined us rather quickly on a small plateau under an outcropping of sheer rocks that was used for rock climbing practice. It was a sport I couldn't imagine anyone being attracted to. Perhaps if you had a death wish...

Police were all over the scene, like bees on a hive. Sheltered by a few trees and perhaps one hundred feet in from the road, the body was covered with a sheet. The hill took a steep rise behind the body.

The detective in charge wore a suit off the rack at Target—a nice contrast to Web's extravagant threads. It was Vic Upsole doing the honors for Angleton's finest.

"How does it look to you, Vic?" Bomber asked. Bomber was always pleasant and respectful when he spoke to cops—unless in an adversarial position in court. I always sensed a touch of awe when cops spoke to him, and it wasn't just the red Bentley that prompted it.

"We'll have to run some tests, of course," he said. "But at first glance it looks like suicide to me."

Bomber looked at the sheet-covered lump on the ground. "One thing certain," he said. "He won't be able to tell us."

Bomber checked out the environs with a wary eye, then turned his attention to the district attorney. "You buy it, Web?" he asked.

"What?"

"Suicide?"

"I don't know. Let's see what they come up with."

"Right," Bomber said, "but if that *is* the murder weapon, it doesn't much matter if it's a suicide or murder—Pia couldn't have done it. I think you should drop the case—only if that was the gun used in the murder of DeWitt Izuks."

"Not so fast, Bomber," Web said. "Your client could have done it and given Lance the gun. They could have done it together. He could have taken the gun to get rid of it *after* she killed Izuks. Lot of possible scenarios. That doesn't in any way absolve your client. This stiff," Web pointed at the body, "could have killed himself out of some Shakesperian sense of love and duty to make it seem like *he* was the killer." Web shook his head. "Not that simple, Bomber, you know that."

"Okay, gentlemen," Judge Fairly said. "Seen enough? Let's head back. We can talk about this on the record."

The trip back was noted for its silence. All were ruminating on how to use the event to their benefit.

The silence was only broken once, when we were almost back at the courthouse, by the judge's, "How do you want to break this news to the defendant?"

"How?" Bomber said.

"Who do you want to tell her? Do you want to, or would you prefer an impersonal officer?"

"That's one you can leave me out of," Web said.

Bomber didn't waste a second. "Tod will do it," he said, and I sank into the leather upholstery of the Bentley.

When we parked on the street at the courthouse, the judge said, "Come with me. We'll let the jury go for the day— admonish them to avoid the news."

"Fat chance," said Web, who had the greater stake in keeping the death of Lance Ludlow secret. Bomber would have been secretly pleased to have *all* the jurors read all about it. It would fan the fires of the conspiracy theories. Always good for the defense.

When we exited the car, the judge hustled ahead and Web practically ran to keep up with him—an action Bomber felt lacked dignity. I had Bomber to myself for a minute.

"Th-thanks a lot," I said.

"Don't mention it," he said, then, after a beat, he looked at me and stopped walking. So did I, naturally.

"Look," he said, "you think we want to be the kind of people who send some anonymous public servant to give that kind of news to our client? We're not. And contrary to what you might think, I didn't propose you as any kind of power play—"

"Y-you could d-do it," I stammered.

That seemed to stop him. He thought about it, then shook his head. "I could," he said, "but you will do it better."

He charged on ahead, and I let him go.

The defense and the prosecution were at their respective tables when the judge came in from his chambers like a matinee idol making his entrance from stage right.

"Before we call the jury and defendant in, I want to tell you both I am ordering the police report of this death for all of us. I hope to have something later in the day, then we'll have a better idea how to proceed."

Judge Fairly looked directly at me. Attention from judges made me uncomfortable. "Mr. Hanson, when do you plan to tell your client about the death of her alibi witness?"

"When we adjourn," I got all of that out without a stutter. I could *feel* the pride oozing from Bomber's pores.

"Very well, there will be no reference in my talk to the jurors. Bailiff, take them to the meeting room when we adjourn."

The bailiff nodded.

"All right, call the jury and defendant."

Pia was brought in, looking mighty confused. She sat between Bomber and me. "What happened?" she asked in a whisper. "Why are we starting so late?"

I patted her forearm. "I'll tell you when we adjourn. It should only be a few minutes."

She looked at Bomber as though he might be more forthcoming.

Bomber stared straight ahead. Wimp. It put me in mind

of when Sis died and I had to take over the emotional fulcrum of the family. Tough as Bomber was—macho Air Force bombardier and all, he was a cream puff with personal tragedy. So when Bomber nominated me to tell Pia her boyfriend was dead, perhaps it wasn't because I would do it *better*, but I was the only one who could do it at *all*.

"Ladies and gentlemen of the jury, there have been some new developments in this case that will necessitate a recess at least until tomorrow morning. Call the jury officer after five tonight to see if you are needed tomorrow. And let me emphasize you are not to look at any newspapers, watch television news, or listen to radio news. Best if you don't turn them on at all. We have a lot invested in this case and I'm sure you will agree we don't want to have to start over because one of you inadvertently listened to the news or glanced at a newspaper. Please ask the cooperation of anyone you are liable to see."

Pia shot me a burning look. It didn't take a psychic to tell something unusual was afoot.

The jury filed out and Pia darted her eyes between Bomber and me. As soon as the gavel struck Bomber was out of there like a launched rocket, without saying a word.

"We'll go into the conference room," I said to Pia, with a gentility that would have put Bomber on guard.

When she was seated at the table, on edge as I had never seen her, and the bailiff stepped outside and closed the door, Pia shot at me, "What is it? What's wrong?"

My first inkling was to ask her what made her think something was wrong, but a quick assessment of the situation told me that might be an insult to her intelligence.

"That's very perceptive of you, Pia—something is very wrong."

"What is it?" she asked, then added with an intuitive dread, "Is it Lance?"

I don't know why that should have shocked me. What else would she have had on her mind? I nodded.

"Oh, no," she gasped. "What?"

"We're not sure what—"

"You're not *sure?*" she pressed.

"I mean, we know what, we aren't sure how."

"He's dead, is that it?"

I closed my eyes. It was all I had to do. She started with a gasp, then accelerating sniffles, then a high-pitched wail, morphing into uncontrolled sobs.

"Oh, no," she cried. "Oh, God, no. Tell me it isn't true. Tell me you aren't sure."

"I wish I could," I said. "I'd like nothing better. We went to the scene this morning. That's why you were waiting. The police say it looks like...suicide..."

"*No way!* Not Lance. Impossible."

I nodded. That was the standard response of a loved one when told of a suicide.

"It was your gun," I said as gently as I could.

"*My gun?* How do you know?"

"Your father ID'd it."

"My *father?* What's he got to do with it?"

"He found him."

"*Found* him? How?"

"Says he's a detective—he couldn't rest until he found Lance. He thinks Lance killed your landlord. And I don't know...maybe since he killed himself with the same gun...it could be..." I said. "We'll know more when we look at the police report."

"Fab is a *snake!*" she said. "I don't trust him. I know I shouldn't say that about my father, and he has been vigilant in taking my side, believing in my innocence, but—"

Now is the time to tell her, I told myself, but the news still stuck in my throat. But I couldn't repress it any longer.

"Pia," I said, "I went to see your mother, you know."

She nodded.

"She told me some things. Made me promise to tell you—I've held off—too difficult for me—"

"What?"

"It's about Fab."

"What about him?"

"Your mother was pregnant when he married her."

Pia shrugged. "That's not so unusual."

"No, I guess *that* isn't, what's *more* unusual is…he was…and is…*not* your biological father."

She was stunned all right. Fell back in her chair as though she had stepped on a landmine.

"That said," I said, "I do think he wants only the best for you. What he did was not meant to be devious, it was really an act of charity."

"Charity?" she said in a daze. "Fab acting in charity?" she shook her head. "Fab never did anything charitable in his life."

"Well, what was in it for him? I mean, I expect he loved your mother."

"Yeah—she was a meal ticket. Not my father? Well, I'll be…"

It seemed that instead of that being a further drag on her spirits, it actually buoyed them—a slight antidote to the news about Lance.

She sighed, drawing in some reality from the air. "Well, there goes my chance," she said. "My witness—my only hope— gone…"

"But he had the gun. Isn't that proof *you* didn't have it?"

She considered. "I guess. But I expect the district attorney will make up something. Like I gave Lance the gun after I shot DeWitt."

"Did you?"

"Of course not."

"Then why make it up?"

"Sorry," she said. "I just feel so…helpless…"

I nodded. It was an echo of my last conversation with Lance.

"Are you going to be okay?" I asked. "I've got to go to the police and get to the bottom of what really happened."

"I'll be okay—do what you have to. I would bet my life Lance didn't kill himself. That's all I can tell you. Fab? I wouldn't put *anything* past him."

The matron came in and escorted Pia out. I sat immobilized watching her go. Life, I thought, sure dealt her some rotten cards, and I wanted to shuffle them into a winning hand.

Angleton was not exactly the murder capital of the world, so you wouldn't expect the town to attract the best homicide detective brains. Now there were two murders on one case. There are a lot of pressures from various sources to solve murders in a timely manner, and they don't all lend themselves to facile solving. Vic Upsole was really as good as any second tier detective in the county. He was bright, resourceful, hardworking, conscientious—all the good stuff. And better still, he was affable. He sat now with his feet propped on his desk in the detective room, where there were four desks. His legs were crossed at the ankles.

"We'll have a report on the judge's desk by five tonight," he said with a smile. "But there are reports, and then there are reports," he said. "How does that saying go? Do you want it good or do you want it Tuesday? Protect and serve is our motto. You want it Tuesday—we can deliver. You want it good, it'll take a little longer."

"Suicide?" I asked.

He shook his head. "I don't think so."

"How long was he dead?"

"About forty-eight hours. Still analyzing his stomach contents. See if we can get any closer."

"Fingerprints?" I asked.

"There were some of the victim's on the gun. How they got there I couldn't say. That's still being analyzed."

"Was he killed where he was found, or was he moved?"

"He appears to have been moved. We aren't sure, but there are some signs."

I didn't press him for details, I didn't question his

pronouncements. I was fortunate he was giving me a preview of the report.

"Think the fellow who discovered the body could be the culprit?"

"That's always our first suspicion. You want to think they might be smarter than that, but you just never know."

"Is this the gun that killed DeWitt Izuks?"

Vic nodded. "Ninety-five percent certain," he said. "Still—"

"—Doing tests," I completed the sentence for him. He smiled affably, made a gun out of his fingers, pointed it at me and pulled the trigger.

"Is there any evidentiary indication that Pia, our client, could not have fired that gun?"

"None that I know of," he said, his brow furrowing. "Theoretically, she could have shot the victim and given the gun to someone—her boyfriend, or her father. Or one of them could have found it somewhere and taken it to protect her. Around here we go with the odds—at least to keep us on the most logical path."

"What are the odds of that?"

"Pretty low."

When I reported this conversation to Bomber, he nodded. "Could have written the report myself without any tests. Now the problem is how to free Pia with this information. Web won't throw in the towel; know him too well for that. He doesn't admit defeat. His case was pretty thin, now it's almost invisible. But he'll go to his grave maintaining there were some shenanigans with the gun. She shot the landlord, and her boyfriend took the gun. We couldn't get him to testify, so it's supposing wild perhaps, but sometimes wild wins the day. Any juror disposed to convict Pia would have enough ammunition to justify it. If he were persuasive enough, he could sway the whole bunch of them," Bomber shook his head. "We have to do something dramatic to pull this one out of the hat."

"What?"

"That's the question, me boy," he said, "that's the question."

A few minutes after five, the police report was delivered to our office. It said basically what Vic told me—though the certainty factors had increased. Forty-eight hours dead before discovery—within a few hours either way—ninety-nine percent certain the gun that killed Lance was the same gun that killed DeWitt Izuks.

I didn't have any dramatic ideas, so I slipped out of the office before Bomber could saddle me with an all night project. I left him brooding in his office.

That night I made some major revisions to my To Die For sonata for the violin and piano. A ponderous, plodding uncertainty entered with severe tempo and key changes. Good wasn't the description that came to mind when I played it for my critical review—accurate, perhaps, but not particularly good. I called Joan that evening, after her rehearsal, to tell her what I'd done.

"Violin tacit," she said, hopefully. She didn't want to play what I'd described. "It would be lovely with piano alone."

"Thanks."

The next morning I met Bomber in court. He had no dramatic inspiration to report. "Bread and butter," he said, meaning he was going to stick with fundamentals—counter the district attorney's inevitable argument and move on from there.

The judge appeared from backstage at the stroke of nine. That was another thing about him; he didn't make you wait as so many judges did in what was sometimes an unavoidable, but sometimes just a thoughtless, display of power.

He called us to the bench.

"We've received the report. I trust you have too, gentlemen?"

Bomber nodded; Web said, "Yes, Your Honor."

"I've taken the liberty of putting the jury off another day, so we can plan and agree hopefully, on our approach. Your thoughts, Mr. Grainger?"

"My thoughts?" Web said. "I don't see any reason to change course and make a circus out of this. I don't find any suggestion the man was murdered to keep him from testifying. It is a completely different case, and should be treated as such. Any introduction into this case will only muddy the waters. Conspiracy theories will find fertile ground here, and we mustn't allow them to take root."

Nice metaphor, Web, I thought.

"Now, Mr. Grainger, you know what we are interested in here?"

The district attorney looked at Judge Fairly as though he didn't have the answer.

"Truth and justice. Winning and losing aren't important in a court of law. No, the important thing is justice. We should all pull together to that end. Am I right about that?"

"Yes, Your Honor, of course. Will you allow for different viewpoints about how we arrive at justice?"

The judge smiled. "Yes, of course, but one of the perks of this job is that I get to decide which point of view will prevail. Now, I understand your argument, Mr. Grainger. Mr. Hanson?"

"Thank you, Your Honor. I salute you for dignifying the prosecutor's gibberish as an argument. I don't see anything to argue about. The state has a duty to my client, just as I do, to see that she gets a fair trial. Suppressing evidence never contributes to that end. Her alibi witness was murdered with the gun that killed the victim in this case. Obviously, she didn't have the gun, obviously she didn't kill her witness. It would seem, on the surface at least, that whoever killed him did it because he didn't want him to provide an alibi for her. Yes, I know there could be other reasons, but when you have the same murder weapon, you have to think there is some connection. At minimum, there is enough suggestion of connection for us to explore in front of the jury."

Web shook his head. "Can of worms," he said.

"Worms, shworms," Bomber said. "Truth and justice

demand we don't sweep this under the rug."

"We won't—but it is a different case. We'll try it separately—as we should."

"Nice arguments, gentlemen," the judge said. "I'm afraid, Mr. Grainger, if I ruled on your side, I'd be reversed in five minutes. The defendant has a right to an unhampered defense, and I intend to see that she gets it. Mr. Hanson, what is your desire?"

"To put the detective on the stand to testify to what he found. Then to put Fabrizio Franceschi on to inquire into what connection he might have had to the murder. What he can tell us about how the gun got from his daughter's drawer to the mountains above Angleton."

"You don't expect him to confess the murder on the stand, do you?"

Bomber smiled—I hope it didn't seem as condescending to Web as it did to me.

"Not very likely, is it?" Bomber asked, more or less rhetorically.

"So ordered," the judge said. "I'll summon the jury and the witnesses for tomorrow morning. We'll see you then."

When Fabrizio Fruta Franceschi took his seat on the witness chair, he presented himself as a man who was beginning the most important day of his life. He was, after all, a private detective, who, by his own account, had solved the case and absolved his daughter Pia, to ultimately free her from the tight spot she was in.

Since Bomber had gotten Fab banned from the courtroom early in the case, he was not on hand to hear the testimony of police detective Upsole, so Fab likely assumed his own version of the events leading to his discovery of Lance Ludlow's body would carry the day.

Bomber seemed in an affable mood. That would have been calculated to fit his game plan, for Bomber came equipped with a mood faucet that he turned on and off at will.

Though there were numerous variations on his themes, Bomber's approach to witnesses could be categorized in two main divisions: hit them between the eyes at the starting gate, or begin as an old pal—lull the witnesses into a false sense of security, then slam them between the eyes.

The latter approach seemed to be presenting itself with Fabrizio Franceschi.

"Good morning, Mr. Franceschi," Bomber greeted the witness with a broad smile, which was returned in kind. And why not? Were they not buddies in this thing together? Wasn't Fabrizio Franceschi instrumental, through his dogged investigation, in solving the case to Bomber's satisfaction? Fab sat tall in the witness box, and why shouldn't he? Was he not, at this moment, at the pinnacle of his career? All his training and dogged gumshoe hard work had brought him to this zenith. He knew it, Bomber knew it, and now everybody would know it.

"Mr. Franceschi, you testified earlier as to your profession?"

"I did."

"And that was…?"

"I'm a private detective." I'd heard many witnesses give their professions over the years, but never with more pride.

"Yes," Bomber said, "and roughly, how long have you worked at that…profession?"

"Going on twenty-five years now."

"Wonderful," Bomber exclaimed. "And you were working in that capacity—as a private detective—on the case of the State of California versus Pia Franceschi, your daughter, in the last several weeks?"

"I was," Fab said, then added, "Not only the last several weeks, but ever since she was arrested. I knew she was innocent—"

"Your Honor," Web said without rising, "may the witness be instructed not to volunteer his opinions unless asked for in a proper mode of questioning?"

Bomber raised an eyebrow while the judge said, "Just answer the questions, Mr. Franceschi. Let the jury decide the guilt or innocence of the defendant. You may proceed, Mr. Hanson."

"Thank you, Your Honor," said the courtly, obliging Bomber Hanson, defender of the downtrodden. "Now, Mr. Franceschi, to acquaint the jury with the magnitude of your work, would you tell us, please, some of the higher profile cases you have worked on?"

"I'd be glad to oblige," Fab said. "I worked on the O.J. Simpson case from the beginning. The Jon Bennett-Ramsey case, the Scott Peterson case. I've been involved in most of the big cases. I'm currently looking for the great granddaughter of Tyrone Power."

I checked the jury out of the corner of my eye. They were impressed.

"How did you get your start in your line of work?"

"The LAPD."

"Los Angeles Police Department?"

"That's correct."

"In what capacity?"

"I started out in a patrol car."

"And you worked your way up to detective?"

"I did."

Rather than badgering Fab to get at the less glamorous truth of the matter, Bomber left the jury with the impression Fab was an ace detective who paid his dues and worked his way up through the ranks. Then he switched the subject. "Mr. Franceschi, the defendant in this case, Pia Franceschi, is your daughter, is she not?"

"She is."

"And you care for your daughter?"

"She means more to me than anything in this world. More than life itself!"

"And have you been lending your considerable investigative skills to her case?"

"I have."

"All right, Mr. Franceschi, you found the body of Lance Ludlow two days ago, did you not?"

"I did."

"Will you tell the jury how that came about?"

"Through my diligent investigation. Detective work is not some result of lucky breaks; it is consistent, hard work. I've been working twenty-hour days on this case from the beginning. I resolved I was going to leave no stone unturned in the pursuit of truth and justice, and I have done just that. From the beginning I suspected Lance Ludlow was the murderer. He had motive—jealousy, method—the gun I gave Pia, and opportunity—there was a party in the park. Pia and her roommates were there, he was watching from this house next door. The victim, DeWitt Izuks, was alone, asleep in Pia's bed on the other side of the observation house. An easy matter for him to slip next door, use the gun and take it with him and hide it somewhere."

"How did you pursue your theory?"

"I hounded Lance—directly and indirectly. As a result of my perseverance, he moved out of his campus apartment into the hills above town."

"Did you share your theory with the police?"

"I did," Fab said, punctuating his testimony with jolts to his posture.

"What was their response?"

"Nothing. They ignored me."

If Bomber had set on breaking Fab, this would have been a good place to reintroduce Fab's arrest for reckless driving with intent to do bodily harm. Instead, he carried on his love fest.

"Mr. Franceschi, how did you happen upon the body of Lance Ludlow?"

"I didn't happen upon it. I did my due diligence—I pounded the pavement, so to speak. When I heard he didn't show for his alibi testimony, I wanted to make sure he followed through on his promise to Pia to come here and tell this jury he was watching her all night on the night of the murder. His testimony seemed vital."

"So how did you go about finding Lance Ludlow?"

"I found out where he lived."

"How?"

"How? I'm a detective, that's how. It's what I do for a living—find people who are missing, among other things."

"Yes, good. Would you mind sharing with us the steps you took in this case?"

"Yes, well. I don't usually give away my trade secrets," Fab said with wide arm gestures. "I mean, if I gave away my tricks, no one would hire me."

Instead of batting him down Bomber chose to indulge him. "All right, did you find out where he lived?"

"Yes, I did."

"Did you go there?"

"Yes."

"And did you speak to Lance Ludlow?"

"No."

"So you started to look for him?"

"Right."

"Can you tell us how you went about it?"

"Of course. I went to the police first and filed a missing person report."

"To your knowledge, did the police look for him?"

"No," Fab said shaking his head. "If you're an adult, they figure if you're missing, you want to be. Unless I could prove foul play—and I couldn't—they said they'd give it at least a couple of weeks."

"That's when you sprang into action?"

"Exactly! My first thought was he was hiding out until the trial was over. If he was hiding in Philadelphia or the Philippines I had my work cut out for me. I frankly wouldn't have had the funds for such an undertaking. If he was close to home that was another story. So I did my famous circle—"

"What is that?"

"That's where I start at the residence and search in an ever widening circle."

"And you found him?"

"Yes, I did," Fab said, not without a display of justified pride, starting with the expansion of his chest and oozing up to a satisfied smile.

"Can you tell the jury his condition when you found him?"

"He was dead. Gunshot to the head. The gun was a few inches from his hand which was outstretched on the ground."

"Did you recognize the gun?"

"I did. It was the gun I had bought for Pia's protection."

"Did you form a conclusion at that time as to how Lance Ludlow had died?"

"Objection," Web said. "Calls for a speculation he is not qualified to give."

Fab looked astonished. "Not qualified? I'm a detective."

"Yes," Bomber said, "he's a detective. No one is more qualified."

"He may answer," the judge said.

"I did form a conclusion."

"What was your conclusion?"

"It was obvious he had shot himself. It was a classic case of suicide."

Bomber paused. "Suicide?" he repeated with a skeptical intonation. "Are you sure of that?" Bomber asked. "Suicide—a classic case?"

Fab displayed a barely perceptible doubt. Did he detect a shift in Bomber's softball tactic? If he did, it didn't change his story. "Yes, sir. I'd stake my reputation on it."

"Did you do any tests on the body?"

"No, sir, that's lab work. I'm a detective. I don't do lab work."

"So you based your conclusion on…?"

"The position of the body—relative to the gun. It was the gun I gave Pia, I'm sure it was the gun used to kill the landlord. I saw no sign of struggle. The bullet wound seemed consistent with self-infliction. I knew Pia didn't do it—she was in jail for this one. I didn't see any evidence the body was moved. I'm a detective. I've seen dozens of these suicides."

"For the sake of argument," Bomber said, "is it possible someone shot him? Say he wasn't expecting it—shot him at just the right place, then arranged the body to look like suicide?"

"Fingerprints," Fab said. "I expect the gun was tested for fingerprints? As I said, I don't do the lab work myself—I hire others for that."

"But wouldn't a clever killer—someone who had seen a lot of these perhaps—wear gloves, then press the victim's fingers on the handle of the gun?"

"But it all fits. It's Pia's gun. Lance had it. He killed the landlord because of his intentions toward Pia. Whatever you say, finding the landlord in Pia's bed could make a boyfriend snap. He is wracked with guilt at seeing Pia arrested. He doesn't want to go to jail, but he doesn't want her to. So he takes the easy way out. He shoots himself with the same gun."

Bomber stared at Fab, and after some tense moments,

bobbed his head in some noncommittal nods. "Are you sure...?" he said, and paused mid sentence.

"Sure as I can be."

"...that it is the same gun?"

"It was the same...or one exactly like it."

"Hmm..." Bomber mused. "Yes...Mr. Franceschi, what would you say if I told you the police detectives and the lab have concluded, one, the same gun used to shoot DeWitt Izuks was used to shoot Lance Ludlow; and two, Lance Ludlow did not commit suicide, but was shot in the head by a murderer, then moved to that rather remote site?"

Fab pondered the question. He also pondered the shift in the dynamic of Bomber's questions. The focus that was suddenly seeming to fall on Fab himself in connection with the murder. "What would I say?" Fab said at last, hiking up his shoulders. "Is that what you found out?"

Bomber nodded gently.

Fab exhaled a ton of air. "Then I'd have to look at the reports to come to my own conclusions. What I said was based on what I had observed. I didn't do any tests. Look, I know I didn't kill anybody—I don't see another explanation, unless it's that someone we don't even know about—"

"You sure?"

"Sure?" Fab was surprised. "Sure of what?"

"That you didn't commit these murders?"

"Sure? Certainly I'm sure. I'm a detective, not a killer."

"Can you be both?" Bomber was still low-key.

"Well, I suppose you can. I'm not, I've never killed anybody."

"It was your gun, was it not?"

"No. I gave it to Pia. I haven't seen it since...not until I found it with Lance."

"Okay, Mr. Franceschi, let me ask you a few more questions about your detective work. You mentioned all these high profile cases you worked on—O.J. Simpson and others. Well, let's just take the O.J. Simpson trial—who did you work for in that case?"

"Myself. I'm an independent contractor."

"Who did you report to?"

"The detective in charge."

"Do you remember his name?"

"I don't offhand."

"So you worked for the prosecution as opposed to the defense?"

"Correct."

"Or the police. In that case, the LAPD?"

"That's correct."

"Who paid you?"

Fab seemed momentarily baffled. "Well, the people I work for pay me."

"In the Simpson case, that was the LAPD?"

"Well, I expect so. That's been some time now."

"Do you remember how much you were paid?"

"How much?" Fab frowned. "No, I don't. I'm not a person driven by money. I'm more interested in serving the public good. Whatever they pay me for it is okay with me."

"That's very noble, Mr. Franceschi, but I suppose you do have to live."

"Of course."

"So how much does your profession bring in, say on average on a yearly basis?"

"Oh, I couldn't say. It varies so much."

"What are the extremes?"

"Well, it's feast or famine, you know."

"What does that mean in dollars? Say, what is the most you have earned in a year?"

"I'm sorry, Bomber, I don't keep track of those things."

"Do you pay income tax?"

"Well, of course."

"How much did you pay last year?"

"I have no idea," Fab said. "My wife handles that."

"Does your wife work?"

"Yes."

"How many jobs?"

"What?"

"Don't you understand the question?"

"I guess I don't know. My wife has a job—"

"How many jobs does your wife have?"

"Just one, as far as I know."

"Really? Which one is that?"

"She's a supermarket checker."

"And a waitress?"

"She may have waitressed at some time."

"A bookkeeper?"

"That's extra work—I don't know."

"Three jobs, would you say?"

"I don't think she has three steady jobs—"

"We can call her to testify, and subpoena your income tax returns. Because you've never made any money as a private detective, have you, Mr. Franceschi? Your wife supports you and Pia, and she has to work three jobs to do it, doesn't she?"

Fab stared blankly at Bomber as though trying to understand why his friend of the early interrogation had turned so hostile. Suddenly he understood without really hearing the next question.

"You killed DeWitt Izuks, didn't you? And then Lance Ludlow…"

"No," Fab said slowly, "I did not."

"Maybe it wasn't planned. Maybe you didn't intend to. Because the landlord in your daughter's bed made something snap inside you."

"I didn't see him."

"Come now, Mr. Franceschi, admit you weren't happy about your daughter carrying on with her landlord."

"That's true."

"So when you saw him in her bed, you reached for the gun you gave your daughter—it was still where you put it in the bottom drawer of the dresser—you reached for it, and killed him."

"No—" Fab was licking his lips; they suddenly seemed so dry.

"So you tried to make it look like Lance was the killer. You were all over this place telling everyone to find Lance, he was the killer—jealousy—understandable in the circumstances, but he was the man to get. So you thought if you staged the suicide it would seem like Lance was the killer, shooting himself with the same gun to cement the evidence. Convincing anybody of Lance's suicide motive seemed a hard sell, but you were desperate by that time. Your daughter's trial for murder was coming to a close, and it looked like she might be convicted, and you couldn't stand that. You were the guilty one. You didn't want her to take the fall. That would not have been manly of you. Lance had to be an afterthought. A convenient victim—" Bomber zeroed in on his prey, and I was so glad at that moment I had never been in Fab's position: victim to that frightening predator.

Fab opened his mouth to speak, then closed it again. Was he going to deny it, was he going to confess? Instead he turned to the judge—"Your Honor," he said meekly, "could I be excused to go to the bathroom? I have to go real bad."

The judge was sympathetic—"All right, we'll take a ten minute recess."

Fab zoomed up the aisle without looking at Bomber.

Bomber watched him go, then returned to the table where he whispered (the whisper heard around the world), "He's probably got to throw up."

40

Back in the courtroom after the recess we awaited the return of Fabrizio Franceschi.

And we waited. The judge had come in and asked Bomber, "Mr. Hanson, is your witness ready to resume questioning?"

"I'm sure he is," Bomber said, "he just hasn't returned yet."

"But it's been fifteen minutes…do you suppose he is sick?"

"I'd be sick if Bomber had given me that treatment," the district attorney whispered so we heard it at the defendant's table. A Cheshire cat smile was on his lips.

We waited some more. I don't know which of us got the queasy feeling first. It could have been me, but in retrospect, it was probably Bomber.

"Bailiff, check the restroom, make sure he's all right."

The Bailiff left the courtroom.

And we waited. The judge was beginning to show some signs of fidgeting when the sheriff entered the courtroom from the rear door and made his way to Bomber at the defendant's table, laid an envelope before him and whispered in his ear, "Your client asked me to deliver these to you. I was supposed to wait twenty minutes." Then he turned and exited the courtroom.

The judge looked inquisitively at Bomber. "What is it, Mr. Hanson?"

"Apparently a letter," he said, tearing open the envelope. Bomber began to read the one addressed to him when a dollar bill fell out of the envelope. He handed the sealed envelope addressed to the judge to the bailiff for delivery to the bench. He kept the one marked for Pia, as he was instructed.

After Judge Fairly had read his letter he summoned us to the bench. Without a word he turned the letter so Bomber and Web could read it at the same time.

The letter, scrawled in an immature hand on a lined tablet read:

> Dear Judge,
>
> I know suicide is a coward's way out but I just don't see any other way. I am guilty of these murders— DeWitt Izuks, my dear Pia's landlord, and her boyfriend Lance Ludlow. I killed them both with the same gun. The reasons are obvious. I can't face Pia going through any more hell than she already has. My motives were pure when I shot DeWitt Izuks. The world is well rid of him. It was panic that caused me to shoot Lance. He was competing with me for Pia's affection. It looked like they were getting back together. I'm not proud of it, but this letter is just to tell you that Pia is 100% innocent of any murder and she must be released.
>
> I almost confessed to Bomber when I was on the witness stand, but the time I spent in your jail was enough to convince me I couldn't face any

242

more of it.

> Please release Pia
> Franceschi and apologize to her
> for all the suffering I have
> caused her.
>
> Very truly yours,
> Fabrizio F. Franceschi

Bomber turned white as an Alaskan snowstorm, pivoted on his heels, said to me, "You take over," and hurried out of the courtroom handing me the letter Fab had written to him.

"Where's he going?" the judge asked me.

"Bomber doesn't handle suicide well," I said, my memory harkening back to when Sis drove off the pier and Bomber went to pieces. Doubtless this was an unwelcome reminder of that tragedy. It was also the first suicide by a witness who Bomber demolished on the stand, though I'm sure others had considered the option.

The judge addressed Web, "Mr. Grainger, may I assume you are recommending we drop the case against Pia Franceschi?"

Web twisted his body as though he were going to look at Pia at the defense table, then thought better of it. "I don't know," he said frowning at the letter, "this could be another of Bomber's tricks. And where is Fabrizio Franceschi?"

Judge Fairly cocked an eyebrow at Web. "Really? You think Bomber would risk disbarment with a trick like this? We both know he couldn't stand Mr. Franceschi—how do you suppose he could have conspired with him?"

"Bomber could do anything," Web said, but without much conviction. "I think, until we find Franceschi's body, I'd put off any directed verdict…"

Judge Fairly was trying to fathom the district attorney and his reluctance to treat the letter as authentic, when the bailiff sent on the errand to locate Fab returned to the courtroom.

Before he spoke, everybody previewed his words on his face. He came to the bench and whispered to the judge, "Your Honor, a search of all the bathrooms in the building failed to turn up our witness. But a citizen found a body slumped over a steering wheel in a car parked in a red zone—with a ticket on the windshield."

It was Fab, who the autopsy later proved had died from a cyanide pellet.

The judge turned to Web, and with an uncharacteristic caustic tone and cocked eyebrow asked, "Still think it's a trick, Mr. Grainger?"

"No, Your Honor," he said, choking on humble pie.

The judge turned to the jury. "Ladies and Gentlemen," he said, "evidence has come to light exonerating the defendant Pia Franceschi and rendering the case against her moot. The district attorney has dropped the case against her and you are free to return to your homes with our thanks for your attentive service." Web and I returned to our tables.

"Miss Franceschi," the judge said to Pia after the jury filed out showing, one would judge, considerable relief at being alleviated of their burdens—for the burden of proof had many nuances and affected the jury as well as the principal in a murder trial—"Miss Franceschi, you are free to go. Our judicial process is not perfect, but we think it is the best in the world. That doesn't keep mistakes from being made, or perhaps make you feel any better—our apologies may ring hollow, but you have them from all of us, and they are sincere." Pia jumped up when it all sank in.

"I can go?" she asked, and before it was out of her mouth, the question changed to an exclamation and she threw her arms around me, sobbing so I felt the thunderous quaking of her chest against mine.

The courtroom was largely cleared by the time she regained control of her emotions.

"How did it happen?" she asked me. "I mean, what was it made them realize I didn't do it?"

"Your father..." I began, but choked and couldn't continue. I handed her the letter addressed to her.

She appeared confused as she opened it. We read it together.

> Dearest Pia,
>   You are the light of my life. Nobody has ever been more important to me. Everything I did, I did for your sake. Now I must take my punishment.
>   This will also serve as my last will and testament and I hereby bequeath to Pia Franceschi all my worldly goods and I am of sound mind.

It was dated and signed,

> Your ever-loving father,
> Fabrizio F. Franceschi

The signature had all the curlicues and flourishes he always made.

Pia broke down all over again. I didn't read the letter Bomber had given me addressed to him until Pia's wailing had subsided to ceaseless sobbing.

Then I gathered Bomber's papers, the letter from Fab and Bomber's briefcase and Pia and I walked back to our office, where my car was parked.

The Chinese red Bentley was not in the lot.

I drove Pia to the prison to pick up her belongings. "I'm going to go back home to mom in San Jose, get my bearings. I can't face school right now. Maybe when I get back on my feet I'll go somewhere else. I don't know—"

After I waved goodbye to Pia, I opened and read the letter to Bomber.

> Dear Counselor:
>
> Enclosed please find the sum of $1.00 in the currency of the United States of America. It is my payment to retain you as my lawyer so that everything I tell you will be privileged information.
>
> Enclosed, please find two more letters, in sealed envelopes. I direct you to give the one marked Judge Fairly to Judge Fairly in open court, and the one addressed to Pia to my daughter in private.
>
> The letter to the court is a full confession of the murders—both of them. I didn't kill either man but have come to the conclusion the only way to save Pia now is to confess. You've led up to it beautifully with your questioning.
>
> You tried to make me a liar in court, but everything I said was true. I didn't shoot the landlord. I wasn't happy about his relationship with Pia, but I didn't shoot him. I was looking for Lance because I really thought he was the murderer. I knew it was not Pia and I knew

it was not me—so that left Lance. Now I wonder if there isn't a connection between DeWitt's murder and what is going on at 1410 Vine Street. I nosed around there, asked a few questions, didn't get very far. Pia's housemates work there. But when I tried to explain that to the cops they ignored me.

All I had left was my self-respect. Now as a result of your questioning, I don't even have that.

Pia is as fine a person as ever walked the face of this earth. The judge has my full confession. Use it to get Pia off. I hope with all my heart she can put this unpleasantness behind her and have the wonderful life she so richly deserves.

Very truly yours,
Fabrizio F. Franceschi

When I thought Bomber had had enough time to get over Fab's suicide, I asked him the question that had been bugging me ever since he made that untenable stand in court, badgering the district attorney for letting Fab out of jail.

"What did you w-want…why d-did you want Fab out of s-sight?"

"Two reasons," Bomber said. "The first is obvious. I couldn't stand him."

"Second?"

"Ah, yes. More subtle. I thought he might redouble his

efforts to prove to me and all involved, that he was a top-flight private detective and we might glean some benefit from that. We made the point. We didn't want him interfering with us—never more effectively than with my five grand invoice. He had something to prove and he proved it. Doubtless this was his finest moment as a private detective."

"If he didn't m-make that f-fake confession, what d-do you think would have h-happened?"

Bomber gave it due thought before he answered. "No telling," he said. "I choose to believe he saved his daughter's life. But verily, we believe what we want to believe."

41

About six months later, fear, anger, rage, jealousy and lust for revenge welled up in the bosom of one of Gillian Izuks' stable of beauties—Erin Winterbottom to be precise. The brew reached its boiling point when his roving eye landed on a newer recruit to the oldest profession, and coincided with a police raid that caught Erin *in flagrante delicto*. Vic Upsole later bragged how easy it was to get Erin to squawk—to sing the terminal tune of her erstwhile boyfriend/employer's clammy hand on the gun that killed first his uncle, then Lance Ludlow.

Immunity from prosecution is a wonderful persuader—the mighty tumble like fallen autumn leaves. The little guys and gals go a lot easier.

It was one night when the alcohol level in his blood reached mythic proportions, that Gillian, his secret boiling inside him, shared that secret with our gal, Erin. He should have kept his mouth shut. Gillian still sits on death row owing to his double whammy. The wheels of justice are grinding exceedingly slow, owing, in part, to Gillian's aptitude for jailhouse appeals.

All the while, Gillian Izuks has been begging Bomber to represent him. And all the while, Bomber has refused.

ALLEN A. KNOLL, PUBLISHERS

Established 1989

We are a small press located in Santa Barbara, Ca,
specializing in
books for intelligent people who read for fun.

Please visit our website at www.knollpublishers.com
for a complete catalog, scintilating sample chapters,
in depth interviews, and thought-provoking
reading guides.

Or call (800) 777-7623 to receive a catalog and/or be
kept informed of new releases.